The Replacement Wife

Also by Tiffany L. Warren

Don't Tell a Soul

Published by Dafina Books

THE REPLACEMENT WIFE

TIFFANY L. WARREN

Kensington Publishing Corp.
www.kensingtonbooks.com

DAFINA BOOKS are published by

Kensington Publishing Corp.
119 West 40th Street
New York, NY 10018

All Kensington titles, imprints, and distributed lines are available at special quantity discounts for bulk purchases for sales promotion, premiums, fund-raising, and educational or institutional use.

Special book excerpts or customized printings can also be created to fit specific needs. For details, write or phone the office of the Kensington Special Sales Manager: Kensington Publishing Corp., 119 West 40th Street, New York, NY 10018. Attn. Special Sales Department. Phone: 1-800-221-2647.

ISBN-13: 978-0-7582-8060-2
ISBN-10: 0-7582-8060-2
First Kensington Trade Paperback Printing: March 2014

eISBN-13: 978-0-7582-8062-6
eISBN-10: 0-7582-8062-9
First Kensington Electronic Edition: March 2014

10 9 8 7 6 5 4 3 2

Printed in the United States of America

Acknowledgments

Writing this book has been such a journey! I want to thank God, first and foremost! I love that He keeps giving me stories, and I am blessed to continue writing them. Lord, I thank you.

I thank God for my family. My husband, Brent, who continues to be a positive force in my life, thank you for your support and prayers. Continue to walk in destiny.

I must thank my children with every release, Briana, Brittany, and Brynn—you all did a wonderful job as Morgan, Madison, and Danielle in the stage-play version of this book. You are wonderful actors and singers! Brent II and Brookie, thank you for being my babies. You are getting so big that I won't be able to say that soon.

To Mercedes, Adeola, and the entire team at Kensington—thank you for your tireless efforts. To my wonderful agent, Sara Camilli—welcome to my world of crazy. Thank you for supporting the art!

Thank you to all the book clubs that have supported me over the years. There are too many to name, but I'd like to give a special shout-out to Pastor Marguritte Johnson and the Godly Girlfriends book club in Mesquite, Texas. (I forgot them last time I was giving shout-outs!)

To the writers I admire and call friends, thank you for your advice and kind words. You know who you are. To my true blues, my homies, my ride or die (why somebody gotta die) chicks—Shawana, Leah, Rhonda, and Brandi! You all know exactly how to pray for me, so let's get to it.

Shout-out to the Lunch Bunch: Margie Faye, Jay, Misty, Lee Lee, Olivia, and Brandi. (Thanks for showing up at my book signing and acting like I was a celebrity.) Much love to Myron

Butler and the Potter's House Choir of Dallas. (I know y'all sick of my testimonies, but oh well.)

I know I am forgetting lots of folk, so please charge it to my head and not my heart!

Blessings,
Tiffany

PROLOGUE

Chloe scanned the incredibly packed sanctuary and groaned. The only seats available were in the balcony, and that just wouldn't do. Chloe wanted to kick herself for not gassing up her Benz the night before. That extra fourteen minutes at the gas station had probably made all the difference. Now, instead of sitting close enough to her next husband that he could smell her Chanel No. 5, she would be in the rafters with the nonimportant attendees . . . unless she could convince one of the ushers to seat her in front, where she so obviously belonged.

Chloe weighed her choices. One of the center aisles was being guarded by a white-haired woman with a body like a Baltimore Ravens lineman and a glare to match. Chloe immediately decided against her. She was likely immune to any of Chloe's charms and would probably have her removed from the sanctuary for trying to sidestep the rules.

The other center aisle was being handled by a distinguished and handsome man of about fifty years. Every few seconds he wiped tears from his eyes. He probably knew the recently departed Chandra Chambers personally. Had probably dined with the family in that gigantic mansion off West Paces Ferry Road, right smack in the middle of Atlanta's old money. He was, without question, Chloe's mark.

Chloe stumbled down the aisle, tears flowing freely, and soft sobs escaping every few seconds. The sensitive usher approached her and touched her arm.

"I'm so sorry, miss, but there are no more seats in the main sanctuary. You'll have to sit in the overflow."

Chloe nodded and placed one hand on her chest. As she'd hoped, the usher's gaze followed her hand to her slightly surgically enhanced, sufficiently heaving and bronzed bosom.

"I know," Chloe said in a throaty whisper, "but I just want to look at Chandra one more time. We were roommates at Spelman, and she was just like a sister to me."

The usher looked unsure, so Chloe went in for the kill. "When she was sick, she asked me to look after her babies for her. How can I do that from the balcony?"

This settled it for the usher. Chloe was sure he believed every word of her emotional speech. And why wouldn't he? Who would lie at a funeral about the wishes of the deceased?

Only a desperate person.

And as much as Chloe hated to admit it, she was desperate, and her socialite status was in severe jeopardy. She had just a couple hundred thousand dollars in the bank, which enabled her to strategize without getting a nine to five, but it wouldn't keep her in the society circles she'd infiltrated with her late fiancé. Walter had been a billionaire. She'd met him on the beach in St. Bart's one holiday. Although he was seventy-eight, Walter was spry and sexy, and he'd given Chloe everything her heart had desired. Well . . . almost everything. He'd never made her his bride, and when he died suddenly of an aneurysm, Walter's children unceremoniously threw Chloe out on her behind. All she had left was the sum of the gifts he'd given her—a fully furnished townhouse, several large diamonds and other jewels, and a car.

Chloe tried not to draw too much attention to herself as she followed the usher down to the front row. She wanted to be remembered by only one person—Quentin. The lineman usher scowled, but Chloe's friendly usher made room for her on the aisle. None of the family paid attention to the extra person in their pew. In fact, the family seemed to be in a tearful haze. Quentin looked especially hopeless, but even still, his incredible good looks made Chloe's heart skip a beat. His caramel skin seemed to glow as tears coursed down his face.

Chloe wanted to reach out and comfort him, pull him to her saline plumped breasts and caress his pain away.

Yes, Chloe did believe she would have her some of Quentin Chambers. And his millions.

CHAPTER 1

Five years later . . .

Chloe walked into the packed nail salon for her weekly pedicure with her best friend, Lichelle. The Nail Spot was always crowded and always cost just a little bit extra. Maybe it was because it was owned by an ex-rapper turned entrepreneur. Or maybe it was because gossip was on the menu, just like the paraffin wax and the acrylic tips.

Lichelle waved Chloe to the back of the salon—the VIP area. She'd saved Chloe a spot, which was darn near impossible to do, but Lichelle, the wife of a wealthy real estate broker, was a regular. And a good tipper.

Chloe slid into the luxurious chair and leaned back, careful not to muss her freshly perfected hairdo. Her short tresses were expertly sculpted, and they framed her face perfectly, softening the potentially strong features created by her excessive workouts.

"Girl, I thought I was gonna have to fight that queen over there. He kept eyeballing your chair like he was about to snatch it," Lichelle said, as she blew Chloe a kiss.

"I am not thinking about him."

Chloe cut her eyes at the man, who gave her much attitude. She didn't have time to exchange words with him, nor did she want to ruin her mood. She was going to Lichelle's yacht party later with Quentin, and it was going to be a blast.

But first she was about to get her feet rubbed and mashed by her favorite nail tech, Trey. He was fine and buff, and his foot massages took her to the mountaintop.

Trey slid over in front of Chloe on his little stool. "Hey, ma. How's your day going?"

Chloe grinned as Trey cracked his knuckles and took her foot into his hand in a miniature caress. "It's going great now, babe. Do your magic!"

"I am telling Quentin," Lichelle said.

Chloe lifted Lichelle's left hand and touched the enormous rock on her ring finger. "You're the only one married. I am still very unmarried."

"But not unattached. You've been with Quentin for an eternity."

Chloe winced at the word. It had been a long time. Five years, to be exact. Quentin didn't seem the least bit interested in marriage. She didn't think he loved her, but he enjoyed her company enough to foot the bill for her every need. He even gave her a small shopping allowance.

Admittedly, she wanted more. Not necessarily marriage, but at least a commitment. A bit of assurance that the fun times were more than temporary.

"Five years is not an eternity. Especially since we got together right after he buried his wife."

"How long are you going to wait for him to marry you?" Trey asked.

"I'm not waiting for him to marry me. I'm enjoying what we have. Savoring the moments."

Lichelle sucked her teeth and shook her head. "What if he wakes up tomorrow and decides he's ready to trade you in?"

"You do have quite a few miles on you, and you are definitely fine—I wouldn't kick you out of bed. But you're not a twentysomething anymore," Trey said.

"Is this attack Chloe day? I'm not feeling this."

Trey laughed. "Sorry, ma. Let me squeeze that stress away."

Chloe closed her eyes and moaned. It was as if Trey had some secret road map that led straight from the middle of her foot to her unmentionables.

"Seriously, though," Lichelle said, invading Chloe's ecstasy, "have you thought about a backup plan?"

"What do you mean?"

"You need to make sure you're financially okay in case Quentin decides you are not his final resting place."

"You could always have Quentin's baby," Trey said.

"Ugh. No! Low-rent women have babies for a paycheck. I do not do that."

Trey shrugged. "Sorry. It was just a thought."

"If you're not going to give Quentin a love child, then you really need to think about your future. Why don't you ask Quentin to help you start a business?"

Chloe considered this. The problem was, she had no idea what kind of business she'd want to start. She didn't want to work that hard.

She wanted to continue to give Quentin what he needed, and she wanted him to continue giving her what she needed.

"Look, Quentin cares about me. He's not going to leave me high and dry. And maybe one day he will ask me to marry him. And maybe I'll say yes."

"Maybe you'll say yes?" Lichelle asked.

"Yes, maybe. Not every girl needs a husband. I'm happy having a sugar daddy."

"You a little old for a sugar daddy," Trey said. Lichelle and Trey burst into laughter, and Chloe rolled her eyes at them both. She and Quentin were in a good place, and she had no intention of rocking the boat. And as long as she kept rocking Quentin's world, she wouldn't have to.

CHAPTER 2

Estelle watched in silence as chaos unfolded in her living room. These children, her grandchildren, were out of control. Her son treated them with kid gloves because they'd lost their mother, but after five years they were no longer mourning—just taking advantage of their daddy.

The worst of the bunch was the oldest girl, Deirdre. From sunup to sundown she was on the phone talking to random thugs. The all-girls private school they spent thousands a year in tuition for did not seem to curb Deirdre's taste for all things hood.

Completely exasperated, Estelle snatched the phone from Deirdre. "Grandma!" Deirdre screamed.

"Deirdre is busy right now," Estelle said, ignoring her granddaughter's pleas. "She will call you back later . . . What do you mean, who is this? It is her grandmother. And as a matter of fact, she will not be calling you back."

Estelle disconnected the call and handed the phone back to Deirdre. The teenager's angry scowl didn't faze Estelle one bit, although the young girl did in that moment look exactly like her mother. That tugged Estelle's heartstrings a little, but not enough for her to tolerate foolishness.

"Grandma, that was my boyfriend."

"He sounded like a thug. You can do better."

"I don't want to do better."

Estelle shook her head and frowned. "Your mother would be . . ."

"Turning over in her grave! I know, Grandma. But since she's gone, she doesn't really get a say on my boyfriends, now does she?"

"Maybe not, but I do." Quentin had entered the room. Estelle grinned when he kissed her on the cheek.

Deirdre rolled her eyes. "Well, if I left it up to you and Grandma, I'd never have a boyfriend."

"A boyfriend shouldn't be your priority, Deirdre. You've got your mind on the wrong thing."

"Nobody complains about your girlfriend . . ."

Quentin raised an eyebrow at the insolent teenager, but Estelle stifled a giggle. It was no secret that neither Deirdre nor the other children were fans of Chloe, Quentin's lady friend. Estelle had gotten a bad taste in her mouth about the woman on the day of her daughter-in-law's funeral. She claimed to be Chandra's college friend, but no one had ever heard of her. Nevertheless, she'd hung around just enough to get Quentin interested in her, and to Estelle's dismay he'd taken a liking to her; he was seen all over town with her on his arm.

Quentin said, "That's the great thing about being an adult. You don't have to answer to anyone about your romances."

"Grandma says we all have to answer to God."

Before Quentin got an opportunity to respond to that statement, eleven-year-old Danielle skated through the living room at breakneck speed. In hot pursuit were the fourteen-year-old twins, Madison and Morgan.

"Give me my iPad!" Morgan screamed.

Danielle laughed and eluded capture by twirling around a very expensive antique credenza. Estelle inhaled sharply at the thought of that family heirloom being harmed by horseplay.

"I think Daddy should know that you are Skyping boys on here," Danielle said.

Madison said, "She is not! We're trying to do a homework assignment."

Quentin caught Danielle on her next orbit of the room and took the tablet from her. "What kind of homework assignment?" he asked.

"It's a social experiment," Morgan explained. "We're trying to figure out what would happen if a totally z-list boy got attention from an a-list girl."

"The ramifications of such a thing are epic. It could change the whole sociopolitical landscape of middle school," Madison said.

Deirdre laughed out loud. "Enjoy the boys while you can! Next year you'll be brutally forced into a world of all girls."

"No! Daddy said we could go to Reese's high school!" Madison said.

Deirdre's jaw dropped. Estelle knew Deidre was going to have an issue with allowing the twins to go to the high school where their brother, Reese, was a graduating senior. Deirdre had been sent to the all-girls school because of her boy-crazy shenanigans in middle school. There was no reason to subject the twins to the same fate because of her actions. Deirdre hated St. Mary's Preparatory School for Girls with a passion saved for first loves and chocolate.

"Is this true, Daddy?" Deirdre asked.

"I haven't made any decisions one way or the other," Quentin said, but his facial expression told a different story.

Madison and Morgan gave Deirdre smug looks, and she sent the twins daggers with her eyes. Estelle knew this battle wasn't over, especially since Deirdre was dead set on seeing boys at school every day.

"Girls, give me a moment with your father, please," Estelle said, as she directed the roller-skating Danielle toward the double staircase, though she wondered how that child navigated the mansion on wheels.

The twins followed their little sister upstairs, but Deirdre remained on the couch, flipping through a magazine.

"You too, Deirdre. Go find something to do that doesn't include boys."

Deirdre gave her grandmother a deadpan gaze. "Well, Grandmother, I have no idea what that would be."

"Deirdre, stop antagonizing your grandmother," Quentin said.

Deirdre stomped toward the entrance to the downstairs game room. "She should stop antagonizing me."

Estelle shook her head as Deirdre exited. "That girl!"

"I know, Mother. I know. What do you want me to do about it?"

"Maybe if you spent more time with them . . ."

Quentin sighed. "You're right. I'm going to make a plan to take Deirdre on a daddy/daughter date right now. Deirdre!"

Deirdre appeared at the top of the stairs with an annoyed look on her face. "Yes?"

"I was thinking that you and I should go to a concert and to dinner. How's Saturday sound?"

Deirdre shuddered. "Or you could just give me money and I could go to a concert with my friends."

Quentin looked at Estelle. "Sure, honey. We'll chat about it later."

Deirdre rolled her eyes and went back down the stairs. Estelle shook her head and frowned.

"That didn't prove anything," Estelle said. "You're not off the hook."

Quentin sighed. "Is this a lecture about the church or about the foundation?"

"It's actually a lecture about neither. I'd like to talk to you about getting a nanny for the youngest three."

"A nanny? The twins will be going to high school next year, and Danielle is nearly old enough to be left alone. They don't need a nanny."

Estelle said, "Not a preschool nanny, but someone who can help them with homework, be here when they have questions about being young ladies, and maybe . . . a friend."

"Isn't that what their grandmother is for?" Quentin asked.

"Besides, they've got Chloe if they want to talk to a younger woman."

Estelle burst into laughter at the mention of Chloe. The children couldn't stand her. "I'm quite busy with the church, and I'm not even going to comment on that woman."

"They don't need a nanny, Mother. Deirdre can watch the younger three."

"And then who is watching Deirdre? Last week one of the sisters at the church thought she saw her in a movie theater slobbering all over that boyfriend of hers."

"Your church snitches are rarely accurate. Last I heard they were saying I'm gay because I haven't remarried."

"This has nothing to do with your marital status."

"Well, what brought all this on, Mother? Are you concerned with that check I had Tippen write to the foundation?"

Estelle stared at her son and gave him a stern expression. The half-million-dollar check Quentin had had his lawyer write to his pet project, the Transitions Foundation, was somewhat disconcerting. The cause, though, a group home for terminal cancer patients without the necessary resources to ease the pain at the end of their lives, was really important to Quentin.

"I would like to be aware of you spending my grandchildren's inheritance, but no, that is not what brought this on. I think it is time for things to get back to some semblance of normalcy. Just how long are you going to stay away from the church? The music ministry isn't the same without . . ."

"Say it. Without me and Chandra. There is no way I can sit at that keyboard without Chandra directing the choir. I can't play. I can't write. I can't sing . . . all of it reminds me of her. So I work with the foundation, and I enjoy my time with Chloe. I'm trying to live."

"And what about the children? Don't they deserve to live too? They need someone around them who isn't grieving."

"Mother, do whatever you want. Get a nanny. I don't care." There was defeat and resignation in Quentin's tone, but at least Estelle had a victory, albeit a small one.

Ms. Levy, the family housekeeper, entered the room with

Chloe. Although it wasn't required of her, Ms. Levy acted as butler, cook, staff manager, and close personal confidante to Estelle. Ms. Levy also chose her own uniform—all black with a straight skirt that came down to the middle of her calf. She was just showing off with the severe bun at the nape of her neck. It pulled her face back so tightly that she looked Asian.

"Ms. Brooks is here to see you, Mr. Chambers," Ms. Levy said.

Chloe's appearance was a stark contrast to Ms. Levy's. Estelle took in her ensemble—a knee-length, tan, vintage Dolce & Gabbana sundress. It was perfect for the warm Atlanta spring day, and it flattered Chloe's perfectly sculpted body. There were a lot of things Estelle could say about Chloe, but she could never take issue with the woman's appearance. She certainly looked the part of a high-society lady, even if her past exploits, spoken of in whispers at the country club, told a completely different story.

Chloe gave Ms. Levy a dismissive wave of her hand. "When are you going to stop announcing me every time I come over? I'm practically a member of the family. We're on our way to a yacht party, for crying out loud. He's expecting me."

"I will stop announcing you when you are an official member of the family," Ms. Levy said, without a moment's hesitation.

"Uh, thank you, Ms. Levy," Quentin said.

Estelle said, "Come on, Ms. Levy. We've got a nanny to find."

"Will I be allowed to interview her?" Ms. Levy asked.

"Of course."

Chloe walked over to Quentin and threw her arms around his neck. She planted soft kisses on his face and lips. Quentin leaned back and smiled.

"Are you sure you're trying to go to a party? You sure you're not starting something else?"

Chloe laughed. "We can always go upstairs and have our own little party inside."

"Upstairs? Nah, but we could go to the Four Seasons."

"Why go to a hotel, when my man has a mansion?"

Quentin untangled himself from Chloe's grip. "You know, babe. The kids."

"Right, the kids. The kids who need a nanny. Aren't your children a little old for a nanny?" Chloe asked.

"Yes, but my mother won't rest until she's got Mary Poppins flying around my home with an umbrella in her hand."

Chloe stared blankly at Quentin, as if she didn't get the reference.

"Don't tell me you haven't seen *Mary Poppins.*"

She cocked her head to one side. "Is that one of those cutesy movies where everyone is sweet, and the sweet sappiness continues until they're happily sappily ever after?"

"Pretty much," Quentin said.

"Yeah, no. I've never seen that, sweetheart."

"Never mind, Chloe. My mother is going to do whatever she wants to do. No one says no to her."

Chloe didn't voice her response to this with words, but if Quentin had been paying attention, he would have noticed the grimace on her face. In her opinion, someone should say no to Estelle. Those girls didn't need a nanny; they just needed an all-girls boarding school. Far, far away. So she could spend time with her man in his home and not at a hotel.

"I'm not sure I agree with your mother, not that anyone asked my opinion. The girls have entered puberty, for crying out loud."

"That's exactly what I said," Quentin replied. "Maybe if you spent some time with them, my mother would change her mind."

"Or m-maybe your mother is right. Who am I to question their grandmother?"

Quentin burst into laughter at Chloe's reaction to spending time with his children. In all the years they'd been enjoying each other's company, she'd never once mentioned becoming his children's stepmother.

"Is this what you're wearing to the yacht party?" Chloe asked.

Quentin looked down at his outfit. "Right, the party. What do you want me to wear?"

"Something that makes you look incredibly hot."

Quentin shook his head. "You're starting again."

"I know. I'm sorry." Chloe giggled.

"While I'm getting dressed, I want you to think about my fund-raiser for the foundation. I'd love to talk about it tonight with Lichelle and her band of millionaires. They should want to support this cause."

"Where's the fund-raiser going to be again?"

"The Georgia Aquarium."

"The Aquarium? Why can't you have it right here? That ballroom is just waiting to have a party."

Quentin considered this idea for a moment. They hadn't entertained in years—since before Chandra had died. There was a time, though, when his mother had thrown legendary parties, and he and Chandra had enjoyed them immensely. What better reason for a party than the foundation that was started in Chandra's honor? Plus, having the party at their mansion would ensure that more of the donations would go directly to the foundation.

"That might be a great idea."

Chloe's eyes lit up. "And I could coordinate it. It will be incredible."

"Maybe you could work with my mother on making it spectacular."

Chloe looked annoyed at this statement, but Quentin was just trying to prepare her for the inevitable. There was no way Chloe was planning a party in Estelle's home without Estelle having the final say on every phase of the plans. The Chambers estate was Estelle's queendom, and she was the only queen.

"I suppose that would be a way for your mother and me to get a little bit closer. I'm not sure she likes me very much."

"She likes you because I like you."

That declaration made Chloe smile and erased any looks of concern regarding working with Estelle. And Quentin needed the peace. He was allergic to drama, and for the most part Chloe didn't seem to come with it. She wanted to enjoy life, and he was trying to learn how to enjoy it again. It had been five years since he'd lost the love of his life, and he was still in a haze. But Chloe helped.

"Hurry and get dressed," Chloe admonished. "And wear something pastel, but not white. It's not quite white season yet."

Chloe watched Quentin rush out of the room and then sat down on the couch with a satisfied grin on her face. Her boyfriend was nearly a billionaire. He didn't even need to hold a fund-raiser for his foundation. She knew he did it because he wanted everyone to care about his cause. She admired him for that. At times she felt herself falling in love with him for that, but she stopped short. There was no way she was going to give her heart to Quentin when his heart wasn't available to her. As long as his money was available, she would be okay. The Chambers family had built an empire of chemical products for the African-American woman's hair. Chloe had never used any of their greasy gels or sprays. She giggled at the irony of how she enjoyed spending that money.

"What's so funny?" Deirdre asked.

Chloe rolled her eyes. The girl had interrupted her thoughts. "Nothing. An inner musing."

"Whatever that means. You and my daddy going somewhere?"

"Yes, sweetie. Your father is taking me to a dinner party on a yacht and probably to see some friends for dessert and coffee."

Deirdre looked Chloe up and down. Unintimidated, Chloe returned the look. The girl did not bother her one bit—or worry her. Deirdre had no idea what she was up against.

"Did my daddy have to pay for this party?"

"No, it's nothing like that. There's no charge for this. A friend is having a birthday party. They love to entertain."

"It's free? Wow! I'm surprised because you usually cost my daddy lots of money."

Chloe tossed her head back and gave a throaty laugh. "Trust and believe, I do not have any problem spending your father's money. That is one of the perks of having a rich boyfriend." Did she say that? Yes she did. "Remember that, honey . . . that advice was free."

As if Deirdre would ever have to worry about a man with money. It annoyed Chloe that this girl had no idea how fortunate she was. She'd never have to wonder if the man she was dating would ever marry her. Deirdre would have more suitors than she could count, because she was an heiress to a ridiculous fortune.

Danielle entered the room and plopped down on the couch next to Chloe. Chloe's lips became a thin line. She guessed it was annoy Chloe time.

"Hello there," Danielle said. "Do you want to play with me?"

"Play? Play what?"

Danielle said, "We could play dolls or Dance Revolution on my Wii."

"It'll have to be some other time, honey. I'm afraid I'm all done up for a party."

Danielle took in Chloe's appearance. "I think you're pretty. I really like your makeup. Did you do it yourself?"

"Oh, no, sweetie. This look, right here, takes an entire team," Chloe replied, as if it was the most ridiculous question she'd ever heard.

"Can you show me how to do it?" Danielle asked. "I want to look glamorous too."

"Daddy said no makeup until you're sixteen," Deirdre said. "You might as well forget about that."

"Sixteen? That's preposterous," Chloe said. "I've known how to properly apply lipstick, mascara, eyeliner, and eye shadow since I was twelve. A woman needs this in her arsenal."

"What's an arsenal?" Danielle asked.

"It's all the tricks that women use to trap their husbands," Deirdre said.

Danielle looked confused. "You have to trap them? I thought the prince comes along and finds his one true love and marries her. Trapping them seems scary. What if they don't want to be caught?"

"No man wants to be caught, honey," Chloe explained. "They're like wild animals that want to roam free. But if a woman is beautiful enough, and skillful enough, they will give in. They don't have the will to fight it."

Danielle gave Chloe a blank stare. Apparently all of this knowledge was too much for her.

"Um . . . can we play now?" Danielle asked. "Tag! You're it!"

Danielle tapped Chloe on the shoulder and skated away from the couch. Chloe didn't move a muscle. Was the girl lacking in cognitive skills? Didn't she say she wasn't going to ruin her yacht party look? After a couple of laps around the room, Danielle gave up trying to engage Chloe in her game of tag and skated out of the room, probably in search of someone else to harass. Chloe sighed with relief when the child had gone elsewhere.

Deirdre laughed out loud. "You do know you're going to have to play with her if you ever finally trap . . . I mean, marry my dad."

"We'll cross that bridge when we come to it."

"We're a package deal, you know," Deirdre continued. "You're going to have to get used to five children."

Chloe laughed. "I don't have a problem at all with motherhood. As long as it includes some very expensive, very elite boarding schools."

"I'm going to tell my father you said that."

"Don't be silly, Deirdre. You'll find that I make a much better ally than an enemy."

As if on cue, Quentin returned, now ready for the yacht party in a dapper sky-blue jacket and gray slacks. Chloe rose to her feet and kissed Quentin on the cheek.

"Look at you! Don't you clean up nicely?"

Quentin smiled and seemed to melt at the attention. "Thank you."

Chloe looked over at Deirdre stealthily and winked. Deirdre seethed and rolled her eyes.

"Deirdre, we're going out for a while, and we'll probably be out late, so don't wait up for us."

"Okay, Daddy, I won't," Deirdre said.

Quentin leaned in and inhaled Chloe's scent. "What is that perfume you're wearing? I just can't get enough of it."

"Oh, it's nothing, love. Just something in my arsenal."

Chloe gave Deirdre another wink as she and her date left the house. She had meant what she said about being a better ally than an enemy. Deirdre would do well to get on her good side, because she intended to have Quentin and everything that belonged to him, and there wasn't a teenager, roller-skating little girl, or sour-faced mother that could stop her.

CHAPTER 3

Deirdre was glad Chloe had gotten her father out of the house, because she had plans for the evening. Her grandmother had choir practice, and getting past Ms. Levy was easy, but it was dang near impossible to sneak out when their father was home. It was like he had supersonic ears or something.

Deirdre pulled out her cell phone and sent her boyfriend, Moe, a text message. I'm ready now. Pick me up at the edge of our drive.

A few minutes later, Moe replied to her text: I'm waiting for you.

Deirdre hopped up from the couch and made a dash for the door. Of course, the snitches Morgan and Madison came into the room just as she was leaving.

"Where are you going?" Madison asked. "Daddy didn't say you could go out."

"You don't know what Daddy told me. Why don't you go play with your little friends on the Internet and mind your business."

"Pay us," Morgan said, "or we'll tell Daddy you snuck out."

"I'm not paying you anything, and I'm not sneaking. I'm just going."

"Really? Let's see what Ms. Levy has to say," Madison opened her mouth to yell, and Deirdre clasped a hand over her mouth.

"Okay, snitches, I am going out with Moe."

Morgan said, "I knew it!"

"But he is really nice, so I need y'all to cover for me."

Madison and Morgan looked at each other. They both turned and stuck their hands out.

"Pay up," they said in unison.

Deirdre reached in her purse and pulled out a twenty-dollar bill. "You'll have to split this. It's all I have."

Madison said, "Twenty bucks? This is enough for us not to initiate a snitch. It's not enough to keep us from telling if someone asks."

"Right," Morgan said. "So you better get home before Daddy if you know what's good for you."

Once Deirdre finally got rid of her little sisters, she quietly left the house and headed to meet Moe. This was one of the few times Deirdre regretted living on their huge estate. It would take her about ten minutes to walk to the edge of their property. Peach and magnolia trees lined both sides of the walkway, their aromatic scents filling the warm spring evening.

Deirdre looked at her watch. It was nine o'clock. She calculated that she had about three hours to spend with her boyfriend before anyone noticed she was missing. Maybe her father would stay out all night with that gold digger Chloe.

Deirdre wondered why no one except her seemed to notice that Chloe was after her dad's money. She remembered Chloe showing up at her mother's funeral in a too-tight dress with her breasts spilling everywhere. She claimed to be a friend of her mother's from college, but no one had ever heard of her. Deirdre's dad was clueless, and he was a mark from day one. A mark with a whole lot of cash.

A huge smile burst onto Deirdre's face when she approached Moe's car. Although it wasn't a baller's ride, the black Nissan would do. Most of the boys who tried to talk to Deirdre couldn't even pick her up. They could only call her on the phone and send text messages.

Moe took two steps toward Deirdre and encircled her in a

hug. She liked the smell of the expensive cologne she had given Moe for his birthday.

Deirdre said, "Hey, Moe. You smell good."

"Oh, you like that? It's some of that expensive stuff. Some rich girl got it for me."

"You got a rich girlfriend?"

"She is paid, fo' sho'."

Moe opened the car door for Deirdre to get in. He might be a thug, but at least he was polite. Well, he was almost a thug. Moe was a member of their church, Freedom of Life, and had known their family since he was a baby. He didn't attend church much, though, which was great for Deirdre. Church boys made her itch.

"So, how were you able to escape? I thought you said your dad was home."

"His old bootleg girlfriend came over, and they went on a boat or something."

"Your dad's girlfriend is fine. She ain't bootleg. I saw her at church and thought, 'she could get it.' "

"What? You better stop playing."

Moe laughed as he pulled away from the mansion. "You know I'm just playing with you."

"Yeah, whatever. She gets on my nerves."

"Why you always gotta sneak out to meet me, though? Why don't you just tell your dad about me?"

Deirdre laughed out loud. "You do know my father is insane, right?"

"The parents always love Moe."

Deirdre doubted this was true. Moe was the type of guy fathers hated. He was dangerously handsome, with his long hair that he wore in a slicked back ponytail and his thick goatee that wanted to be a beard but wasn't quite there yet. A star athlete at his school, Decatur High, Moe had a muscular body. He looked like he was ready to lose his virginity or, worse, take some girl's virtue.

"Maybe some parents love you, but my dad is a lunatic. He already has me at an all-girls school with a bunch of lames. I don't want to be on total lockdown."

"At some point you're going to have to let us meet. You can't hide me forever."

Deirdre's smile beamed in Moe's direction. "You're planning on being around forever?"

"Forever, ever."

Deirdre reached across and held Moe's free hand while he drove. She'd never felt this way about any other boy, and while she knew most people didn't stay with the people they dated as teens, she hoped they'd be the exception.

"So where am I going?" Moe asked. "You didn't say where you wanted to go."

"I don't know."

"You wanna go skating?" Moe asked.

"No. The last time we went to the rink, someone from church saw us and told my grandmother. I almost got grounded."

"So . . ."

"I just want to do something exciting."

Moe laughed. "I mean what you trying to do? Sneak in the club?"

"Maybe . . ."

"Well, we could go over my cousin's house in Decatur. They're having a little house party."

Deirdre clapped her hands. This was exactly the type of thing she was talking about. She was sick of church skating parties and shut-ins where a bunch of church kids sat around pretending not to be bad when they really were, or wanting to be bad when they were incredibly scared to do anything other than read the Sunday school primer. Deirdre wanted to experience life outside of church. Her father had given his entire life to church, and look at what it had gotten him.

"I definitely want to do the party. Let's go!"

"All right. Okay. Party it is," Moe says.

"Do you know what time it's going to be over?"

Moe shook his head and laughed as he pulled onto I-20. "You can't want to kick it hard and then worry about what time you're gonna get home. These kinds of parties don't have an end time. They go until."

"Until when?"

"They're over," Moe said. "Forget it, I'm about to take you to IHOP to eat. You ain't ready."

Deirdre slumped in her seat and crossed her arms across her chest. "I am ready. I was just trying to see if I was gonna have to sneak back in or walk through the front door."

"If I take you over my cousin's house, you gonna have to sneak in."

"Okay, then, let's go."

Moe still seemed hesitant, so Deirdre repeated, "Let's go. I'm serious."

"We'll go, but don't be trying to blame me if you get in trouble."

"They don't run me like that."

"Oh, you a boss now?" Moe laughed so hard that he snorted.

Deirdre rolled her eyes and pounded the dashboard. "Just drive!"

When they pulled up to his cousin's house, Deirdre tried to hide her nervous energy from Moe. There were cars parked along the side of the house and in the yard. There weren't any cars in the driveway, because there were three very frightening-looking dogs there in a huge, cage-like contraption. It was too late, of course, for Deirdre to change her mind, but she wished she'd let Moe talk her out of this.

"You okay, baby girl?" Moe asked when she paused before stepping out of the car.

Deirdre gave him her fakest smile. "I'm cool. Just afraid of dogs."

"They're on lockdown. They can't get you."

Deirdre and Moe walked into the party with his arm around her waist. She couldn't have been more ecstatic. He was claiming her to his friends and cousins, and not just to the lame boys he knew from church. These were his hood friends. That meant she was down enough and fly enough, no matter how much money there was in the Chambers fortune.

The small house was dimly lit, and it was very hard to see through the foggy, smoky haze that filled the room. For half a second Deirdre was scared. The whole scene reminded her of one of those Lifetime movies where a teenage girl wakes up clutching her tattered clothing, unable to remember the previous night. But then, as she focused on each face in the room, her nerves calmed. These were regular teenagers getting together for fun, and even though the room was smoky, only one person seemed to be actually partaking in the weed. Everyone else drank soda out of cups and balanced plates with spaghetti, chips, and burgers on their laps.

"Hey, y'all, this is my girl Deirdre. Can y'all make her feel like family?"

"Yeah," shouted one of the guys. "Just like kissin' cousins."

Deirdre chuckled nervously as Moe led her to a tiny love seat near the back of the living room. At least everyone wasn't paired off. There was a boxing match playing on a big flat-screen TV that was mounted on the wall. Deirdre glanced around at the other meager furniture and decided the TV was out of place.

"You okay?" Moe whispered, as he put his arm around Deirdre. "You seem a little uptight."

She nodded and repeated her words from earlier. "I'm cool."

Deirdre felt herself relax even more when one of the cousins brought her a plate of food. The spaghetti looked incredibly greasy—there was actually a puddle of orange-tinted grease around the glob of food, and the burger was cold, but she ate it with all the enthusiasm she could muster. She wanted Moe's cousins to know that she accepted their hospitality.

The undercard boxing match ended, and the main fight started. Deirdre had no idea who the boxers were, so she cheered when Moe cheered. He seemed happy that his down, fly girlfriend was taking an interest in the sport.

"Who you got? Ruiz or Lopez?" one of the cousins asked Deirdre when she cheered again.

Since she hadn't bothered to learn their names, Deirdre said, "I've got the guy in the white shorts!"

"Lopez! Good choice. He's gonna put Ruiz to sleep in a couple of rounds."

Deirdre assumed that "putting to sleep" included winning the boxing match. She wondered if the party would be over then, because it was getting late, and it had taken about twenty minutes to get over here. She wanted to make it home before her father and be safely in bed by the time he got home.

Lopez delivered those winning punches just a few moments later. As everyone in the room cheered, Deirdre saw a gigantic cockroach scurry across the floor in her direction. It was almost as if the monstrous bug was charging. Deirdre closed her eyes tightly and gasped.

"What?" Moe asked.

"It's a r-roach!"

Moe burst into laughter as the roach scurried on past their feet and under the love seat where she and Moe were sitting. Deirdre immediately started squirming, because now all she could picture in her mind was the roach crawling up the back of the couch and jumping on her neck. Did roaches attack? Did they jump? She didn't know, but she was getting the heck off that love seat.

When Deirdre jumped up, Moe's laughter intensified, and now the others were looking in her direction with questions on their faces. Deirdre was beyond embarrassed, but she couldn't make herself sit back down.

"What's wrong witchu?" The pretty, round girl who asked the question looked Deirdre up and down like she was crazy.

"Nothing," Deirdre replied. "I just like standing up. My legs get restless sometimes."

"She's scared of a roach!" Moe blurted. His giggles made Deirdre want to choke the sound out of his throat.

"You ain't never seen a roach before? Girl, bye." The round girl gave Deirdre a disgusted look. So much for fitting in with Moe's family and friends.

Deirdre didn't want to admit that she hadn't ever seen a roach up close before. It wasn't her fault that the Chambers family exterminated.

"Well . . . uh . . ."

"Deirdre?" A loud and very recognizable voice boomed behind Deirdre. She spun on one heel and found herself eye to eye with her brother, Reese.

"What are you doing here?" Reese asked, his voice not lowering one bit.

Deirdre was in utter shock. Her legs were shaking so badly that she could feel her knees knock. Then she took in her brother's appearance. His clothes were disheveled, and there was a girl with him who definitely looked like she'd just done something the mothers of the church would get all up in arms about.

"What are you doing here, brother? Looks like you're doing more than I am."

Moe jumped up from the love seat. "Reese, she just wanted to hang. Nothing popped off."

Reese looked Moe up and down. "Don't think my sister is about to be your next little freak. It's not going down like that."

"Stop it, Reese. He really likes me." Deirdre didn't like the sound of her voice when she said that. It seemed too desperate, and she thought that maybe she should've let Moe proclaim his honorable intentions.

Reese grabbed Deirdre's arm too roughly for her liking. "Come on. Let's go."

Finally, Reese's girlfriend spoke up. "You're leaving? I thought we were gonna hang."

"Sorry, babe. I gotta take my sister home. I'll call you later."

The girlfriend sucked her teeth and gave Deirdre an evil glare. "You better."

"You don't have to do this, man. I'll make sure she gets home okay," Moe said.

Reese narrowed his eyes and gave a tight head shake. "This is my sister. I know how you roll. Stay away from her."

Still holding on to Deirdre, Reese pulled her toward the door. She looked back at Moe, wishing he would rescue her from her brute of a brother. Deirdre had to go with Reese—there was no way she could let him go home without her. He'd tell their dad on her.

Once they were in Reese's car, he started yelling. "What are you thinking, Dee? Do you know what happens to girls like you at those kinds of parties?"

Deirdre ignored him. He wasn't her daddy.

"For real, Dee. You trying to be a baby mama out here?"

"I know you are not talking. Are you trying to have a baby mama out here?"

Reese didn't answer the question as he sped back toward the safety of their mansion.

Deirdre gasped when she saw her father's Benz in the garage. It was the car he'd driven to the yacht party. She knew because she'd watched him as he drove off, and he was definitely still awake because the barracuda's Lexus was parked in the circular drive. Chloe never spent the night, but sometimes their father drove her home. He hardly ever went to pick Chloe up for their outings, which in Deirdre's opinion said something about their relationship, and it wasn't something good.

"Reese, Daddy is still up . . ."

"Good. I need to tell him where you been hanging out."

Deirdre shook her head in confusion. "Reese, you were there too."

"Totally different."

"Why you gotta be a snitch?"

" 'Cause you my little sister, and you not about to be a ho out here. If I hadn't been there, Moe would've had you in the back room."

Deirdre jumped out of the car and slammed the door. If Reese was planning to snitch, she wasn't going to give him the pleasure. She was going to walk into the house and deal with her dad herself.

Although their mansion was huge, there was only one way

upstairs, and that was the big double staircase. Unfortunately, the main parlor was the highest-traffic area of the home.

All of Deirdre's boldness faded when she saw her father pacing the floor a few feet away from her. He hadn't noticed her sneak in, but Reese was on her heels, so it was only a matter of moments before her life was over.

"Who is that? Reese?" Quentin asked when he heard Deirdre try to tiptoe upstairs.

"No. It's me, Daddy." Deirdre's voice shook as her father stormed out of the sitting room with Chloe on his heels.

"You were out at this hour? Where have you been?"

Deirdre's first inclination was to lie, but she knew that would never work. "I was hanging with Moe, at his cousin's house in Decatur."

"I must be in the *Twilight Zone* or something. Did my sixteen-year-old daughter just tell me she went out with a boy without my permission? Are you out of your mind?"

Chloe followed Quentin and gave Deirdre an irritated glare. Deirdre was sure she had interrupted some conversation about something Chloe wanted to buy—with her father's money.

When Deirdre didn't say anything, Quentin continued, "No child of mine is gonna be out in the street at night like she's tricking for dollars."

Reese walked through the door and gave his sister a sympathetic look. Deirdre wondered if he had forgotten, while he was planning his snitch festival, how their father acted when he was angry.

"Dad, she wasn't doing anything bad."

"You were with her?"

"We just kind of ended up at the same place, I guess."

Quentin lifted both hands to the sky. Deirdre wondered if he was praying. "So both of my kids are hanging out in the hood?"

"Quentin, babe, maybe you're overreacting. Everyone is safe. Didn't you ever do anything like this when you were their age?" Chloe said, while stroking Quentin's back.

Quentin shrugged off Chloe's touch. "These are my children. I didn't ask for your input."

"I was just trying to . . . help."

"You're not helping," Quentin said.

"Well, since I'm not part of this little family affair, I'm going home. Will you at least walk me to my car?" Chloe asked. "It will give you some much-needed time to calm down."

Quentin said, "Yes, of course. Deirdre and Reese, if you know what's good for you, you'll be out of my sight by the time I get back in here. And don't even think about going out anywhere."

Deirdre pouted as her father walked out the door with Chloe. The daggers coming from Chloe's eyes could have cut through a boulder.

"You so stupid," Reese said. "I wasn't really gonna tell on you."

"Whatever, Reese. How was I supposed to know that?"

Deirdre ran the rest of the way up the huge staircase and into her bedroom. She threw herself onto her bed and bawled into her pillow. No one understood what she was going through. If she just had someone who would speak up for her. She knew it would be different if her mother had lived. Everything would be different.

But Deirdre knew, just as her dad and her siblings knew, that there was no amount of crying, praying, or shouting that would bring her back.

CHAPTER 4

Montana belted out the solo to "Encourage Yourself" by Donald Lawrence and the Tri-City Singers as if it had been written just for her. Even though it was only rehearsal, the entire choir at Freedom of Life Church had gone into worship from the rousing rendition of the song, and even though Montana was feeling pretty hopeless, she had to admit that singing always made her feel better.

The day had started out all wrong, with a notice to move within three days plastered on her door first thing in the morning. She'd begged her landlord to give her more time to come up with the rent, but it had been a month and a half since she'd had any money to give. She'd been laid off from her job three months ago and had yet to find another one. If only that call center had waited just a few more months until she'd gotten her teaching certificate before they'd sent her packing, then she might have been able to rebound more quickly.

Anyway, in a few days she was going to be homeless in Atlanta, the last thing she'd ever wanted. Of course, she could go home to her family in Ohio, but she was getting too old to keep running back home every time she lost a job—or a man.

She needed encouragement, and a miracle.

When the choir director, Brother Odom, asked for any prayer requests, the usually timid Montana jumped out of her seat. She was desperate for a breakthrough, and that desperation broke down every bit of her shyness and inhibition.

"What's your prayer request, Montana? Or do you have a testimony?" Brother Odom asked.

Montana shook her head sadly, and before she began to speak, tears started to trickle down her face. "Maybe soon I'll have a testimony, but right now I'm in the middle of a test. Some of you know I've been unemployed for three months. I do receive unemployment, but I'm about to be evicted from my apartment. Y'all, please pray for me. I have a few job interviews lined up, but I won't be able to get a substitute teaching job until the beginning of next school year. I need this like yesterday."

Montana slowly eased herself back down in her seat. She felt lighter after sharing her struggle. The hugs and words of prayer and encouragement helped too.

After rehearsal, Montana's friend Emoni, the daughter of the pastor, came up to her and gave her a hug. "Girl, you sang that song, for real! You know that God's got you, right?"

Montana nodded and hugged her friend back. There was no one in Atlanta that Montana was closer to than Emoni, but even she didn't know the extent of Montana's financial problems.

"I know He's got me. It might not feel like it sometimes, but . . ."

"But nothing. Things are going to change for you. I feel it in my spirit," Emoni said.

"Okay. No buts. I just wish He'd hurry up."

Emoni stroked Montana's arm lovingly and squeezed her hand. "We're all going to Houlihan's. You want to ride over with us? Trent's going to be there . . ."

Montana rolled her eyes playfully and chuckled. Emoni was always trying to hook her up with someone. The current eligible bachelor was a guy named Trent. He was nice enough, but Montana wasn't attracted to him at all. He was the opposite of everything she liked physically. And while she knew looks weren't everything, they were something. Plus, she didn't have McDonald's money, much less Houlihan's.

"I'm gonna pass, okay? Don't be mad at me."

Emoni twisted her lips into a frown. "It's Saturday night. Are you just gonna turn into an old maid hermit?"

"Why I gotta be an old maid and a hermit?"

"Come on, girl. I know your money is tight. I'll spot you for dinner."

The thought of a real meal made Montana's mouth water. She hadn't had a steak in about six months, since her ex-boyfriend Rio had taken her out for a reconciliation dinner.

Rio. Montana's stomach flipped at the thought of him. If she wanted to resolve her financial problems instantly, all she had to do was call Rio and welcome him back into her bedroom. It would be as easy as stepping into a pair of Victoria's Secret panties and teddy.

Montana remembered the day they'd met. It replayed over and over in her mind like a video stuck on repeat.

It was raining that day, but it was still scorching hot. A downpour on day four in a week of record-breaking temperatures. Montana was on her way home from an interview for a job she was sure she wouldn't get, but she'd stopped at Caribou Coffee for her favorite drink, a Caramel High Rise with a pump of cherry. The drink would make her feel better and give her the energy to comb the Internet classifieds again when she got home.

When she stepped into the line for coffee, Montana slipped on a puddle of rainwater and fell directly into Rio's arms. She'd been embarrassed. He'd given her a smile that melted her heart. Then he said the words that changed the next three years of her life.

"Don't you think you should learn my name before you fall for me?"

That witty humor had captured her attention from the very start. Not to mention his smooth, buttery-gold skin and huge, expressive eyes. She'd starting falling for him that very moment.

Rio had been Montana's first grown-up relationship. Before him, her boyfriends were as sporadic as her jobs. She'd dated a string of guys in college and beyond, but none of those relationships had ever gone past a few months and a few rolls in the hay. She hated to think of the number of guys she'd been with; it wasn't a number she was proud of. When she hit the age of thirty and had to count her partners on more than her two hands, she knew she was tired of being a "get around" girl, but how could she know that the next guy wouldn't be the one?

Montana hesitated for several dates before finally acquiescing and giving Rio the goodies. To her surprise, he stayed. Rio told Montana that he wanted to be monogamous, and that one day they would get married.

Three years later they were still dating, and halfway shacking. Montana's family would have a fit if they knew. Shoot, as far as she knew, they all thought she was still a virgin.

When Montana joined Freedom of Life, Bishop Prentiss had preached a series for single women called "Far Above Rubies." Montana remembered going home and telling Rio she couldn't sleep with him anymore until they were married. His response broke her heart.

He'd said, "You can't just cut a brotha off like that. You can't change the rules in the middle of the game. If I had known you were going to go celibate, I wouldn't have taken your phone number."

And that night she'd slept with him like she'd never heard the message.

But God kept pulling at her heartstrings, and she'd finally broken up with Rio and rededicated her life to the Lord. They had been practically living together, although he maintained his own apartment. And since Rio was an engineer who clocked a six-figure income, he supplemented Montana's income and kept her afloat.

It broke Montana's heart that Rio wouldn't respect her newfound faith. She loved him and had imagined walking down the aisle to meet him at the altar. She had seen herself having his children.

When she cut Rio off for good, she knew it was going to be tough financially, but she'd budget, eat sparingly, and stop having her specialty cups of coffee. She didn't have to be Rio's kept woman—God would keep her.

Tonight, in fact, God was gonna hook her up with a nice steak dinner.

"Okay, I'll go!" Montana said. "But do not try to hook me up with Trent. He is not my type. Just because you and Darrin are getting married doesn't mean we all have to pair off."

Emoni raised her eyebrows. "Girl, I've been wearing this engagement ring for two years. If we don't hurry up down the aisle my daddy is gonna start interviewing new suitors."

"Well, then, you need to stop being a runaway bride. I know it's all you."

Emoni waved over at her very fine fiancé. "You're right. It is all me. I just want to be sure. Come on and ride with me. I'll bring you back to the church to get your car when we're done."

"Okay." Montana was glad Emoni offered to drive. Her gas had to stretch until her unemployment check came on Wednesday, and she didn't have any extra for recreational trips.

As they were leaving, Estelle Chambers stopped Montana and Emoni. Emoni hugged and kissed the older woman, who was very good friends with her parents. Montana had heard that the Chambers family had helped found the church with their fortune.

"Sweetie, can I talk to you for a moment?" Montana was shocked when Estelle took her hand and pulled her away from Emoni.

Emoni winked at Montana. "I'll be waiting outside."

Montana watched Emoni walk away and wished she'd stayed for the conversation. Montana barely knew Estelle, and having a one-on-one conversation with an almost stranger caused Montana's heart to race.

"Mother Chambers, can I help you with something?"

Estelle burst into laughter. "Girl, if you call me Mother Chambers one more time, I don't think we'll ever be friends."

"I'm so sorry. I didn't mean . . ."

"It's all right. I'm joking. But please call me Estelle."

Montana nodded. "Okay."

"I was listening to you testify, and I'm so glad you did. I came to choir rehearsal tonight with a heart to bless somebody."

"You did?" Montana felt her heart leap. This lady was rich. She could solve all of Montana's problems with one check.

"I did. I'm hiring for a position in my home, and I was wondering if you'd be interested."

Montana swallowed twice. Was Estelle about to ask her to be a maid in that big old historical mansion?

"A position."

"Yes. Have you ever been a nanny?"

Montana sighed with relief. Estelle didn't want her to clean her floors; she wanted her to be a . . . wait. Estelle's grandchildren were hellions, and none of them seemed young enough for a nanny.

"I've never been a nanny, but I could sure try. Would it be for your grandchildren?"

Estelle smiled. "Yes, and I guess it isn't really a nanny that I'm looking for. I don't know the name for it now, but years ago they used to be called governesses. I just need someone who can assist with their homework and make sure they aren't tearing down Atlanta. My grandchildren aren't babies, but they're missing a woman's touch."

"They have you, don't they?"

"They do, but as much as I hate to admit it, I'm old. They need someone they can relate to. Do you want the job or not?"

She had never been a nanny or a governess a day in her life, but wouldn't it be like teaching? How could she say no? What if this was a blessing? What if this was God not leaving the righteous forsaken?

"Oh, I forgot to mention, it's a live-in job, so part of your compensation package would be room and board," Estelle said.

Montana felt tears well up again for the second time this evening. She sat down on the closest pew, because her knees were shaking so bad that she could barely stand. She was going from her apartment to the Chambers mansion? In Buckhead?

The one you couldn't even see from the street because there was so much land in front of it? The one that looked like a European castle?

"So, do you want the job?"

Montana nodded. "Yes, I do, but I think I should say that I'll be getting my teaching certificate soon. I hope to teach elementary school in a year or so, so it would be short term."

Estelle smiled. "A year? That sounds like just the right amount of time. Here's my address. Stop by tomorrow after church. We'll do all the paperwork and the background check next week, but I want you to meet my son."

"Your son?"

"Yes, the children's father. You've only been a member here for a few years, so you've never met him."

"Thank you so much, Estelle! I will definitely see you tomorrow."

Montana looked down at the card in her hand and smiled. How could she have ever doubted God?

CHAPTER 5

"Okay, give me the scoop on the Chambers family." Montana decided to grill Emoni for information on the way to the restaurant.

Emoni tapped the steering wheel and shrugged. "Well, they're filthy rich. No, let me take that back. They're wealthy."

"And the son? There's nothing weird going on there, right? Why doesn't he come to church with the rest of the family?"

"Quentin's wife, Chandra, died from cancer five years ago. She directed the choir, and he was the minister of music. He was pretty devastated."

Montana's lips formed a small *O.* "So that's why they need a nanny. I didn't want to ask what happened to their mother."

"You're going to be their nanny?"

Montana nodded. "Estelle just offered me the job, and told me I could move in too."

Emoni cheered and gave Montana a high five. "God is awesome!"

"Well, let's see how it's gonna work out first before you start testifying. What if they don't like me?"

"What's not to like? And Quentin is fine! I remember all the girls in the youth choir had a crush on him."

Montana considered this. "But he's a widower. Too much baggage."

"Yeah, you're right. And he's got that wretched Chloe as a girlfriend too."

Montana scrunched her nose at the mention of the socialite, heiress, or whatever she was. Chloe pranced around the church in her designer clothes as if she was blessing everyone with her presence. Montana never could understand people who didn't come to church for God, but the pews were full of Chloe types who only cared about socializing with the wealthy members of Freedom of Life.

"Well, I wonder why she doesn't spend time with his kids," Montana said. "Estelle acted like they needed a female role model or something."

"Think about it. Would you want that diva being any girl's role model? Plus, you love kids."

"I do! It just scares me to have a live-in job. If they don't like me, then I'm out on the street."

"They will like you. I promise. And this could be great for you."

Emoni pulled into Houlihan's parking lot. It was packed, but that was to be expected on a Saturday night. Montana almost wished she'd stuck to her guns and gone home. They had to be at church early, and she didn't want to be out all night kicking it. But since she'd let Emoni drive, she was trapped.

The guys were waiting outside the restaurant—Darrin, looking exceptional as usual, with his sidekick Trent. Trent was about five feet tall and loved to sport a tweed fedora, even if it didn't match his outfit. Instead of making him look hip and trendy, his black-rimmed glasses made him look like an extra from a civil-rights-era movie. Montana took a deep breath and prepared herself for his ridiculous attempts at flirting.

"Montana!"

The voice stopped her in her tracks. It was Rio. It was like she'd thought him up or something. She'd managed to avoid him for six months, but here he was about to witness her being set up with the man of no one's dreams.

Montana tried to wave from across the parking lot, but Rio was already jogging over. He'd even left his date standing next to his car. What kind of man does that? But then, Rio had always done exactly what he felt like doing at any given moment.

Instead of saying a polite hello, Rio scooped Montana into his arms and spun her around. The smell of his cologne was as dizzying as the spinning. He placed a soft kiss on her neck as he placed her back on the ground. It was not welcome at all. Montana hoped the scowl on her face communicated as much.

"Montana. I have missed you, girl."

"How have you been, Rio?" Montana asked, avoiding his declaration.

He cocked his head to one side and grinned. "Lonely. Why don't you let me come and see you?"

Montana panicked and then glanced over at Darrin and Trent. "Um . . . my new boyfriend wouldn't appreciate that."

Rio followed Montana's line of sight and focused in on Darrin. "I guess he's all right if you like that pretty model, Boris Kodjoe–lookin' type brotha."

Emoni cleared her throat. "That is my fiancé. Montana's . . . boyfriend . . . is the other one."

Rio's jaw dropped when he let his gaze fall on Trent. "Stop playing, Montana."

"What? He respects my faith, so he's exactly what I need."

Rio took Montana's hand and stroked the inside of her palm—a move that always drove her mad. She swallowed and snatched her hand away.

"Stop, Rio."

"Your man didn't even run over here to defend your honor. I'm blatantly hitting on you. If I was him, I'd be running up on me right now, hitting me with a two-piece."

Montana narrowed her eyes and blew an angry breath out of her nose. "He knows I can handle myself. Why don't you go take care of your date? She's waiting for you."

Rio scoffed. "Date? She knows exactly what she is. She's a maintenance chick. I need some, she needs some, so it's on."

"Rio, I'm gonna go now," Montana said, frustration punctuating her words.

"Okay, babe. It was good seeing you. Don't be a stranger." Rio said these words to Montana's back, because she'd snatched Emoni up and moved on.

Emoni whispered, "You were not believable at all. And, oh my glory, he is gorgeous. Is that your ex?"

Montana nodded. "Yep, that's Rio. The devil's nephew."

"How did you ever get the nerve to walk away from him?" Emoni asked. "He looks like one of those men who get you strung out."

Montana nodded in agreement. "He is one of those men, and seeing him just made me feel like I need a hit. Can you pray for me?"

"Right now?"

Montana nodded. "Yeah, now."

Emoni glanced over at the guys, who now looked a bit impatient, but then she took both of Montana's hands in hers.

"Dear God, I ask, in the name of Jesus, that you strengthen my sister. Help her to know that the enemy only shows up right on the brink of a breakthrough. You've blessed her this evening with a job and a home, and now the enemy wants to take her testimony. We rebuke him right now in the name of Jesus. We don't know what your plan is for Montana, but we know that whatever it is, it's going to be awesome. Thank you, in advance. Amen."

Montana nodded and whispered, "Amen."

"Let's go get something to eat, now," Emoni said. "I'm starved. And since you just claimed Trent as your boyfriend, maybe you spoke it into existence."

"Boo," Montana said.

"You could've said anything, but you claimed him. I think that was a Freudian slip. You like him, don't you?"

Montana got a really serious look on her face. "Emoni, you're going to force me to thrash you."

Both of the young women burst into laughter at the mention

of a line from Montana's favorite movie, *Coming to America.* She knew it was a comedy, but it was the only fairy tale she knew about where a random black girl marries a handsome and sweet African prince. Montana could recite the lines word for word, and she forced all of her friends to watch it with her at least once. Emoni had been a victim on several occasions.

"Okay, you better stop dissing my boy Trent. How do you know he's not from some rich kingdom in the Motherland?" Emoni asked.

Montana sighed. "Because if he was, he'd have absolutely no interest in me whatsoever."

Emoni linked arms with Montana and pulled her toward their dates. "You have got to start thinking more positively."

Montana grinned. She was thinking positively. She was positively sure that she was going to try her best and make the Chambers family love her. Maybe they'd give her a permanent position. Maybe living with them would give her a new sense of security and erase all the vestiges of her former life with Rio.

CHAPTER 6

Quentin looked down at his friend Alexis as she slept. It wasn't a peaceful sleep. Her snore rattled like an old car in dire need of a tune-up. But at least she wasn't in pain, not now anyway.

There were currently five residents at Transitions; they'd had up to ten in the past. All were referrals from a social worker or agency, and all had terminal cancer in its last stages. Quentin remembered how bad it had been in Chandra's final days. She'd been in so much pain that one morphine dose barely held her over until the next.

The medical bills were very expensive, but because of his family's wealth, Chandra was as comfortable as it was possible for her to be. But there were unfortunate souls, like Alexis, who didn't have a penny to their name. Alexis's final days would've been much worse than Chandra's had been if she hadn't been referred to Transitions.

Alexis finally stirred. She squinted her eyes and said, "Q-Doggie-Dog. How long have you been here?"

"Just a few minutes. I was just about to leave with all that snoring."

Alexis let out a weak chuckle. "Was I loud?"

"Yes. You sounded like you were hibernating."

"Yo' mama."

"Does absolutely snore, but not as loud as you. How are you feeling?"

Alexis sighed. "About a five."

The Transitions residents had a pain scale from one to ten, with one being a great day, and ten being a steady morphine drip. Alexis's doctor had given her a three-month prognosis, and she'd been at Transitions for two months. Her condition hadn't worsened, but it hadn't improved, either.

"You need meds?" Quentin asked.

She shook her head. "No. I'm writing in my journal this afternoon. I have some stuff I need to get on paper today."

"Make sure you ask for them before the pain gets too bad."

Alexis gave him her lopsided smile. "Hey, if I'm in pain, it means I'm still alive."

"But don't suffer, okay? That's why you're here."

"I think I'm here because God wanted me to have a caramel angel at my bedside while I waste away."

Quentin shook his head and grinned. Alexis had no problem openly flirting with him or talking about God like He was someone who actually cared about their day-to-day lives. Quentin was convinced that God paid as much attention to humans as humans did to ants building an anthill.

"I'm at your bedside because I want to be. God didn't tell me to do this."

Alexis shrugged. "Okay then. I was just giving you an excuse for your little girlfriend about all the time you spend with me. But you can keep it real if you want. Tell her you just can't get enough of me."

"You are a mess, Alex."

"Where is she anyway? Why haven't I met Miss Thang? Is she too good to visit us?" Alexis covered her mouth with her hand to contain her giggle.

"Maybe I haven't invited her."

Alexis laughed out loud. "Why wouldn't you invite your fiancée here?"

"Because she's not my fiancée. Where'd you get that from?"

Alexis shrugged. "I guessed because you've been dating her for a long time that you'd marry her. Maybe you don't have the nerve to propose to her."

"Nerve?" Quentin said with attitude. "You don't think I have the nerve to propose to Chloe?"

"Terminally ill people are pretty candid. Don't take it personal."

"It has nothing to do with nerve."

"Then why haven't you asked her yet? You're not getting any younger."

Quentin said, "Maybe I'm waiting on you to get better, so I can leave her and we can run away together."

"Shoot, we can do that now. Where you wanna go?"

"I don't know," Quentin said. "Barbados?"

Alexis pressed the remote control next to her bed and the television came to life. She clicked through the channels—all with some peaceful scene—until she got to the channel with the white sand beach and waves crashing over the shore.

There were about twenty channels for the residents to choose from as a form of pain management. It was all about meditation and relaxation. Alexis used the television more than the other ladies, but then she also used less morphine.

"You know, on a serious note," Alexis said, "why don't you get a couple dudes up in here? It gets pretty boring with all this cancer-ridden estrogen floating around."

"I'm not enough man for you?" Quentin asked, as he stood up from his chair. He kissed Alexis on the top of her head. It wasn't something he did with all the residents, but he and Alex had become close. If he'd ever had a little sister, he imagined she'd be like Alex.

"You're about to make me blush," Alexis said. "Don't go home smelling like me; your girlfriend might get mad."

Alexis burst into laughter at her own joke. She smelled like a mixture of menthol, oatmeal, and sickness. There was nothing appealing about the scent of decay.

"I'll be back to see you tomorrow. I've got to meet some new nanny my mother hired."

Alexis raised her sparse eyebrows. "I'll be counting the seconds until you return. Except after I take my meds. Then I'll be out like a light until your return."

"Yes, you better take your medication, Alex."

"I will. I promise."

Quentin squeezed her hand. "Don't suffer."

"You either."

Quentin kissed Alexis's head once more before he left the room. He couldn't promise her he wouldn't suffer, though. Quentin witnessed the pain of every resident at Transitions and felt an emotional drain every time one of them passed on.

Sometimes Quentin asked himself how many times he would watch someone die before he stopped feeling guilty for being alive. And he couldn't answer the question. He didn't know when it would be enough, or if it would ever be enough. As long as his pain enveloped him like a woolen shawl, he'd continue to watch their transitions, while he stayed the same.

CHAPTER 7

Montana stood outside the Chambers mansion, feeling tiny in comparison to its grandeur. Although it was the biggest house she'd ever seen up close, the white brick and blue shutters gave it a welcoming feel.

Montana lifted her hand to ring the bell, but the door swung open before she got the chance. Standing in front of her stood a sour-faced woman in all black, with her hair pulled back in a mean-looking bun.

"Oh, hello," Montana said, unable to hide her surprise.

The woman's gaze swept over Montana from head to toe. "You're late."

"I know, and I'm so, so sorry," Montana gushed. "I just ran into horrible traffic on the way from church."

"Come in. Mrs. Chambers is expecting you. I am Ms. Levy. If you do get the job, you will report to me."

If she got the job? Montana thought their meeting was a formality. She didn't know she was still being tested. She approached this prospect with some trepidation. Her tardiness had already put her on her potential supervisor's bad side.

Montana couldn't help but gasp as Ms. Levy led her through a large foyer with ceilings that seemed to stretch into infinity.

"I bet the acoustics in here are great," Montana said.

Ms. Levy said, "The late Mrs. Chambers swore by the acoustics in this foyer. She'd have Mr. Chambers wheel a piano right in here and play for her while she sang."

Montana smiled at Ms. Levy's musing, thrilled that she'd evoked a good memory instead of a bad one. Perhaps it would erase her earlier faux pas.

Ms. Levy showed Montana into a parlor filled with pretty peach and silver furniture. She motioned for Montana to sit, and she did.

"Wait here," Ms. Levy said. "It shouldn't be long."

Montana gazed out the room's bay window at the wonderful view. The sun danced on a lake surrounded by small peach trees. A little family of ducks traveled across it as if they had major business to accomplish.

"It's beautiful, isn't it?"

Montana turned to answer whoever belonged to the deep, rich, baritone voice. "It is. Very."

And so was he. Montana's breath caught in her throat at the sight of him. On first take, she couldn't find one flaw. He had smooth caramel skin, dark curly hair that fell across his forehead, and light brown eyes. Those eyes were what had Montana feeling flustered. The contrast of their color and the heavy, long eyelashes overwhelmed her. It was as if God had said, "Let there be romance" and then drew those eyes.

He offered his hand for Montana to shake. "I'm Quentin Chambers. I think I'm supposed to be meeting you."

Montana jumped to her feet. "Mr. Chambers, I'm Montana Ellis. I attend church with your mother."

He chuckled. "Don't be nervous. I'm not the one in charge here. It's my mother and Ms. Levy that you have to worry about. And my mother obviously likes you already or you wouldn't even be here."

"I love your mother. We sing together in the choir."

Quentin lifted an eyebrow and cleared his throat. Montana panicked. Had she said something wrong?

"But I'm not sure about Ms. Levy," Montana continued, trying to recover. "I don't know if I've impressed her."

Quentin's warmth seemed to return. "Her bark is bigger than her bite. I'm sure you're fine."

Montana looked at her feet for a moment to gather her wits. She couldn't match Quentin's steady gaze.

When she felt ready, she looked back up at him and asked, "Do you have any questions for me? They're your children."

Quentin ran one hand through his hair while he pondered, and it was then that Montana noticed his biceps. She swallowed hard. He wasn't just fine. This man was incredible.

"For the life of me, I can't think of one thing to ask you. That's horrible, right? Maybe if you looked more like a nanny, I'd have a question or two."

Montana looked down at her clothes. She'd worn what she'd had on at church—a white blouse, a black skirt, and a red rose. Well, she'd moved the flower from her lapel into her massive headful of curls, but other than that it was the same outfit.

She shrugged. "How should a nanny look?"

Quentin looked stumped again, but this time he was saved by his mother, who burst into the room, breaking the uncomfortable silence.

"Well, I wanted to introduce you," Estelle said, as she gave Montana a hug. "This is the young lady I was telling you about. What do you think?"

"Um . . . what do I think?" Quentin asked.

Estelle shook her head slightly as if he was irritating her. "Yes, don't you think she's perfect?"

"Oh, yes. Whatever you say, Mother. This was all your idea."

"And after Deirdre's shenanigans you agreed with me."

Montana felt like she should say something, but she didn't know what, so she looked from Estelle to Quentin with curious glances, hoping they'd remember that she was standing right there in the room with them.

"Montana, I will have Ms. Levy show you around the house, and to your room."

Montana's eyes lit up. "So, I'm hired?"

"Yes, honey. If you'll accept the offer. We're paying fifty thousand a year, plus room and board. I think that's fair, don't you?"

Fair? That was more money than she'd ever made in her life. Just to watch some children who were half grown already? Montana felt like she should make a counter offer of something lower.

"It's very generous. Thank you," Montana replied.

Estelle nodded her approval. "I remember your testimony during choir rehearsal. Do we need to send movers to your apartment?"

Montana blinked back tears of joy. "Yes, ma'am, that would be really, really helpful."

"We have lots of storage here if you want to keep your furniture here, or I can have Ms. Levy locate a local storage facility if you don't feel comfortable with that," Estelle said.

Montana was in awe of Estelle. Had she thought of everything?

"Before she accepts, don't you think she should meet the children?" Quentin asked.

Estelle gave him an irritated glance. "Oh, Quentin, I declare. As if they would deter her from accepting this offer. I'll go and get them, though. It will be love at first sight."

"Ms. Levy can get them, right?" Quentin asked. Montana wondered if he didn't want to be left alone with her again.

"Ms. Levy is off for the afternoon. She is going to visit her aunt in Marietta. I will be right back."

Estelle left the room, and Quentin gave Montana a nervous smile. She returned the gesture with what she hoped was a warmer smile than the one Quentin had managed.

"Thank you so much for the opportunity, Mr. Chambers. You don't know how badly I need this."

He shrugged. "It's my mother. She probably thinks this is ministry. And you can call me Quentin."

Montana shook her head. "I'd rather call you Mr. Chambers. I don't want the children to think I'm unprofessional."

Quentin chuckled. "Sure, that's fine."

Ms. Levy popped her head into the parlor. She was out of her all black and in a colorful shapeless dress. The bun was still there. Montana did not think the dress was an improvement. The black suited her better.

"Quentin, Ms. Chloe has arrived. Should I tell her to join you in here?"

"Um, yes. Of course. Enjoy your afternoon."

A few moments later Chloe walked into the room looking stunning in a red sleeveless dress and red pumps. Montana was sure designers had made every piece of her outfit.

Chloe gave Montana a charitable glance. "Is this a new staff member?"

Montana's jaw dropped. She was wearing her Sunday best, and Chloe's first assumption was that she was the help? True enough, her skirt had come from T.J. Maxx and her blouse from Target, and yes, her comfortable Nine West pumps had been on sale at Ross, but she clearly wasn't dressed like staff.

"Chloe, meet Montana. She's the new nanny. Montana, meet Chloe. She's . . ."

"Quentin's future wife," Chloe finished his sentence. "I am very glad to meet you."

Chloe daintily extended her hand for Montana to shake. Montana responded with a hug. This seemed off-putting to Chloe, who took two steps backward to separate herself.

"We're not quite engaged yet, Chloe," Quentin said with raised eyebrows. Chloe promptly ignored him and continued to smile at Montana.

Montana said, "I've seen you in church. Do you recognize me from the choir?"

"Typically I arrive in time for the sermon, so I don't usually get to see the choir," Chloe said. "But if you're a member of Freedom of Life, I guess a 'Praise the Lord' is in order."

"Yes it is," Montana replied. "He's worthy."

Estelle walked back into the parlor with five children in tow. She looked at Chloe with an unreadable expression. Montana tucked that reaction away into her memory.

"Well, here's the surprise," Estelle said, as she took Montana's hand.

The child who was apparently the youngest looked at Montana with a confused look on her face. "She is so not a pony."

One of the identical twins said, "Grandmother never said it was a pony, you said it was a pony."

"Well, what is it exactly?" the other twin asked.

"She, not it, is your new nanny," Estelle beamed. "How would you like the children to address you, dear?"

"Uh, I guess Ms. Montana will be fine."

The oldest girl burst into laughter. "Are you serious? You really went out and got a nanny. This is un-freaking-believable."

"Deirdre! Manners, please. Ms. Montana is going to think you were raised by a pack of wolves," Estelle snapped.

"Oh, I'm sorry, Grandmother," Deirdre snapped back. "How do you do?"

Deirdre did an elaborate curtsy that made her younger sisters laugh out loud. Montana bit her bottom lip to contain her own giggle. This one would be a challenge, Montana was sure about that.

The only boy said, "You stay clowning. Hello, Ms. Montana, I'm Reese. I'm sure we won't have too much contact, since I'm hardly ever here, but welcome."

"Thank you." Montana beamed in his direction. "And you might just need me every now and then. Are you a senior?"

He nodded. "Yep. Almost grown."

"Almost," Montana said. "Do you take calculus?"

Reese frowned. "Yes. That class is whipping my butt."

"Who was in the math club in high school?" Montana raised her hand. "Oh, that would be me."

"Well, then, Ms. Montana, we might be best friends. But you're not my nanny."

"No, no. You're almost grown. You absolutely don't need a nanny."

Deirdre rolled her eyes at Montana. "And neither do I."

"But I'd love to be your friend too," Montana said.

Deirdre scoffed. "Friends aren't on the payroll."

Deirdre turned and ran out of the room before anyone

could stop her. Montana bit her lip again. Deirdre was going to be more than a challenge. She was going to be a prayer request.

"I'm sorry," Quentin said. "She's angry with me and taking it out on everyone."

"No need to apologize. She'll do it later," Montana said.

Chloe chuckled, and Estelle cut her eyes at Chloe, immediately shutting that down. Quentin wasn't lying about who was in charge.

"So what are your names?" Montana asked the twins, and the youngest. "I've got Deirdre and Reese."

"We're Madison and Morgan," Madison said. Morgan nodded. Montana decided that Madison was the mouthpiece of the two girls.

"I'm Danielle, and I like you already," Danielle said.

Montana gave the youngest child a hug and spun her in a circle on her roller skates. "I remember you from Vacation Bible School. Do you know I love roller skating too? I have my own pair."

Danielle hugged her back. "Okay, you are better than a pony. Can we keep her?"

Quentin said, "Yes, we're keeping her. Isn't that right, Montana?"

"Yes, this is going to be fun," Montana replied.

"But temporary," Chloe said.

Estelle said, "I will determine the length of Ms. Ellis's employment."

"I was just thinking we wouldn't need a nanny anymore once Quentin and I are married," Chloe said.

Estelle chuckled. "Yes, well, that may be true, but the children may be off and married themselves before that happens. Let's not get ahead of ourselves."

"I'm just speaking those things that are not, as if they are. Isn't that a Scripture, Ms. Montana?"

Montana wanted to say, "Now if you had to ask, maybe you shouldn't quote it." But she did not.

She said, "It is. It's about faith."

"And I've got lots of that! And patience," Chloe said.

"Yes," Quentin said. "The patience of Job."

Quentin gave Montana a look that was on the verge of amusement but didn't quite make it there. She assumed he was teasing Chloe, but the joke seemed to go right over her head.

Estelle said, "Welcome, Montana. Let's get you settled in."

Montana happily followed Estelle out of the parlor. There was too much tension in there, and she wanted to be as far away from that as possible.

When they were upstairs in the hall, Estelle said, "So are you ready for this adventure?"

Montana smiled eagerly. "I am so looking forward to getting to know the entire family."

Especially Quentin.

CHAPTER 8

"What was all that about?" Quentin asked as he floored the gas pedal in his drop-top red Benz. He was driving like he was angry.

"What was all what about?"

Chloe answered his question with a question in an attempt to stall. She didn't know why she'd introduced herself to that nanny as Quentin's future wife. The words had just fallen out of her mouth before she could stop them. There was something about that girl that had immediately caused her antennae to rise. Maybe it was her vixen-like curves, or maybe it was the way Quentin's kids were falling all over her like a bunch of lost puppies. Or perhaps it was the fact that Estelle seemed to like Montana.

All of it added up to the nanny being a threat.

"Future wife, Chloe? Where'd that come from?"

Chloe cleared her throat, knowing she'd have to give an answer. "Well . . . one day, right? Aren't you ever planning on getting remarried?"

"I mean . . . I don't know. I haven't thought about it too much. Are you unhappy with me? I thought we were having fun."

"We are! I enjoy our time together."

"Then what is it?"

"Sometimes I think about getting old, you know? We're young now, but I don't know. Maybe I think our fun might have an expiration date. And then what's going to happen to me?"

There was a long, uncomfortable silence, as if Quentin was carefully choosing his words before responding. Chloe felt a twinge in the pit of her stomach. This wasn't good.

"Look, I'm not in a hurry to get to the altar, Quentin," Chloe said when Quentin's pause went on for too long. "I guess I just saw that curvy nanny and got jealous that she's going to be under your roof and I'm not."

Quentin squeezed Chloe's hand. "Don't be jealous, Chloe. I had nothing to do with hiring her, and if anyone has an expiration date, it's her. My kids are going to grow up soon."

Chloe smiled, and Quentin kissed her hand.

"What matters most," Quentin continued, "is that we're still having a great time. I thank you for making these past five years bearable."

Chloe's heart warmed at Quentin's words. He'd never acknowledged that she'd stood in the gap for him all this time, during his grieving. She wondered if he'd ever move past it. She wondered if there would ever be a place in his heart for her.

"You're welcome."

Quentin let go of her hand. "All right, then. I feel like eating something incredibly bad for me. You want steak? Pasta?"

"Whatever you want, babe," Chloe said, a little bit disappointed that their tender moment had passed.

Quentin blasted music from the speakers of his car. A Jay-Z song. Not really Chloe's type of music, but as long as Quentin was in a good mood he was in a spending mood. Mama needed a new handbag.

CHAPTER 9

Chloe sat on her leather sofa, stroking her new Louis Vuitton bag. It was one of the new ones for the summer season and would draw many compliments and envious stares from women who couldn't afford one. And Quentin had purchased it without blinking.

So why didn't it make her feel any better?

Maybe it was because after they were done dining and shopping, Quentin had taken her back to his mansion to get her car and then followed her back to her condo in Vinings. He hadn't asked her to stay over and spend more time, and he hadn't offered to stay at her place. He'd kissed her on the cheek and made sure she got inside, and then he'd left. Just like he always did.

Chloe wondered if she would've even seen Quentin at all if she hadn't gone to the mansion after church. He hadn't called her to make any plans, even though it was a beautiful day.

Sometimes Chloe felt like she was chasing Quentin. Like she'd been chasing him for five years. She wondered if he'd ever allow himself to be caught.

She remembered their very first conversation. It was at the mansion during the repast following his wife's funeral. Chloe had waited patiently for everyone to pay their respects. The crowd had thinned, and only a few remained. Quentin sat in the sitting room that everyone said was Chandra's favorite room in the house.

Chloe recalled walking over the threshold into that room and it feeling surreal. There was a moment of hesitation, because of what she was about to do. Some people might've thought she was the lowest type of woman, but she'd reasoned with herself. His wife was gone to heaven, not on vacation. She wasn't coming back. As far as she was concerned, she was staking a claim on property that was no longer claimed.

"Excuse me, Quentin?" she'd said.

Quentin's first glance at her had been through tear-filled eyes. She'd never seen anyone look so sad. "Yes?"

"I just wanted to tell you how sorry I am for your loss. My name is Chloe. I knew Chandra in college. She was beautiful."

"Were you good friends?"

"Not good friends, but we knew each other around campus, and in some society circles. She was always a beautiful spirit."

"Thank you for coming. I appreciate it."

"Listen, I'd like to come and check on you and your children. Would that be all right?"

There had been a weak smile from Quentin. "Sure."

"It's nice to meet you, Quentin. I wish it had been under different circumstances."

Quentin had looked at the floor then. She'd seen a tear splash to the ground. Finally he'd looked up again.

"It's nice to meet you too, Chloe."

And then Chloe had done something neither she nor Quentin had expected. She'd stepped nearer to where he was sitting and hugged him tightly. He'd sobbed into her chest for a few minutes, and she'd held him. She'd been a stranger but had become an instant friend.

"I'm so sorry," Quentin had said.

Chloe remembered how she'd gone into her purse and had given him a tissue. "You buried your wife today. You're supposed to be sad."

She'd patted him on the back and left him then, sure the seeds had been planted for their future. But five years had gone by, and the only fruit had been gifts, vacations, and thrilling times in the bedroom.

There was something about that nanny that made Chloe feel a sense of urgency. Maybe Montana was planting new seeds over her failed crop. Maybe she was planning her own harvest. Whatever it was, Chloe didn't plan to go down without a fight.

CHAPTER 10

Quentin didn't want to admit it, but something had stirred deep within him when he'd seen Montana sitting in what had been Chandra's favorite room, staring out the window at those ducks who'd laid claim to the lake.

Even though he'd spent the afternoon eating and shopping with Chloe, and the night in Chloe's arms, he hadn't been able to shake the image of Montana from his mind.

He wasn't lying when he said Montana didn't look like a nanny. She looked like a petite package of fineness. Especially that headful of wild, auburn-colored curls. The carefree hairdo was begging to be touched and dying to be fondled. And the rose Montana had pinned to the side of her 'do complemented the style perfectly.

Montana's smooth caramel skin had the translucent glow that you see on babies, innocents, and very happy people. But while her face seemed innocent, her body belonged to a grown woman. She was curvy in all the right places, but fit and trim where she needed to be. Compared to Chloe's hard athletic body, Montana's was lush and inviting.

Quentin pushed the thoughts of Montana far from his mind. He had a good thing in Chloe. She had class and style, and she was a freak in the bedroom. But most of all, she didn't require a commitment. Well, she hadn't up until this point. Now, all of a sudden, she was talking marriage.

Quentin preferred swimming in shallow water when it came to the women in his life. It was for the best—no one would ever replace Chandra in his heart. There would never be another Mrs. Chambers.

Quentin had left Chloe's condo in the wee hours of the morning, as he always did. He never spent the night. Quentin's lifestyle was one thing, but he didn't want his children, especially his son, to think that what he had was the ideal thing. He wanted them to find love like he had with their mother.

After his morning run was complete, Quentin jogged back to the house, his head clearer than when he'd started. The quiet and fresh air always had that effect on him, so it was how he always started his day.

Quentin entered the house through the kitchen patio door, where he found the subject of his thoughts—Montana. She was wearing a cute pair of yoga pants and a T-shirt, and drinking a glass of juice.

"Good morning, Mr. Chambers. Is it warm enough out there for me to go without a jacket?"

"Good morning. It's warm enough if you're running. Are you?"

Montana laughed. "No, I'll be taking a stroll, but not running. The grounds are so beautiful! I've never lived anywhere like this."

Montana's excitement tickled Quentin. She was also very cute when her eyes lit up like that every time she laughed. He knew he should try not to, but Quentin was enjoying the view.

"Well, it is very pretty this morning, but I think you might need a jacket. Enjoy your walk."

"Okay, Mr. Chambers, I will."

"Will you please call me Quentin?"

Montana shook her head as she pulled on a jacket that matched her yoga pants. "Nope."

"Well, if we're not on a first-name basis, then maybe I should call you Ms. Ellis."

She grinned. "Suit yourself, Mr. Chambers. I'll answer to both."

Quentin watched Montana walk through the door. She smiled and waved at him on her way out. He felt a little silly waving back, but he did anyway.

"Hey, Dad," Deirdre said, as she stomped into the kitchen in her school uniform. Her friendly tone immediately put Quentin on the defensive and erased all his thoughts of Montana.

"Hey. You need a ride to school?"

"No. Reese is dropping me off."

"Cool."

Deirdre laughed as she took a cereal bowl out of the cabinet. "Dad! Can I talk to you about something serious?"

"No."

"Daddy! When are you going to let me off punishment? I've learned my lesson."

Quentin leaned back on the counter and folded his arms across his chest. "Really? What lesson have you learned?"

"To always let you know where I'll be and to not sneak out. Now that we have a nanny, we don't really have to worry about me leaving Danielle here with the twins. She'll always be supervised."

Quentin shook his head and sighed. Deirdre had apparently learned nothing. He was upset she had snuck out, but he was more angry that she was hanging out with thugs in Decatur. He knew that she was getting older and that boys were now part of the equation, but why couldn't she pick a nice guy from parents with money? The family absolutely knew enough of them.

"You don't even know what the lesson is, so how could you have learned it?"

"Daddy! I have learned! You can't keep me on punishment forever."

"Yes, I can."

Deirdre huffed and pouted. "What about Reese? We were at the same house party. He's not on lockdown."

"Reese is older than you."

"So he can hang out in Decatur because he's older?"

Quentin nodded. "Yep. He can. And he did the right thing by getting you out of there. I'm proud of him for having your back, because apparently you don't have enough sense to have your own back."

Deirdre slammed her hand down on the counter, causing cereal and milk to spill out of her bowl.

"This isn't fair! You make me go to an all-girls school, and you're not making the twins go there. And now you're locking me up like I'm a nun."

Quentin calmly grabbed a bottle of water from the pantry while Deirdre continued her outburst. Nothing she said would change his mind about that thug she liked, so she was wasting her breath.

"I think you hate me! You hate me because I look like Mom!" Deirdre yelled.

Now it was Quentin's turn to slam the bottled water down on the counter.

"You don't get to use your mother to win an argument. I'm done talking about this. You're on punishment until I say so."

Quentin watched Deirdre storm out of the kitchen and let out a tired sigh. One thing she was right about was how much she looked like her mother. Deirdre was Chandra's twin—in looks, but not in temperament.

Chandra had been Quentin's partner with the children. The more disconnected he became from Deirdre, the more he missed Chandra's levelheaded calmness.

Quentin thought about Montana and her peaceful, sweet, sunny disposition. He wondered if she'd have an effect on Deirdre. He hoped so, because something had to give. If not, Deirdre was in danger of not surviving her teenage years.

CHAPTER 11

It was nearing the end of Montana's first week with the Chambers family, but Montana still felt like she was interviewing for the job. This afternoon, Ms. Levy had invited her into the kitchen under the guise of having an afternoon cup of coffee, but Montana quickly found out it was really a quiz.

"So are you ready to handle the pick-up and drop-off schedule on your own?" Ms. Levy asked.

Montana nodded slowly as she tried to remember it all. "Madison has dance at the studio downtown, and Morgan has soccer at her middle school. Danielle needs to be dropped off at her piano lesson. I stay at the lesson with her, because Danielle will be done first. Madison and Morgan get out at the same time, but I pick up Morgan, and Madison gets dropped off at practice by her friend's mother."

Ms. Levy paused for a long moment with one of her eyebrows raised. Montana held her breath waiting for the woman's answer. She'd been with the Chambers family for only a week, and she wanted to stay on.

"I'm impressed," Ms. Levy finally said.

Montana let out a sigh of relief, but she wasn't off the hook yet. That was only the first day of the kids' schedule. She had the rest of the week to remember.

"It seems like these kids need a chauffeur instead of a nanny," Montana said, after rattling off two more days of the schedule.

Ms. Levy shook her head. "What they need is a mama. As much as I love Quentin and Estelle, they are making a mistake with these children. They're trying to keep them busy every moment of the day just to keep them from realizing they don't have a mama."

Montana didn't know how to reply to this. She hadn't been around the family long enough to truly have an opinion. So she decided to remain quiet.

"And that Chloe ain't got any mama qualifications," Ms. Levy continued. She sucked her teeth to punctuate her sentiment.

It was true, Montana was curious about Chloe and Quentin's relationship. Every time Montana and Quentin were in a room together, she got nervous flutters in her stomach. And every time, she chided herself for being attracted to another woman's boyfriend. Montana knew she couldn't let herself go down that fantasy road.

"She might not have any mama skills, but she sure knows how to land a man, right?" Montana asked. "She's his future wife, right? That's how she introduced herself."

Ms. Levy scoffed. "I guarantee that was the first time Quentin had heard about that. If she's planning a wedding, she's planning it all by herself."

Estelle walked into the kitchen and poured herself a cup of coffee. Montana bit her lip nervously, wondering how much Estelle had heard. She didn't want Estelle to think she was snooping into the family affairs.

"Who's planning what all by herself?" Estelle finally asked after neither Montana nor Mrs. Levy spoke up.

"We talking 'bout Ms. Chloe," Ms. Levy said, "and her future wife declaration."

Estelle burst into laughter, and Montana breathed a sigh of relief.

"I thought you all were talking about this fund-raising ball Quentin is having for the foundation."

"Foundation?" Montana asked.

Ms. Levy replied, "Yes. Mr. Chambers takes care of terminally ill cancer patients in a big country house outside of Douglasville. It's called Transitions."

Montana couldn't hide her surprise. She was very impressed by this. But she was saddened at the same time. It made her want to get to know Quentin better, and she knew that was out of the question.

"Yes, my son's pet project that he insists on running himself," Estelle said.

"I think it's awesome!" Montana said. "It must be very rewarding for him."

Estelle inhaled deeply and exhaled a heavy breath. "What he does for those women is wonderful, but I don't know if it's rewarding. I think he's reliving his pain over and over again."

Montana considered this and understood Estelle's sadness. Quentin surrounded himself with the dying, and life was happening all around him. Especially with his children.

The doorbell rang, and both Montana and Estelle looked at Ms. Levy. She frowned at both women.

"I suppose it is my job to answer the door, but I get sick of looking at Chloe, the duchess of bougie."

Estelle and Montana burst into laughter at Ms. Levy's joke. After a few moments, Ms. Levy returned, with Chloe in tow.

"Mrs. Chambers, I present to you Ms. Brooks."

Chloe shook her head and rushed over to Estelle to hug her. "Will you please stop announcing me like that?"

Ms. Levy pursed her lips together tightly. "I will if you ever become a member of . . ."

"The family," Chloe interjected. "I know."

Chloe stretched her arms in Montana's direction. Montana lifted her eyebrows in surprise, not exactly sure what she should do. Then Chloe wiggled her fingertips in a "come here" motion. Did she want a hug?

Montana rose from her seat and hugged Chloe. It felt weird, but Chloe was being so nice that she couldn't resist. Maybe it was best if she was friends with Chloe. It just might keep her from fantasizing about Quentin.

"Ladies, if you'll excuse me, I'm going to study the children's pick-up and drop-off schedules. I'm on call this afternoon, and Ms. Levy is going to be so disappointed in me if I don't get it done."

Chloe pouted. "I thought you were going to stay and help us. I'd love to have another perspective, and maybe a tie breaker in case Estelle and I can't agree."

"I would volunteer to be your tie breaker, but I've got Bible study to prepare for," Ms. Levy said, as she placed a previously prepared tray of sweet tea, sandwiches, and cookies at the center of the table, and turned to leave.

Chloe's eyes pleaded with Montana. Montana felt sorry for Chloe. She eased back down at the kitchen table.

"Okay, I will stay for a while," Montana said. "In a few hours I have to pick up Danielle, though."

"We'll be done before then," Chloe said. "I promise."

Estelle said, "So, Chloe, I'm excited to see what you've already come up with."

Chloe's eyes widened with surprise. "The planning is absolutely in its infancy, Estelle. I wanted to get your thoughts first instead of going down a wrong path and having to change everything later."

"Change everything? How unreasonable do you think I am?" Estelle asked.

Montana pinched herself to keep from giggling at Chloe's facial expression. There was probably no safe way to answer Estelle's question, so Chloe just stared at Estelle and blinked.

When Chloe didn't reply, Estelle asked, "How much money are we trying to raise with this event?"

"I was thinking that if it's grand enough we can raise two hundred fifty thousand dollars. That seems like a safe number."

"I can get that amount by calling up a few friends and asking them for donations," Estelle said. "If we're going to go all out for this event, we should be thinking around one million."

"Well . . . okay, if you say so," Chloe replied. "I just wanted to give us a realistic goal."

Montana was confused. She knew the Chambers family was beyond rich. So why were they holding a fund-raiser for a million dollars?

"Can I ask a question? I hope I'm not being rude, but can't you just write a check for the million dollars and forget about the party?"

Estelle threw her head back and laughed. "Of course I could. And truthfully, everything at Transitions is currently being paid for by Quentin. Some of those women have medical bills in the hundreds of thousands of dollars when they get there."

"But Atlanta's elite like to have parties," Chloe said.

"We party for a cause, and this is a great one," Estelle said. "What is the theme for the ball?"

Chloe bounced in her seat. She was clearly excited about this part of it. "It should be a masquerade ball! At Transitions the women always have to wear a figurative mask to hide their pain and suffering. We will honor their struggle with our masks and donations."

"I like that," Montana said. "And masquerade balls are always fun to plan."

Estelle cleared her throat. "They are fun, indeed. What is your budget for the ball?"

Chloe flipped through a few pages in her little notebook. "The biggest expense will be the catering, of course, since we don't have to worry about a venue. I was thinking close to fifty thousand for the dinner with onsite chefs and wait staff. Also, the decorations will be expensive, but I've reached out to a couple of art and jewelry galleries that are willing to provide some tasteful pieces for our use."

"And how do you intend to cover these expenses?" Estelle asked.

"The cost per table will be ten thousand dollars, and individual tickets will be one thousand. We will also have a jewelry auction and a rich eligible bachelor auction."

Montana lifted her eyebrows at this suggestion. It would be

nice to rent a prince for a day. "Do you think Mr. Chambers would participate?"

"I don't know," Chloe said. "He's not really a bachelor."

Estelle said, "But it would be fun. It's his organization, and I'm sure some cougar would love to drop a mint to be seen on the town with Quentin. It would be harmless."

"I suppose . . . ," Chloe said. She did not seem pleased with the line of reasoning.

Montana regretted speaking her mind.

"Someone would have to convince him first," Estelle said.

"Of course, I'll do it," Chloe replied, although she didn't look the least bit thrilled about the task.

"What about flowers?" Montana asked, trying to change the touchy subject. "I love flowers. Wouldn't it be lovely to have different arrangements in various stages—from bud to full bloom? It could also be symbolic of transition."

Estelle clapped her hands. "That is perfect! I just love that idea, and I'm sure Quentin will agree."

Chloe narrowed her eyes at Montana, and Montana swallowed. The look was so subtle and quick that Montana wondered if she was imagining it. Estelle was gushing over her idea when she'd been indifferent, at best, to Chloe's suggestions. Maybe she should've let Ms. Levy stay instead.

"I'm sorry," Montana said. "Am I talking too much?"

"Absolutely not. That's why I asked you to stay, I want your suggestions," Chloe said.

Montana smiled. "Okay, well feel free to let me know when I'm out of line."

"I will let you know," Chloe replied, in a tone that let Montana know she most certainly would let her know.

Estelle's cell phone rang. She looked down at the caller ID and smiled. "This is First Lady Prentiss. Please excuse me for a moment. You all continue with the planning."

Estelle left Montana and Chloe sitting across from one another at the kitchen table. Montana grabbed a cookie from the tray and took a bite to keep from putting her foot in her mouth again. Chloe simply stared at Montana, as if she was assessing her. It made Montana uncomfortable, but she thought maybe Chloe wanted her to feel that way.

"So tell me about yourself," Chloe said. "Since it looks like we're going to be working so closely together, we should probably get to know each other."

"Um . . . well . . . okay. I'm a teacher—well, I'm going to be soon. I just have one more test to pass, and then I'll have my certificate. I sing in the choir at church. I'm originally from Ohio, but I've been here in Atlanta since college. What else do you want to know?"

"Are you seeing anyone?" Chloe asked, without a moment's hesitation.

"You mean like a boyfriend? No. Not right now."

Chloe gave a look of surprise. "Really? You're so pretty and bubbly and sweet. Why don't you have a boyfriend? Someone should be ready to give you a bunch of babies."

Montana looked down at her lap. "I can't have my own children. I guess that's why I decided to be a teacher."

"Well, just because you're going to be a teacher doesn't mean you have to be an old maid. You can still get a husband, so you can . . . you know . . ."

Montana burst into laughter. "I said I wanted to be a teacher. Not a nun. And I'm not a pure maiden, unfortunately. I wish I was, though."

"Oh, honey, most of us left behind that purity when we stepped on a college campus. I'm sure God's forgiven you."

"He has definitely done that. He's also going to send me a husband someday. You're so lucky to have someone like Mr. Chambers."

"Yes, I am. He's right out of a fairy tale, isn't he?"

"He is!" Montana gushed.

Chloe snapped her head to one side. "You sound more excited than I am."

"Oh no, I didn't mean it like that. I just meant that he's a great man. You are blessed to have him."

"A blessing is a gift. I worked hard for what Quentin and I

have," Chloe said triumphantly. "If ever there was a man who loved his wife, it's Quentin."

"He must've been devastated when she passed. I can't imagine."

Chloe nodded. "He was, and I was the one who helped put him back together again. I encouraged him when he wanted to start his foundation, and the children love me. We're a perfect match."

Montana wasn't sure about the children loving her, but as long as she had Quentin's affection, it would probably fall into place.

"Well, that's wonderful for both of you," Montana said, not sure how to respond to Chloe's speech.

Chloe nodded emphatically. "But we have to find a guy for you. Do you want someone rich, because I know a few . . . Oh, who am I kidding? Every girl wants a rich man."

"I wouldn't really mind if he wasn't rich. I just want someone who loves God and then loves me. I don't need a lot of money."

"How about if he loves God and you, and he's rich? That would be perfect, right?"

Montana grinned. "Can he be handsome too? Can he be tall, caramel-colored, and muscular with beautiful eyes?"

Montana stopped cold when she realized she was describing Quentin. "He could be short, though," she added. "I'm tiny, so he doesn't have to be tall."

Chloe gave Montana a strange look but did not get a chance to respond because Estelle came back into the kitchen.

"I would like for some of the church members to attend," Estelle said, "but they won't all be able to afford that one-thousand-dollar ticket price."

Chloe frowned. "This is supposed to be a society affair. The cream of Atlanta society will be here. If we wanted it to be a church picnic, then we would've had it at the church."

"Freedom of Life is very important to me, and Bishop Prentiss continues to pray for my son and family. I would never exclude them from any event in my home. I also will have the ladies from our Steering Committee, and the Nurse's Guild.

And, of course, Bishop Prentiss's children. Just make room on your guest list."

"But . . ."

"No buts," Estelle said. "I won't hear any objections to this. Now on to the menu."

Montana watched Chloe's expression darken. She didn't know if Chloe looked angry or just plain frightening, but Montana was sure of one thing. She didn't want to cross her path. Montana pushed all thoughts of Quentin to the back of her mind.

God would have to send her another prince, because this one was already attached to his prospective queen—by her claws.

CHAPTER 12

Chloe was annoyed by her meeting with Estelle and Montana. So much so that she called Lichelle to meet her at Neiman Marcus for some serious retail therapy. While Chloe waited for Lichelle to arrive, she tried on a pair of Louboutin peep-toe ankle booties. They made her toned legs look phenomenal, but it still wasn't enough to lift her spirits.

Chloe almost didn't recognize Lichelle as she sashayed over to the shoe department. She was wearing a new mid-back-length red wig with big barrel curls. It was loud and garish—something that Chloe would never wear but that was perfect for Lichelle.

"Hey girl," Lichelle said in her bubbly voice. "You like my new do?"

"It looks good on you," Chloe said truthfully, as they shared a hug.

Lichelle looked down at the shoes. "Those are fierce, girl. Get them. In every color."

Chloe laughed out loud. It wasn't unusual for Chloe to use her entire shopping allowance on shoes. Quentin loved to see her in heels—especially red bottoms—whether she had on clothes or not.

"What was the emergency?" Lichelle asked. "You called me

sounding crazy. All I heard was a bunch of noise about a chunky nanny."

Chloe shook her head. "You don't listen to me. This chick has stars in her eyes when she talks about my man. That is a problem."

"I mean, but she's the help. Quentin wouldn't get with the help. He's got too much class for that."

"Yes, I agree, but his mother just loves her. She sings in the choir at church, and you know Estelle has been dying for her son to come back to that church."

Lichelle shrugged. "So what? You go to church too."

"But I can't sing."

"What does that have to do with anything?"

"He used to be a musician, you know. I don't want that girl to have anything on me."

Lichelle tapped her acrylic nails together and seemed to ponder this possibility. It certainly worried Chloe that she didn't have that music thing going. What if Quentin did decide one day to play that piano again? Would that heffa be draped across the piano in a negligee, playing the part of the muse?

"Chloe. Chloe! Where'd you go? I thought we were having a conversation here!"

Chloe shook her head and exhaled. "I'm here. I just thought about that woman under the same roof as Quentin! He won't even let me spend the night."

"So she goes to church, and she's curvy. Is she a buttaface?"

Chloe scrunched her nose. "What is a buttaface? Your hood slang is so troublesome."

"A buttaface is a chick with a nice body and a jacked-up face, like a smashed stick of butter."

"Oh. Well, no. She's cute if you like rosy cheeks, big eyes, long eyelashes, and plump red lips."

"Wait, it sounds like you're the one trying to holla at her!"

"Lichelle! I need your help, and you're just mocking me."

"I'm sorry, girl. I don't think you need to worry, but it is always good to have some dirt on her, just in case."

"You're right."

Just as Chloe was deciding whether to get one or two pairs of the booties, Deirdre walked into the shoe department and picked up a pair of designer pumps. Something about a teenager being able to buy thousand-dollar shoes bothered Chloe. She remembered life before her first sugar daddy. Back then, Chloe was lucky to get a pair of last year's fashions out of Marshall's or T.J. Maxx.

"Look at her," Chloe said.

Lichelle shrugged. "Her daddy is a baller. What do you expect?"

"It makes absolutely no sense at all."

"I keep telling you to get that ring, so you can have an all-access pass to them dollars too. He's got you on the same budget as his teenage daughter."

Chloe narrowed her eyes, and her nostrils flared a bit. "I'll be right back."

Chloe dropped her shoes onto the floor and stormed toward Deirdre. As she stomped she rapidly formulated a plan.

"Where are you going that you need shoes like that?" Chloe asked, as she walked up to Deirdre.

Deirdre turned and smirked at Chloe. "Wouldn't you like to know?"

"I don't care, but your father would want to know, especially since I heard him place you on punishment indefinitely."

"Who says I'm going anywhere? Maybe I need these shoes for a school program."

Chloe laughed out loud and took one of the silver shoes from Deirdre's hand. "A school program? What are y'all doing? A reenactment of a night at the club?"

"Why are you bothering me? Are you spying on me so you can run back and tell my father?" Deirdre asked, as she snatched the shoe back.

"I am not the one you need to be worried about, honey. It's the jail keeper they hired. She's your problem."

"I know," Deidre said with a sigh. "She was interrogating me this morning."

"I could help with that."

Deirdre lifted an eyebrow; her skepticism apparent. "How?"

"I can help you get around her and your father's punishment if you really want to see your little boyfriend in the hood. I'll pretend to mentor you or something. Then I'll drop you off wherever you want to go."

"Will you bring me home too?"

Chloe rolled her eyes. "I suppose I'll have to."

"Wait a minute. Why would you do this for me?"

"I'm not sure yet, but I may need your help."

"With what?"

"Listen here, don't question me. Just tell me if you want to do it. I'll get you to your boyfriend, and you'll help me later, if and when I need it."

Chloe grinned at Deirdre, as she waited for the words to sink in. She could tell that Deirdre didn't trust her, but she still didn't refuse the deal.

"If I do this and you try to play me, I'm telling my dad."

Chloe laughed out loud. "Ditto."

Deirdre snatched up her shoes, spun on one heel, and marched away. Her hesitation tickled Chloe, but it also made her careful. She was in just as much danger from a betrayal as Deirdre, maybe even more so. After all, Quentin wouldn't disown his daughter over this treachery, but he might just break things off with his fun buddy.

Chloe sighed. She had to move quickly, before her window of opportunity passed. Operation "Ditch the Nanny" was in full effect.

CHAPTER 13

A loud crash of thunder woke Montana from a deep sleep. She'd been dreaming about Cinderella, of all things. In the dream she and Cinderella were wearing rags and running through a huge mansion, and they were being chased by something unseen. It was crazy, because in the dream, Montana was a real woman, but Cinderella was a cartoon, like in the film she'd watched over and over again as a child. She touched her stomach and wondered if that late-night plate of shrimp fried rice was the cause of her strange dream.

Montana decided to make herself a cup of lavender tea. It always settled her stomach and made her sleepy. At least she got to sleep in a little bit in the morning. The kids were on spring break, so no drop-offs. As soon as she got the schedule down, they were out of school for a week. She was going to have to learn everything all over again.

Montana slipped a robe on top of her nightgown and put on a pair of furry slippers before quietly descending the spiral staircase to the kitchen. As big as the Chambers mansion was, it seemed like almost everything took place in the kitchen and the media room. The rest of the house went mostly untouched.

On her way into the kitchen, Montana peeked into the parlor that used to be the favorite place of the late Mrs. Chambers.

It was a warm and friendly room, even in the dark in the middle of a storm. Occasionally, Montana would see Quentin in the room, standing in front of the window staring out at the pond, but tonight he wasn't there. The mansion was silent—even the floor creaks were drowned out by the sound of the rain.

In the kitchen, Montana quietly heated her tea water in the microwave. She preferred using a teapot, but she didn't want to break the silence with the whistle of the pot.

When the tea was ready, she sat down at the table and closed her eyes. The house was so peaceful with the rain pattering against the roof. She was tempted to go outside and splash around in the puddles.

In Montana's robe pocket there was a buzz. Her cell phone. Who would be texting her at this hour? Immediately she thought of her elderly aunt in Cleveland and snatched the phone from her pocket.

She breathed a sigh of relief when she saw that it wasn't her aunt, but let out a low groan when she saw who the text was from. Rio. Why hadn't she changed her number after they split up?

His text said, Montana, it was so good seeing you. I know I said I wouldn't contact you after you broke up with me, but I can't stop thinking about you. You look like you've gained a few pounds, but trust me when I say it's in all the right places. I'd love to feel you in my arms again. Don't you miss me at all? Did I really lose my favorite girl to Jesus?

Montana shook her head and deleted the text message. There was a time when she had missed him. She'd missed him so badly that she'd almost given up going to church. But she prayed for God to remove her craving for Rio and all of the carnal things he'd done with her and to her.

God was faithful, because she didn't have those cravings for him anymore. He was like a drug that had been flushed from her system. She'd been detoxed.

Montana finished her cup of tea and quietly rinsed her cup, dried it, and put it back in the cupboard. She had turned off the light and headed back to her room when she heard a loud thump behind her in the kitchen. Then there was a yelp that sounded like a child, but it could've been an animal. She pondered for a moment, grabbed a poker from the fireplace, and headed bravely back into the kitchen.

Montana threw on the light switch and there, sprawled out on the floor, clutching her ankle, was Deirdre. She was soaking wet from head to toe, and wincing from pain.

"Deirdre, are you okay?" Montana asked.

She nodded and put a finger to her lips. "Will you be quiet? Are you trying to wake up the entire house?"

Montana put the poker down and kneeled next to Deirdre. She touched the ankle that Deirdre was nursing. Deirdre winced in pain again.

"I think your ankle is swelling."

"Thank you, Captain Obvious," Deirdre said.

For some reason, this made Montana giggle. "Sorry, I know you're in pain, but that was funny."

"I'm glad you're so easily amused," Deirdre said.

"What were you doing out there anyway?"

Finally, Montana noticed what Deirdre was wearing. A tiny jean skirt, cute heels, and a snug knit blouse. She also had on a face full of makeup.

"I was just taking a walk," Deirdre said.

Montana held up one of the red five-inch heels. "In these?"

"Yes," Deirdre said as she snatched her shoe. Montana tilted her head to one side and swept the wet hair from Deirdre's face. "You can trust me, you know. I'm not your enemy."

"You're my warden. That's why they hired you."

"Maybe we could be friends."

"Isn't that called fraternizing with the prisoners? I'm sure it's against the rules. Plus I don't need any more friends. I've got enough."

"That's crazy. Why don't we get to know each other first before you decide."

Deirdre rolled her eyes. "What do you want to know?"

"Well, let me think. What do you want to be when you grow up? Where are you going to college?"

Deirdre laughed loudly and then quieted herself. "Why do I

need to go to college? It's not like I'll ever need a job. We've got more money than I can ever spend. I should just drop out of school right now and go shopping every day."

"I can't believe what I'm hearing!" Montana fussed. "Not everyone has the opportunity to have the kind of education your family can afford. I scraped my way through school, but it was the best thing ever. You don't just go to college to get a job. You go to discover who you are."

"I know who I am," Deirdre said. "I'm a trust-fund brat."

Montana tilted the girl's chin upward and smiled at her. "You're more than that! God's called you to do something."

"God doesn't care about me. If He did, my mother would still be here."

Montana's heart ached for Deirdre. "I felt that way when I lost my mother, but I hope someday you'll feel differently."

"Whatever," Deirdre said, slowly rising to her feet. "I'm going to bed. My walk has tired me out."

"Well, don't you want to know anything about me?"

"Nah. You're the one trying to be friends. Not me."

Montana sighed as Deirdre hopped out of the kitchen. Quentin wasn't the only one in the Chambers family who needed healing. Montana might have to leave his wounds to Chloe, but she would see to it that Deidre got healed.

CHAPTER 14

Quentin was having a rough morning. The previous night's storm had interrupted his sleep multiple times, and his alarm clock was annoying him with its incessant buzzing. When he finally did get out of bed, he stubbed his big toe on the corner of his solid oak armoire, sending ripples of pain through his foot and profanities through the air.

The last thing Quentin needed this morning was excitement. He just wanted to have his protein shake and go to Transitions for a while.

He looked all over his bedroom for his cell phone and couldn't find it. Then he remembered; he'd left it in his office the night before on purpose. He hadn't felt like talking to Chloe, so if she'd called he could truthfully say he'd missed it.

Quentin stepped inside his office to take his phone off the desk and noticed a pretty bouquet of flowers. As grumpy as he felt, the blossoms made him smile. It was a pleasant surprise, and he wasn't used to getting those very often.

Now in a better mood than when he rolled out of bed, Quentin went downstairs to make his protein shake. It was his normal breakfast, along with some fruit. He ate healthy during the week, for the most part, and let loose on the weekend. It was how he'd avoided that middle-age gut some of his friends had acquired.

As he neared the kitchen, Quentin's senses noticed two things. Noise—a lot of it. And the scents of cinnamon and vanilla. All of a sudden that protein shake was incredibly unappetizing.

When he heard the children's voices, Quentin expected his mother to be in the kitchen with them, but instead it was Montana. Four of his children, all except Deirdre, were hanging out in the kitchen with Montana while she flipped French toast on the griddle.

Quentin also noticed the vases on the countertops and on the table, filled with vibrant fresh flowers. But as stunning as those flowers were, they didn't come close to outshining Montana's beauty. She was wearing sweats, and her big hair was pulled into a high ponytail. The sight of her caught Quentin completely off guard.

There was something about her—a glow. Something that radiated from inside. Maybe she was just a happy person. No, Quentin thought, it's more than that. It looked as if she'd never been sad. It was a quality most people lost when they experienced a heartbreak or suffered a loss.

The children were playing a game of charades with Montana, and they were laughing and keeping up such a racket that they hadn't noticed Quentin in the doorway. He quietly observed them from his post and enjoyed the fun.

Danielle was the first to notice Quentin. She ran over and hugged his waist. "Daddy! Are you hungry? Ms. Montana made French toast. I told her it was your favorite."

"Good morning, Mr. Chambers. I hope we didn't wake you."

Quentin walked arm in arm with Danielle over to the table. "No, you didn't. This house is so big, a fireworks show could've been going on down here and I wouldn't have heard it in my room."

"Oh, good," Montana said. " 'Cause we were getting a little rowdy in here."

"Rowdy is cool. It's spring break, y'all are supposed to be cutting up." Quentin motioned toward the flowers. "Did you do this too?"

Montana smiled. "The twins and I went out and gathered flowers this morning. They're from the property. You like?"

"I guess I could use some floralization. It's nice."

Danielle scrunched her nose. "Daddy, floralization is not a word."

"He made that up on purpose, dummy," Morgan said.

"Don't call your sister a dummy," Montana said. "She is very, very smart!"

Danielle stuck her tongue out at Morgan, and Morgan laughed. Quentin sat back in his seat and folded his arms across his chest. The kids seemed to really like Montana. Quentin had to give his mother credit for this whole nanny idea.

"Should we give your daddy the first French toast?" Montana asked.

Reese said, "You should give both men some first."

"You are not a man," Madison said.

Madison took the plate from Montana and sat it in front of Quentin. "Eat up, Daddy. I know it's not those nasty shakes you usually have, but it's better!"

Quentin picked up a fork. "I'll be the judge of that."

He took one bite and shuddered at the deliciousness of the French toast. There was a nutty flavor in addition to the cinnamon, and it was the perfect combination of crispy at the edges and soft and buttery in the middle.

"This is really good, Montana. Thank you!"

Montana smiled, and Quentin felt butterflies in his stomach. Then he felt ridiculous for the butterflies. He was a grown man. Grown men didn't get all twisted about a pretty girl.

But the butterflies continued.

Quentin ate a few more bites and stood to his feet. He couldn't take Montana and her smiles anymore this morning. She was making him feel lame.

"You leaving, Mr. Chambers?"

Quentin paused before answering Montana's question. The tone of her voice made him think she wanted him to stay.

"Um . . . yes. I've got some runs to make."

"You should stay and hang out with us," Morgan said.

"Do you all have anything planned?" Quentin asked.

"They want to go to the mall. Girl stuff," Reese said. "Save yourself, Dad."

Quentin frowned. "The mall? How about I just give y'all a credit card?"

"That's what's up!" Madison said. "Hand it over!"

Quentin said, "Okay, I was thinking you were gonna be like Mary Poppins, but you're a chef too? What don't you do?"

"There's quite a bit I don't do! I'm just putting my best foot forward. I want you guys to like me."

"Well, we definitely like you. Keep up the good work." Quentin wished he had a rewind button to press. He thought he sounded way too enthusiastic on that last comment.

He was rewarded with another big smile from Montana. "Maybe you can hang out with us another time, Mr. Chambers. We'd be glad to have you."

"Okay, y'all. Enjoy the day."

On the way out of the kitchen Quentin ran into Estelle, who was still wearing her lounging robe. "Mother, are you feeling well?" he asked. Estelle always got dressed when she woke up.

She nodded. "I'm just feeling lazy today, and I smelled breakfast cooking, so I came down. I thought it was you cooking."

"No, it's Montana and the kids."

Estelle lifted her eyebrows in surprise. "They sound like they're having fun."

"They are."

Estelle made a satisfied little noise before stepping around her son and continuing to the kitchen.

"Quentin," Estelle called when Quentin was at the bottom of the staircase.

"Yes?"

"You're welcome."

Quentin laughed out loud. Estelle never waited for thanks. She commanded it.

"Okay, Mother. Okay. You were right! The kids needed a nanny."

Estelle gave Quentin a knowing smile as if she knew about the butterflies. She couldn't possibly. Could she? Quentin put one hand on his stomach in an effort to calm them and rushed away from his mother.

He was a grown man. He didn't need a nanny or insects in his stomach.

CHAPTER 15

Montana happily cleaned up the kitchen after making breakfast with the children. The Chambers family had a maid, of course, but Montana was taught to always clean up after herself. Her values hadn't changed when she'd moved into a mansion.

Singing always helped her work go by more quickly, so she practiced the song they were going to sing at church on Sunday. It was an old Andrae Crouch song called "We Are Not Ashamed." Montana simply loved the song, and she felt so honored when the choir director asked her to lead it, along with one of the brothers.

When she got to the chorus part, Montana belted, "We are not ashamed!" at the top of her lungs. Then she caught herself and lowered her voice. She remembered Quentin wasn't all that fond of church, and that probably included gospel music. He was gone on his errands, but maybe one of the staff would tell him. Things were going well with Ms. Levy, and Montana wanted to keep it that way.

"Ms. Montana?"

Montana jumped at the sound of Morgan's voice. "Yes, honey? Do you need something?"

She shook her head, and then Madison tipped into the

kitchen too. Morgan said, "Please don't stop singing. Our parents used to sing that song all the time."

"They did? Mr. Chambers can sing too? I knew he could play, but I didn't know he could sing."

"He doesn't sing anymore," Madison said. "No one sings anymore in our house."

"Well, I sing! Only I do it in my room with the door closed," Morgan said.

Montana's heart ached for these children. It was like they were all trapped in cages waiting for the jailer to arrive with the key and set them free.

"Singing should be heard," Montana said. "I'm going to sit down, and I want you to give me a concert."

Morgan covered her mouth with her hand and giggled. "What should I sing?"

"Whatever you want!"

Morgan cleared her throat, closed her eyes, and launched into a beautiful rendition of "Killing Me Softly." It was a take on Lauryn Hill's version, and Morgan's voice was perfect for it. Then, on the chorus, Madison came in on the harmony parts. Their voices blended seamlessly.

When they were done, Montana gave them a round of applause. Danielle had joined them in the kitchen, and she was clapping too.

"You girls sound incredible! Why aren't you in the youth choir at church?"

"Daddy won't let us," Danielle said. "I can sing too."

Montana gave the youngest girl a hug. "You can?"

"But Deirdre sings the best," Madison said. "Her voice is ridiculous. One time she sang at a talent show at school. We went, but no one told Daddy."

"Go and get Deirdre. I want to hear her sing too," Montana said.

Danielle scurried out of the kitchen to get her sister. Montana beamed at the twins.

"I can't believe you guys have been keeping all this good singing to yourself!"

Deirdre limped into the kitchen behind Danielle. She looked annoyed.

"What?" Deirdre asked.

"Your sisters tell me you are an awesome singer! I want to hear it!"

Deirdre rolled her eyes at her sisters. "Y'all better be glad Daddy isn't here with all this singing y'all doing."

"Sing! Sing! Sing!" Madison, Morgan, and Danielle chanted and giggled at the same time.

"Okay, rugrats."

Deirdre cleared her throat and started snapping her finger. Then she sang Adele's "Rolling in the Deep" like the song was written for her. She sounded so good that if she wanted a record deal, she could get one that very day.

"Wow," Montana said when it was over. "That was incredible."

"I know," Deirdre said with a laugh.

Everyone burst into laughter at Deirdre's cocky reply. Deirdre did a little dance where she bobbed her shoulders up and down.

"How do y'all feel about not being able to sing around your father?" Montana asked, changing the lighthearted mood.

The twins looked at each other and then the floor. Danielle had a sad face as well, but Deirdre looked angry.

"It's like he's trying to take away the one thing I remember about my mother," Madison said. "She was always singing, and she sang with us too. She taught us songs, and we sang them together."

"Remember this one, y'all?" Deirdre asked before singing "The Shepherd Song."

Morgan said, "Yes! We were little when she taught us that one."

"I don't remember it," Danielle said. "Why can't I remember?"

"You were a baby," Deirdre said.

Montana had a great idea. "You could learn it now! How would you all like to sing at your grandmother's brunch on Sunday?"

"All of Grandmother's friends come to her Sunday brunch," Deirdre said. "Daddy wouldn't want us singing in front of them."

"I know. That's why we won't tell him about it. It will be a surprise."

Morgan's eyes widened. "Ms. Montana, you are gonna get in so much trouble."

Montana smiled. She wasn't worried about getting in trouble with Quentin Chambers. Not if it was going to bring music back into this house, where it belonged. The children wanted—no, needed—to sing. It was their legacy, gifted to them by their mother.

Montana also had a sneaking suspicion the music would reach Quentin too. If he fired her after that—well, then, Montana was sure that bringing the music back was her purpose in this household. She had to follow God on this, and her spirit was telling her to lead a miniature Chambers choir. God had never led her wrong before.

CHAPTER 16

Chloe was determined to have the perfect birthday. It started off well with a morning at the day spa. She had a full-body hot-rock massage, pedicure, and facial, and she tipped very well—on Quentin's black American Express card.

Next she took herself on a shopping spree and treated herself to a new Hermès Birkin bag and several new pairs of Louboutin heels—of course, all paid for by Quentin. He was being quite generous on her special day, and Chloe felt as if she deserved every bit of it. It was exactly what she deserved for being a great girlfriend and future wife.

Speaking of which, since her birthday would be the perfect time to pop the question, Chloe made sure to choose a very romantic new French restaurant called Le Grand Château for her birthday dinner. In case Quentin was feeling matrimonial, the beautiful setting might push him to go ahead and do the inevitable.

Quentin had agreed to dress up for her birthday dinner, and he was looking very delicious in his suit. Chloe was going to have a taste of caramel for dessert too if Quentin played his cards right and came correct on the birthday gift.

"What did you buy me?" Chloe asked Quentin, as the maître d' showed them to their table.

Quentin laughed out loud. "Didn't you just take yourself shopping?"

"That's not the same, and you know it! I'm not going to be a happy camper if you don't have a tiny box of something on your person."

"Why does it have to be a tiny box?" Quentin asked.

"The best presents come in tiny boxes, sweetie."

Quentin smiled at the waiter as he approached. "Wine, sir?" the waiter asked.

"Yes, bring me your best Pinot Noir, and Riesling for the lady."

"Excellent choices, sir. Would you like to order your dinner?"

Quentin nodded. "We'll have the five-course seafood with stuffed rockfish and lobster tail."

"That comes with dessert, sir. What would you like?"

"Ask the lady. It's her birthday."

The waiter smiled at Chloe. "Mademoiselle, would you like to try our flan? It is regarded as the best in town."

"Do you like it?" Chloe asked.

"Oh, I love it," the waiter gushed.

She doubted he liked it that much, but nodded. "I will try the flan."

"Wonderful choices. I will be right out with the wine."

"He's working hard for his tip, isn't he?" Quentin asked. "I thought he was about to start tap dancing and sing us a song."

Chloe laughed at Quentin's dry humor. "He would if you ask him. He knows a wealthy man when he sees one. Your tip would probably pay all of his expenses for the month."

Sometimes it bothered Chloe that Quentin didn't seem to understand the power that came with his wealth. He'd never been poor and never would be, so the idea of a life without luxuries was foreign to him.

Chloe knew exactly what it meant to struggle. Her family came from a little town in Alabama called Leeds, and they were dirt-poor. Chloe's grandmother's house had had indoor plumbing for only about fifteen years. She remembered going over there during the summers and enduring the God-awful heat and that disgusting outhouse.

She'd come to Atlanta to reinvent herself, and she'd been successful at it. Now she could send her grandmother money from time to time. When she went home to her family reunions, everyone said she was big-time, and she was—compared to them.

But marrying Quentin would be the ultimate come up. She'd provide everything he needed in a wife, and he'd make her rich beyond her wildest dreams.

She decided to change the topic of conversation from her gift to something Quentin actually seemed to care about—his foundation.

"So I met with your mother a few days ago on the plans for the ball. We're shooting for the beginning of June."

"That doesn't give you much time to plan, but I trust you to pull it off."

Chloe beamed. "Yes, I think your mother and I make a great team. We've also enlisted the nanny's help."

"Montana? She's a party planner?"

"Not really, but she's sweet and eager to please. Plus, she's the tiebreaker between me and Estelle."

Quentin threw his head back and laughed. "I'm surprised my mother is allowing you to think that. The only employee who might overrule Mother is Ms. Levy, and that's only because they've become friends over the years."

Chloe was thrilled to hear Quentin refer to Montana as an employee. That's exactly what she was, and Chloe had to keep reminding herself that the young girl wasn't trying to steal her man.

"Yes, well, maybe I'll befriend Montana, and it'll be young Mrs. Chambers and the nanny versus the elder Mrs. Chambers and the housekeeper."

Quentin's laughter abruptly stopped. "You slid that on in there, didn't you?"

"What?"

"I'm going to let it pass, since it's your birthday. Everybody gets to make wishes on their birthday."

"I don't make wishes. I make plans," Chloe said.

Quentin shook his head wearily. "Do you have a theme for the party?"

"We're having a masquerade ball. What do you think?"

He shrugged. "If you all like it, I love it."

"We do love it. And Montana made the suggestion of having flowers all over the house in different stages, from buds to blooms."

"Transitioning flowers for Transitions," Quentin said, nodding thoughtfully while he took in the idea.

"I like the idea too," Chloe said, although she was slightly annoyed that Quentin had figured out the reason for the flowers without being told. She didn't want him in sync with Montana.

The waiter came back and presented them with two bottles of wine. He poured each of them a glass and bowed deeply as he backed away from the table.

"You know something funny," Quentin asked, as he took his first sip of wine. He closed his eyes and savored the taste before swallowing. "Montana has been leaving fresh flowers in my office every day. I thought it was one of the children, but it was her!"

Chloe lifted an eyebrow. "Really? Why does she do that?"

"She said that my office is pretty boring, and that she was trying to brighten the place."

"I could decorate your office if you'd like. Bring in some great interior designers, maybe even tear down a wall. Would you like that?" Chloe asked.

There was a hint of irritation in her tone. She didn't like Montana noticing anything about her man's space. First of all, what was she even doing in Quentin's office? And then to take the liberty of leaving fresh flowers for a man? It sounded flirtatious to Chloe. It sounded like something she would do to get a man's attention.

"No, no. I don't want to redecorate. It was just nice of her to think of that. I appreciated it. Then the kids told her I like

French toast. Do you know she and the kids got up and made me breakfast?"

Chloe pouted. "You're going to make me jealous! She's there to take care of the children, not my man."

"You're jealous of Montana? That's crazy."

Chloe took a huge gulp of her wine. She hadn't meant to swallow so much, and she choked a little. When Quentin jumped up to help, she waved one hand in the air.

"I'm fine. I'm fine. But yes, I am jealous. I'd like to do those things for you. I want to be there for you. She's known you a couple of weeks, she's under your roof, and already she's doing nice little things for you."

"She was just spending time with the kids. She's the nanny . . ."

"Yes, but in five years you haven't once mentioned wanting to wake up to me on the other side of your bed."

Quentin chuckled. "I've woken up many times next to you, Chloe. You're being silly."

"Yes, in hotels, villas, cottages, bed and breakfasts, and châteaus. But never your home."

Quentin gave her an incredulous look. "I can't believe we're having this conversation. You know why you can't spend the night. My children live in the mansion."

Chloe looked down at the table and sighed. "I don't want to spend the night. I want to spend my life."

Suddenly remorseful, Quentin took Chloe's hand. "I'm sorry if it seems like this is going nowhere. I do care for you very much, but I wouldn't be angry with you if you decided to move on."

Quentin flipped Chloe's hand over and placed a little box in it. She knew there wasn't a ring inside, based on Quentin's presentation. Instead she opened the box to find a pretty pair of emerald and diamond earrings. They were beautiful, but not what she was hoping for.

"Thank you, Quentin. They're lovely."

He stroked her face with one hand. "Just as you are."

Chloe looked up into Quentin's light brown eyes and exhaled. How long would she be able to stand being his woman without the benefit of being a wife? There weren't any other eligible multimillionaires beating down her door. She'd invested too much time in Quentin. Out of common courtesy, none of the wealthy men in Quentin's circle would touch her with a ten-foot pole. And the thought of finding another wealthy, elderly white man, after she'd sampled Quentin's caramel goodness for five years, turned her stomach.

One thing she did know, that French toast was the last meal this nanny was going to cook for her man.

"So how would you like to order some strawberry crêpes?" Chloe asked.

"Oh, they have crêpes? I didn't see that on the menu," Quentin replied.

Chloe grinned. "I mean at the Ritz. For breakfast."

"Can we get this fancy French stuff to go?"

Chloe cackled as Quentin flagged the waiter down. There was one thing she did have on the sweet, flower-bearing, breakfast-cooking Montana. Chloe had spent five years learning everything that turned Quentin on, and all the things that didn't.

In Chloe's book, a black lace teddy trumped breakfast any day.

CHAPTER 17

Quentin's head throbbed as he made a cup of coffee in the kitchen at home. No doubt, Chloe was going to be furious when she woke up to find him gone, but he'd promised Alex he was coming over for a visit. At least Quentin had shared the strawberry crêpes with Chloe at three in the morning. Quentin was barely interested in the entire evening—the carnal activities or the crêpes—but Chloe seemed to be enjoying herself, and that's all that mattered since it was her birthday.

Chloe would've been furious to know that Quentin's thoughts kept drifting to Montana during her birthday celebration. He kept imagining her smile and that big wild head of hair that begged him to touch it.

There was something about Montana that made him want to pursue her. He felt like a sleepy lion that'd been having his meals brought to him. Then suddenly a young gazelle crossed his path, and he remembered that he was a hunter.

That was exactly it. Chloe had offered herself up on a platter, but Montana just skipped back and forth, taunting him, stirring his true nature. Quentin was a man's man. He liked to hunt for his food.

He closed his eyes and sipped the coffee. It was good, a Jamaican roast he'd bought when he and Chloe had spent a week in Montego Bay.

Quentin wondered if Montana had ever been to Jamaica. Then he imagined her curves in a two-piece swimsuit.

It completely jarred Quentin when he opened his eyes and Montana was opening the sliding kitchen door. She looked like she'd been in a fight. Her hair was flying out of its ponytail, she was drenched in sweat, and she clutched the wall, huffing and puffing.

"What happened to you?" Quentin asked.

Montana held up one finger. She inhaled deeply and exhaled a few times before replying. "You inspired me, Mr. Chambers. I tried to go running this morning."

This made Quentin burst into laughter. "You just woke up one day and decided to go running?"

"Yeah, well, I figured I've got two legs and two feet. How hard could it be?"

When Montana started to slide down the wall to the floor, Quentin helped her over to the table. Then he gave her a glass of juice and a bottle of water.

"Drink both. You've probably sweated out every electrolyte in your body."

Montana guzzled the juice. "Thank you. I feel okay, except that my feet are killing me."

"Let me see your shoes."

Montana stuck out her feet and immediately Quentin saw the problem. The shoes weren't running shoes. They were walking shoes, definitely not made to take the impact of running on the hard ground.

"Are they okay?" Montana asked.

"Not for running. They look a little cheaply made, too."

Montana scoffed. "I beg your pardon! I paid twenty-nine dollars for these at Target."

"If you're gonna run, you need better shoes."

Quentin took out his cell phone and flipped it open. He started dialing a number.

"What are you doing? Calling the sneaker police on me?" Montana asked.

He shook his head. "Sneakers? Therein, my friend, lies the problem."

"There is nothing wrong with my shoes."

Quentin held up one finger as he spoke into the phone. "Hey, Gerard. Yeah, man, can you open a little early today? I've got an emergency. A friend of mine is trying to run in some no-name walking shoes. . . . I know, man. She don't know no better. . . . Nah, not Chloe. Chloe doesn't run, she zumbas or whatever. Yeah. . . . Okay, we'll be there in forty-five minutes."

Montana furrowed her brows. "Who will be where in forty-five minutes? I don't have money for any expensive running shoes. I will stick to my Target specials."

"Let me help you. I don't want you to hurt yourself out there. My friend has a sporting goods shop, and he will fit you with the best running shoes you've ever had."

Montana folded her arms across her chest. "And how much is this going to cost me?"

"Just a couple of hours."

"You can't buy me shoes, Mr. Chambers. That's not part of my salary."

Quentin shook his head. "Okay, then let's call it your clothing allowance. Go shower really quickly, though, because you stink."

"I do not!" Then, Montana sniffed herself. "Okay, so I do, but that was rude."

"No, it would be rude if I let you go out and about smelling like that. A friend wouldn't do that."

"We're friends, Mr. Chambers?"

Quentin smiled at her. "Anyone who cooks me yummy food for breakfast is my friend. And since we're friends, I have another request."

"What's that?"

"Call me Quentin."

Montana gave him a thoughtful look. "Okay, I'll call you Quentin. But only when I'm off the clock."

"Okay, I'm giving you the morning off to go shoe shopping. Most women would be ecstatic about this. You have given me nothing but push back."

"I am not like most women."

Quentin nodded his head in silent agreement. He was going to enjoy taking her shopping. He wished it wasn't just for shoes. He'd love to buy her a dress. Something bright to flatter her figure. Then he wouldn't mind sporting her on his arm.

His cell phone buzzed on the table. It was Chloe. What a way to get knocked back to reality.

Quentin shooed Montana from the kitchen. "Go and get changed before the kids start harassing you for stuff."

When Montana was gone, Quentin answered the phone. "Don't be mad."

"I'm not mad. I'm hurt." Quentin cringed at the whining tone in Chloe's voice. Had she always whined like that and he hadn't noticed it before?

"We had a great time, didn't we?"

"Yes, but I'm lonely and cold in this big bed."

"I'm sorry, Chloe. I've got a million and one things to do today. My mother is forcing me to go to her brunch on Sunday. I'm trying to escape."

There was a long pause before Chloe replied. "I will be there."

"I can't endure her church friends."

Chloe let out a sad chuckle. "I know you can't. That's why I'm coming. I've got your back."

"I know. Call me later?"

"Yep. Bye, baby, love you."

Quentin swallowed. "Okay, talk to you soon."

He disconnected the call and shook his head. Every time Chloe said, "I love you," he felt like a massive jerk. Who deals with a woman for five years, sleeps with her whenever he wants, parades her around town, and doesn't tell her he loves her? He didn't think he was that guy. But ever since Chandra had died, Quentin couldn't bring himself to say those words to a woman—especially not Chloe.

Chloe was not who he wanted to spend the rest of his life with. He knew that about two years into the five-year affair, but she was determined and he was lazy. That's what having meals served up to a lion did to him—it made him sluggish.

Was it time to end things with Chloe? The thought made Quentin feel like an even bigger lowlife. But he just couldn't pursue Montana while he had Chloe biding her time and waiting on a ring. He definitely wasn't that guy.

So the lion was awake. But did he remember how to hunt? Would he have to learn the rules all over again? Would the gazelle outrun him and leave him famished and unsatisfied? Maybe the lion wasn't fully wide awake yet. Coffee first, gazelle hunting in the afternoon.

CHAPTER 18

Montana stood in her bedroom, freshly showered and wondering what to wear on her shopping trip with Quentin. She couldn't tell if he was flirting with her, or if he was truly just concerned with the welfare of her feet.

It was a very warm morning, so she chose a sundress that fitted snugly at the top but flared out at the bottom. It didn't show off her best asset, but she'd caught Quentin doing a double take of her backside when she left out of the kitchen earlier. If he was flirting with her, she didn't want to seem like she was encouraging it. She was simply accepting a very generous offer from her wealthy employer.

She pinned her hair up and put a yellow flower in over her right ear. A friend once told her that Hawaiian women signaled their availability to men by the position of their flower. On the left meant married and spoken for. On the right meant single and ready to mingle. In the middle meant up for negotiation.

Montana had no idea if the explanation was true, but just in case Quentin had heard it too, she wanted him to be clear that she was absolutely single. Just in case it was the beginning of something.

Montana was bothered by the fact that Quentin was not single, though. At least she didn't think he was. But maybe he and

Chloe had called it quits and hadn't told anyone yet. Why else would he be flirting?

There was a knock on her bedroom door. She asked, "Who is it?"

"It's Deirdre. Can I come in?"

Montana grinned and opened the door.

"What can I do for you?"

"I was going to ask you a question about this song, but it looks like you're on your way somewhere."

"Oh, we're going to practice this afternoon. You can ask me then."

Deirdre inhaled deeply and gave Montana a suspicious glare. "You smell good! Where are you going?"

"Oh, nowhere, really. Your dad is taking me shopping for a pair of running shoes."

Deirdre's mouth made a little *O* shape. Montana shook her head and laughed.

"Does Chloe know he's buying you shoes?" Deirdre asked.

"He just felt sorry for me, because he says my shoes are raggedy."

Deirdre pushed her way into the room and sat down on Montana's bed. "Why would you go out with a guy like my dad to get running shoes. How about some Louboutins? I'm sure you don't have any red bottoms."

Montana gazed at Deirdre and tried to figure out where the conversation was going before it got there. Deirdre's expression was completely innocent, although Montana sensed that the questions were not.

"Are you trying to get Chloe really mad at me? What business would your father have buying me designer shoes?"

"What business does my father have buying you any shoes?"

"It's like I said. He felt sorry for me."

"Mmm-hmm," Deirdre said. "That still doesn't explain why you gotta smell so good, but okay."

"Um . . . okay."

"Can you remind my dad that Chloe is taking me to lunch

today? Just in case he thinks I'm trying to sneak off my punishment. I might not be here when you get back."

"Why don't you go downstairs and tell him?"

"Because if he looks guilty about this little running shoe trip, I'd feel weird during my outing with Chloe."

"There's nothing to be guilty about."

Deirdre hopped up from the bed. "Sure. I got it. You've got your hair pinned up, you're drenched in perfume, and you've got a dress on that's hugging your boobs. It's nothing."

Deirdre skipped out of the room like it was Christmas morning and she'd just opened a new toy. She was too happy about her insinuations.

The conversation left Montana feeling uneasy. The last thing she needed was for Deirdre to say anything out of pocket to Chloe, but to ask her not to mention it might make it seem like they did have something to hide.

And if Chloe was taking Deirdre to lunch, then obviously things were going fine between her and Quentin. So he wasn't flirting, then, and it really was all about the shoes.

Finally, Montana headed back downstairs to meet Quentin and go. He was standing just at the bottom of the staircase, and he watched her descend the stairs. Quentin's face seemed mesmerized, and immediately Montana thought that maybe she'd overdone it with the dress and the flower in her hair. What if he thought she was pursuing him?

"Wow. Am I taking you to a photo shoot on the way to the shoe store?" Quentin asked.

Montana blushed. It was too much. "I can change. I didn't know where we were shopping. I thought it was some rich people's store. I didn't want to look bummy."

Quentin doubled over with laughter. "Oh boy. Let's go, Montana! I don't even know what to say to that."

They walked through the house to the attached garage, where there were multiple luxury vehicles, all in different shades of red. All shining brightly.

"Someone is a collector," Montana said.

Quentin smiled. "I am. It's the only thing I really splurge on."

Montana grinned to herself. She'd also heard he splurged on Chloe, but she wasn't about to bring her up.

"So which one you want to go for a ride in?" Quentin asked.

The burgundy Aston Martin convertible was calling her name, so Montana pointed to it. "What kind of car is this?"

"It's an Aston Martin, and you have great taste. Let's go."

Quentin went to a lockbox on the wall and punched in a code. He opened it and removed a set of keys. Then he opened the passenger-side door for Montana and she got in.

The buttery leather felt good on Montana's skin, and the car smelled like it had just left the showroom. There wasn't a crumb, scratch, or nick inside—a far cry from the inside of her Nissan Sentra. This car felt like money. And she was riding shotgun.

"You ready?" Quentin asked.

Montana nodded, and Quentin opened the garage. He turned on the car, dropped the top, and zipped to the edge of the property in what felt like three seconds.

"Wow!" Montana said breathlessly.

"That's nothing," Quentin said. "Maybe I'll take you out to the country one day so you can see it really move."

Montana looked at the floor and tried not to smile. Was he making plans for their next outing already? She wanted to ask him about Chloe, but couldn't think of how to do it without sounding presumptuous. What if he was just trying to be friends?

"What is that scent you're wearing?" Quentin asked. "It's nice."

"Oh, it's just some cheap Bath and Body Works spray. It'll probably be worn off by the time we get back."

"It doesn't smell cheap."

Montana cocked her head to one side and narrowed her eyes at Quentin. Why couldn't he just come out and give her a compliment? He said she looked like she was going to a photo shoot instead of telling her she looked nice. And instead of saying she smelled good, he said her perfume didn't smell cheap.

He was being very careful with his words and careful not to flirt. Maybe he was just trying to be a good boyfriend to Chloe.

Or maybe he wasn't flirting at all. Montana didn't like not knowing.

Montana thought of a safe question to ask. "I didn't see you come in last night. Were you out late?"

"I was," Quentin replied.

Dang! That wasn't enough information to go on, and any additional questions would seem like she was being nosy.

"Were you worried?" Quentin asked.

Montana detected some amusement in his tone. "No! Why would I be worried? Honestly, I was just being nosy."

"Well, why didn't you just say so? I took Chloe out for her birthday, and then we went to the Ritz."

Montana nodded slowly. The guys she'd dated in the past had taken her, at best, out to eat and then to the Marriott, or back to their home. Quentin was just like any other unsaved guy—dinner, then a hotel. He just had more money.

She felt silly for getting done up. It was stupid anyway to get even a little bit carried away over Quentin when he clearly had a girlfriend.

Montana was quiet the rest of the way to the shoe store, and Quentin didn't try to engage her in conversation. The wind whipping through the car seemed to be enough noise for both of them.

The sporting goods store was definitely one of those places where the wealthy spent their money. There were no price tags on any of the shoes, and there were items Montana had never seen before.

The owner came from the back and hugged Quentin, then gave him a fist pound. "Frat! What's going on?" he said.

Quentin said, "I can't call it! Gerard, meet my friend Montana. Montana meet Gerard. We go way back, and he's gonna hook you up."

"Well, aren't you lovely," Gerard said, while sweeping his eyes from the top of Montana's curly head to her feet.

"Thank you," Montana said. She glanced at Quentin out of the corner of her eye to gauge his reaction. She didn't see anything out of the ordinary. He didn't seem to mind the compliment.

"She needs outdoor running shoes. She was trying to run on my estate today and had sore feet afterward."

Gerard nodded. "A lot of uneven terrain on your property. Some rocky areas. Did you ever put in a running path?"

"No, but I might do it now. I have been the only one running all these years."

Gerard's eyes widened, and he gave Quentin the strangest look. Quentin burst into laughter. "Oh, man! You are funny. Why didn't you just ask? My mother hired Montana to be the children's nanny."

"Ah!" Gerard nodded. "I was about to trip. I was up here asking myself when you traded Chloe in for the younger model."

Gerard and Quentin shared a hearty laugh that was complete with slaps on the back and more fist pounds. Montana frowned and felt she was the butt of a joke somehow. Was Quentin teasing her?

"Okay, Ms. Montana, I'm going to ask you to stand on this contraption here. It's going to tell me how you distribute your weight on your feet, so I'll know the best kind of support for you." Gerard took Montana's hand and led her over to the machine in the corner.

Montana took off her sandals and stood on the machine while it buzzed and whirred and made clicking and beeping sounds. She hoped all those noises meant the machine knew what it was doing.

After a few moments, a small printer attached to the machine printed out a sheet of paper. Gerard read it and nodded. Then he had her step down.

"Looks like you have flat feet, Ms. Montana. I'll need to get you a shoe with a lot of shock absorption and stability support."

Montana looked confused. "Um . . . I have no idea what you just said."

"Sit here. I'm going to bring you a shoe that will make love to your feet."

"Well, it's a good thing I don't have a boyfriend, because he'd be jealous."

Montana chuckled as she walked barefoot over to the brown leather couch. When she sat, her entire body sank into the cushions. Yep, she was definitely in a rich establishment.

When Gerard left the showroom floor, Quentin asked, "Why don't you have a boyfriend?"

"That's a personal question, Mr. Chambers."

"We're back to Mr. Chambers?"

Montana nodded.

"But why? I thought we were having fun."

It had gone back to Mr. Chambers in the car when Quentin talked about spending the night with his girlfriend at the Ritz. Then it was absolutely settled when Quentin and his boy had a good laugh about her being the "younger model." What was so funny about that? She wasn't as glamorous as Chloe, but she definitely held her own. Admittedly, she'd thrown out some bait with her sundress and the flower in her hair, but Montana decided that this was a dangerous game she was playing.

Quentin was obviously a forever bachelor, and Chloe was his long-suffering girlfriend. No matter what she'd been dreaming about, Montana was no Cinderella and Quentin was no prince. He was just an incredibly handsome man with a fat wallet.

"I thought we were getting running shoes," Montana said.

Quentin gave Montana a mischievous smile. "Well, I will just have fun all by myself then."

Montana tried to give him a serious glare, but had to look away when his gaze turned intense. She felt like a ball of yarn in the paws of a tom cat, and it wasn't a good feeling at all. After getting delivered from Rio, Montana was determined not to be anyone's toy.

CHAPTER 19

"So, what should I tell my dad we talked about on our outing?" Deirdre asked Chloe.

Chloe rolled her eyes and stared at the road. She had agreed to drop Deirdre off at the Cracker Barrel restaurant in Conyers, a place that none of her grandmother's friends would ever go for lunch.

"You can tell him we talked about your taste in boys," Chloe replied. "You need to find someone who can take you to a nicer place for lunch if they're trying to be your beau."

"My beau? You mean my boo?"

Chloe blinked slowly. This girl was in need of so much grooming. Even though the whole "mentoring" idea was a ruse, Chloe almost wanted to do it for real. She knew Deirdre didn't have a mother, but she did have a grandmother. What in the world was Estelle teaching Deirdre about the opposite sex?

"No, I mean your beau. You're getting to the age where you should start thinking about your future. Like what kind of man you'd like to marry."

Deirdre burst into laughter. "Stop playing, Chloe! I am sixteen. I am not thinking about a husband right now."

"Well, you should. You could end up making a mistake that could jeopardize your future."

"My future is real bright, Chloe. Bright and rich."

"You think you know everything, don't you?"

Deirdre laughed again. "No, not everything. But your man advice is suspect, so I think I'd rather listen to an expert. Maybe I should ask Montana for some advice."

"What is that supposed to mean?" Chloe slammed on the brakes at the red light and glared at Deirdre.

"You are awful touchy about Montana, aren't you?" Deirdre asked. "Well, maybe you should be, because my dad took her shopping this morning. Right before you came to pick me up."

"He. Did. What?"

"Apparently she needed new running shoes or something. They hopped in the Aston Martin with the top down and left the mansion."

Chloe swallowed and tried to determine how much of what Deirdre said was fact and how much was fiction. Deirdre's smirk didn't help matters, because it was so cocky and know-it-all.

"He's going to buy her running shoes? Maybe he thinks she's fat and is just trying to help her get in shape."

Chloe tried to convince herself that this was the case. Even as she said the words, she felt her heart stop racing. Yes, that's what it was. That ba-donka-donk was too big for her man's liking. Montana probably was at risk for high blood pressure, and Quentin didn't want to be responsible for paying any of her bills.

"She sure didn't look fat with that tight sundress she had on. It wasn't something I'd wear, but I guess it was cute on her."

Horns honking behind Chloe made her look up at the light. It had changed, but she was still sitting there. Chloe pressed the gas a little bit too hard and the tires squealed.

"You okay, Chloe?" Deirdre asked.

Chloe narrowed her eyes at Deirdre. The heffa knew exactly what she was doing. She was enjoying this way too much.

Chloe squeezed the steering wheel tightly, trying to channel her frustrations there. She couldn't believe that her man was out shoe shopping with Montana, and that she was wearing an outfit trying to entice him.

"Why wouldn't I be okay? I'm not concerned with that low-class domestic worker," Chloe finally said.

"Well, I would be if I was you. I was just telling you because I don't think you should let her move in on my daddy like that."

"You think she's moving in on him?"

Deirdre nodded. "Of course she is! She's broke and single!"

"I guess you do have a point."

Chloe pulled into the restaurant's parking lot and up to the front door. Deirdre jumped out of the car and smiled at Chloe.

"When are you coming back to get me?"

"You're going to have to find your own ride home. I have something to take care of."

Deirdre's eyes widened. "What am I gonna tell my dad?"

"Don't worry. I'll cover for you. Just make sure you get home before five."

"What are you gonna do?" Deirdre asked. "You're about to go off on Montana, aren't you?"

"Oh, no ma'am. I don't do that. I do not have hood-rat tendencies, but I would like to see Montana's new shoes."

Deirdre tossed her head back and laughed. "I want to be there for this! It's gonna be like an episode from *Real Housewives.*"

Chloe waved good-bye to Deirdre as she drove off from the restaurant. She couldn't believe she'd let that nanny get in her man's radar. It was time to pull out her full arsenal and let this nanny know that she was the boss.

CHAPTER 20

Quentin and Montana rode in silence after their shoe shopping was finished. He was kicking himself for even initiating the outing to begin with. His initial thought was that she needed shoes, that she probably couldn't afford the right ones, and that in some way he wanted to thank her for the French toast and the flowers.

Then he saw her come in the house from running, noticed how those sweat pants hugged her curves and found himself looking forward to spending time with her. When she'd changed into the sundress he wanted to spend the whole day with her. He enjoyed how excited Montana had gotten when she'd seen his automobile collection. Chloe was rarely impressed with him anymore. She'd seen it all.

"Have I offended you, Montana?" Quentin asked.

"No, Mr. Chambers. Oh, thank you for the running shoes. Please forgive my bad manners."

"You're welcome. As long as you're with our household, you can have anything you need. Don't hesitate to ask."

"Well, I better get while the getting is good. It sounds like Chloe plans on giving me my walking papers as soon as the two of you walk down the aisle."

Quentin wondered how he should respond to this. Of course, Montana had no idea he was thinking of ending things with Chloe. He wasn't even sure if he wanted to go back to being alone.

"I'm not sure what Chloe communicated to you, but I haven't proposed marriage to her. So . . . um . . . your job is safe for now."

Montana nodded and glanced out the window.

"Montana, what's wrong? Why are you upset all of a sudden? Tell me what I did wrong!"

"Nothing, Mr. Chambers! I have a lot on my mind. You didn't do anything."

Now she was lying. Quentin could tell.

"Okay, well, if you aren't angry with me, then I'd like to take you somewhere else before we go back home."

Montana frowned. "You're playing games with me, Mr. Chambers. It's very unkind."

"No, no, no! I'm not. I promise! I just want to thank you for what you've done with the kids. They're happier somehow."

"You pay me to take care of the children."

"But I also want to thank you for the French toast, the flowers in my office. For everything. I was . . . well, I was hoping we could be friends. I don't have many. You just met one of them."

"What about Chloe? She's your friend."

Quentin drew in a sharp breath. He chose his words carefully. "Chloe has been a good friend over the years."

"Okay. I'll be your friend. But where are you taking me? I don't like being surprised."

"First, stop calling me Mr. Chambers. My friends use my first name."

Montana cracked a tiny smile. "Quentin, where are you taking me?"

"To Transitions, the foundation house. Would you like to go?"

Finally, a real smile from Montana. One that lit up her face and the entire car.

"I'd love to visit there, Quentin. Thank you for the invite."

For the rest of the way to the country house outside of Douglasville, Georgia, Montana's chatter filled the car. Quentin heard all about her college days at Clark Atlanta University, and how she couldn't wait to be a teacher. He found out that she had family in Cleveland, Ohio—an aunt and cousins. Her mother had died while she was in high school.

It was information overload for Quentin, but he was okay with it, because Montana was smiling again—and he sure enjoyed that.

"Is this the house, Quentin? Oh my goodness! It's beautiful!"

Quentin looked out at the house with Montana. It was a grand sight to behold on the first time seeing it. It was two stories and white, with huge roman pillars and porches that wrapped around the entire house on both stories.

Montana didn't even wait for Quentin to open her door when he stopped the car. She wanted to see more, and he was excited to show her. This was his life's work.

One of the nurses opened the door as Quentin and Montana approached. She looked surprised to see Montana. Quentin usually came alone, so this would be different for everyone.

"How's Alex today?" Quentin asked, as soon as they got to the porch.

The nurse shook her head. "Not so good, sir. But she won't take any meds right now. She says she's writing. She suffers for no reason."

"Not being alert enough to write is even worse to Alex than the pain. Charlene, this is my friend Montana. Montana, Charlene is the head nurse here."

Montana hugged Charlene, and it caught her off guard. "It's nice meeting you."

"I'm gonna show her around, Charlene."

"Okay, Quentin. Let me know if you need anything."

Quentin showed Montana the reading room. The walls were covered with books, and the lighting was soft. There was one woman reading with a bandana wrapped around her head—Ola. She'd been at the home for a month and had stage-four pancreatic cancer. Most days she didn't leave her bed, but today she was full of energy. Ola was near the end. They always got energized at the end of the battle.

"Hey, Quentin. Who's this?" Ola asked.

"She's my friend Montana."

Montana waved. "Hello."

"Well, hello, beautiful. I was pretty like you a long time ago. My name is Ola."

"You're still beautiful," Montana said. "Can I . . . can I pray for you? Is it all right?"

Montana looked at Quentin when she asked, but Ola replied, "Yes, chile. Pray for me. I'm gonna see Him soon, so I can use all the prayer I can get."

Quentin watched in awe as Montana went over to Ola and laid her hands on her. He had no idea what Montana was saying in the prayer. She whispered so that only Ola could hear her. When she finished, Ola had tears in her eyes, and she hugged Montana with the little amount of strength that she had.

"Thank you, sweetie," Ola said.

"You're welcome."

Montana walked back over to Quentin. "Who else do I get to meet?" she asked.

"Come on. I want you to meet Alex."

Ola laughed. "Alex ain't gonna like her."

"Yes she will. Ola, you are a mess."

Quentin showed Montana all the rooms on the way upstairs to Alex's bedroom. They could hear Alex's low moan as they approached the room. Alex didn't even realize she made the sound, but she was in so much pain without her medicine that she made it without meaning to.

"Alex, babe. Look who's here."

Alex looked up at Quentin and Montana. "Oh, you done brought your girlfriend up in here. You real bold, Q."

Montana's eyes widened. She didn't know whether to laugh or be nervous.

"Alex, stop! This is my friend Montana."

Alex's eyebrows went up. "Oh. The nanny. I've heard lots about you."

"You have?" Montana asked.

"Yes, Q tells me everything. One day, he's gonna take me out of here, and all you groupies are gonna have to fall back."

Montana clapped her hand over her mouth to contain her laughter. "Groupies?"

"Yeah, all of y'all trying to get with my boo. But he built me this big old house out in the country. He lets my staff live here too."

Quentin crossed the room and kissed Alex on the forehead. "How you feeling today?"

Alex paused. "Let's just say, I am one hundred percent alive today."

"It's pointless to tell you to relax," Quentin said, and then he motioned for Montana to come over. "Could you do for Alex whatever you did for Ola?"

"Do what?" Alex asked. "You some kind of voodoo lady? I'm a Christian. Well, mostly. Somebody needs to help me repent for lusting after Q, but other than that I should be straight."

Montana looked at Quentin.

"If I can stop laughing long enough," Alex continued.

"Alex! Stop playing and let her pray for you."

Alex frowned at Quentin. "What you doing? Giving me my last rites? I'm not Catholic."

"Do I look like a priest?" Montana asked.

"Ooh! She tried it! Was I talking to you, groupie?" Alex asked.

Quentin sat down in the chair next to Alex's bed. "I should've known she would be difficult. See, Alex here believes that she and I are going to run off into the sunset together."

"We would if it wasn't for that gold digger Chloe," Alex said.

"Oh my," Montana clutched the necklace around her throat and giggled.

Alex cleared her throat and laughed. "I'm just playing. I don't get to have much fun around here. Everyone is a fun stealer up in this piece. Please pray for me. I'm in a lot of pain, but I'm trying to finish my writing before I leave. Q says he's going to publish my stuff posthumously."

Quentin nodded at Montana. "I keep telling her that she's got plenty of time to finish it, but she pays me no attention."

"Now we both know that's not true," Alex said. "So if you've got some prayer skills, then lay it on me."

Montana stepped up to Alex's bedside and laid her hands on Alex's body. Then she said another quiet prayer. Quentin could hear bits and pieces of her words. He heard enough to know that she was anointed for this. He wanted to bring her to Transitions every time he came.

After Montana was finished praying, Alex said. "Thank you. I feel like I can get through this for a couple hours. As much as I love looking at your pretty face, Q, can you go spend some time with this girl? I've got work to do, and I don't want to be rude."

Quentin kissed her head again. "Stop teasing me, Q," she said.

"Come on, Montana. Let's allow Alex time to finish her masterpiece."

"Bye, Q. Bye, groupie," Alex said.

Montana sucked her teeth. "Bye, Alex."

"I'm just playing. Bye, Montana. Nice meeting you. Q," Alex said. "You ought to bring her again."

Quentin smiled. "I hope she'll come back again, Alex. See you later."

Once they got outside Alex's room, Montana burst into quiet tears.

"What's wrong?" Quentin asked.

She waved her hands in the air. "I'm sorry. I'm okay. It's just . . . she's so young."

"Cancer doesn't discriminate."

Montana nodded. "I know."

"You want to see the rest of the grounds?"

Montana nodded. "Yes."

Quentin showed her all around the outside of the house, including the pool area with the saltwater whirlpools that had been put in for pain control. There was a picnic area and a little playground.

"Why is there a playground?" Montana asked. "Do you have children here?"

Quentin shook his head. "No, but sometimes the women who stay here have children."

After they were done touring, Quentin said a second goodbye to Ola and Charlene and checked in on the other two residents, Carmen and Layla.

When they were back in the car, Montana was silent for a while. But it wasn't an angry silence this time. She really did seem like she had a lot on her mind now.

"Quentin, Transitions is a blessed place. Thank you for bringing me here."

"I don't know what made me want to show you, but I'm glad I did."

"I'm really excited to help with the fund-raiser ball now."

"How is that going, by the way?" Quentin asked. "Are my mother and Chloe driving you crazy yet?"

"We only met one time so far, and it was okay."

Quentin nodded as he drove away from Transitions and headed back up the long road that led to I-20.

Montana said, "I've never been friends with a boss before."

"I've never been friends with a nanny before," Quentin said. "We're even."

Quentin stopped the car at a tiny ice cream stand. He didn't want the time with Montana to end, and he loved the peach ice cream that the small establishment made.

"You want some ice cream?" Quentin asked. "It's homemade and delicious."

Montana hesitated. "Don't you think I should be getting back to the children? Maybe they need something."

"Did anyone call you?"

"Well, no, but that doesn't mean . . . well, it is a weekday, so I'm on the clock."

"But the kids are on spring break, so you're fine. Plus, I'm the boss."

Montana smiled again. "You're right, Quentin. Ice cream it is."

Quentin jumped out of the car and rushed to open Montana's door. She rewarded him with another smile. He thought he'd go on all day doing nice things for Montana if she'd keep smiling like that.

"Do you like peach?" Quentin asked, as Montana delicately stepped out of the car.

"Yes."

"Then you have to get theirs. It's incredible."

Quentin got two cones and led Montana over to a little table next to a blossoming magnolia tree. He sat next to her on the side of the bench facing the trees so that there was a magnolia-scented breeze. The fragrance of the trees along with the sweet aroma of the ice cream—not to mention the even sweeter view—made Quentin want to sit there all day.

"This is so good, Quentin," Montana said. "I would get so fat if this place was closer to home. I'd be here every day."

Quentin laughed. "You could just run off the calories. Those shoes you have are going to make you think you can run a marathon."

"I hope so. I've never had to work out much before, but the older I get, the more I spread. I'm hoping this helps."

"There is nothing wrong with your . . . spread. But running will make you healthier."

"I don't know how I feel about the direction of this conversation," Montana said with a chuckle.

"I didn't mean to be out of pocket. It's just that I don't think your figure is a problem. That's why I asked why you don't have a boyfriend. You just don't seem like you'd be single."

"Well, I'm at a place in my life where I want a meaningful relationship, and that hasn't materialized yet."

A meaningful relationship. Quentin wondered if he was capable of that again. He was absolutely available for shopping sprees, vacations, and every kind of fun imaginable, but he didn't know if meaningful was in the cards for him again.

"I hope you find someone. You're too much of a gem to be alone."

In that moment, Quentin was struck with the awareness of how close he was sitting to Montana on the bench. He inhaled her perfume, and sighed.

Quentin leaned in until his lips nearly touched Montana's. After a long moment, he tilted his head to one side in preparation for a kiss. Suddenly, Montana jumped up from the bench.

"Quentin. What are you doing?"

Dang. He thought the moment was right, but he'd screwed up. "I'm sorry, Montana. I'm an idiot."

"Were you trying to kiss me?"

"Yeah, I was, but I'm so sorry. It won't happen again. I was out of line."

Montana sat back down on the bench, this time putting space between herself and Quentin. He grimaced at his own stupidity.

"Quentin, I'm not the kind of girl who kisses someone else's boyfriend."

He nodded. "And no matter what it looks like, I'm not the kind of guy who cheats on his girlfriend."

"So . . . do you want to forget this ever happened?" Montana asked.

Quentin's entire body relaxed. Montana would forgive him, and that was a good thing. But he didn't want to forget that it had ever happened. He wanted to finish what he'd started.

"I promise you, I won't ever try anything like that again. I really want us to be friends."

Montana's smile lifted Quentin's spirits even more. "I do too."

Quentin stood and held his hand out to Montana, and he helped her to her feet. "Let's go, before anyone notices we've been gone this long."

"Okay."

Quentin threw the rest of their now soggy cones in the trash can and watched Montana walk back to the car. He was afraid of what he felt with Montana. He was scared that even with all his money and status he wasn't good enough for her. She deserved a guy who wouldn't make a move on her while he still had a girlfriend.

But even though he didn't feel worthy, he still hungered for the type of relationship he knew he could have with Montana. Leaving Chloe would take a leap of faith. Quentin wondered if he had any of that left.

CHAPTER 21

Chloe tapped her foot impatiently on the marble floor in the parlor of the Chambers mansion. She resisted the urge to text or call Quentin—even though her blood was close to boiling, and even though it was almost four in the afternoon and he hadn't returned from his shopping trip with the nanny.

Ms. Levy walked into the parlor for the umpteenth time, wearing a frown on her face.

"You know I can call you when Mr. Chambers returns."

Chloe rolled her eyes at the nosy woman. "It's fine. I can wait."

"Well, was he expecting you?"

"I don't need an appointment to see my man, Ms. Levy."

"Did you call and tell him you were here?"

"No. I am surprising him."

"Why? It's not his birthday."

Chloe balled and unballed her fists.

"Well, if you insist on waiting, you might as well sit down," Ms. Levy said.

"I like standing."

"You've been standing for three hours."

"And I will continue."

Ms. Levy shook her head and walked back out of the parlor.

Chloe felt herself begin to tremble with rage. What could Quentin and Montana be doing? How long did it take to buy shoes?

When Chloe finally heard the door in the kitchen open, she spun on one heel and gathered her composure as best as she could. Then she saw Quentin place his hand at the small of Montana's back to help her inside. Her composure unraveled.

"Here you are!" Chloe squealed.

She barreled into Quentin, threw her arms around his neck, and hugged him. She felt him stiffen beneath her touch. Montana stepped to the side and looked away.

"Hey! Is everything okay?" Quentin asked.

"Yes. It is now." Chloe glanced at Montana out of the corner of her eye. "Hello."

Montana looked up and smiled. "Hey, Chloe."

"Did I miss an engagement or something?" Quentin asked. "Please tell me we didn't have plans."

"No, I just wanted to see you today. Montana, please excuse us."

"Oh, of course!" Montana said. "How rude of me."

"Yes," Chloe said.

Montana smiled nervously and rushed out of the kitchen, carrying her shopping bag. Chloe narrowed her eyes at Montana and then Quentin.

"Were you out shopping with her?" Chloe asked.

Quentin shook his head. "It's not what you think. She was trying to run in shoes from Target. She was going to hurt herself."

Chloe searched his face for deception and found none. "If I was a jealous girl, I'd think you were lying to me."

"Well, I'm happy you're not a jealous girl."

Quentin untangled himself from Chloe's near choke hold and grabbed a bottle of water from the refrigerator. He held one out to her, and Chloe shook her head.

He took the top off and swallowed about half of the bottle in a few gulps. Then he said, "To what do I owe this visit?"

"I just wanted to spend some time with you, love."

Quentin chuckled. "Okay, now tell me the real reason you're here."

"You don't think I like spending time with you?"

"Yes, of course I do, but Ms. Levy texted me and said you'd been waiting for hours. You wouldn't do that for no reason. What's up?"

Chloe shook her head. Ms. Levy was a hater. "Well, I had this great idea I wanted to share with you."

Quentin pulled a chair from the kitchen table and motioned for Chloe to sit. "An idea about what?"

Chloe waited for Quentin to take a seat across from her. "Well, I was dropping Deirdre off for a study group at the library, and something occurred to me."

"Wait. Deirdre's at the library?" Quentin asked.

"Yes."

"And you took her there? Why?"

Chloe shook her head. "She didn't tell you? I'm going to be her mentor. She asked me to do it. She really wants to be back in your good graces."

Quentin frowned. "Okay, continue."

"Well, when I was dropping her off, I got to thinking it was something that her mother would've done. Then I started thinking about all the things she was probably missing out on by not having a mom."

"She's got me, and her grandmother," Quentin said.

"Hear me out, Quentin. I was thinking that maybe as an offshoot of Transitions, you have another group called Transitions Kids that focuses on the children left behind when their mothers lose the battle to cancer."

Quentin's eyes widened. She had his attention.

"What do you think?" Chloe asked. "It's a good idea, right?"

"It's a great idea, Chloe."

Chloe clapped her hands. "You won't have to do anything at all. I'll run the entire program. I'll get sponsors and raise money. We'll introduce it at the masquerade ball."

"I never knew you were this interested in the foundation."

Chloe reached across the table and took Quentin's hand. "How could I not be interested in something that's so important to you? I want to work with you on this."

Finally, Quentin smiled. It had taken long enough. Chloe was almost annoyed that he was so shocked. He acted as if she didn't have a heart. She did. And she wasn't going to let him break it by running off with the nanny.

"This is going to be incredible, Quentin. Wait and see."

CHAPTER 22

Montana sat in the choir loft at Sunday morning worship service and watched the congregation members file in. Attending a megachurch gave her the opportunity to meet a lot of people, and at their church almost everyone was welcoming and kind. That spirit came straight from their leader. Bishop Kumal Prentiss was one of the most relatable pastors in the country.

Emoni sat down next to Montana and poked her in the side. "What are you thinking about? Your face looks twisted about something."

"I made a new friend," Montana said.

"Okay, and why would you be looking all crazy because you made a friend?"

"Because the friend is Quentin Chambers, and I so don't want to just be friends."

Emoni laughed out loud. "Girl, I told you he was fine. How did y'all get to be friends?"

"You're gonna laugh. He bought me some running shoes."

"What?"

"I was trying to be like him and go jogging outside, and I tore my feet up. So he bought me shoes."

"He's practical. Saw a need and fixed it. This is a good thing."

"It would've been, except the fact that he brought up spending the night with Chloe at the Ritz."

"Ooh, bummer. Well, you knew he was dating her."

Montana nodded. "I did. He also took me out to his foundation for cancer patients."

Emoni's eyes widened. "He's inviting you into his world. Maybe he does want to be more than friends."

"He has a girlfriend, though."

"It's been five years. Maybe he's thinking of kicking her to the curb."

"And he tried to kiss me."

"What? So he did break up with Chloe?"

Montana shook her head sadly. "No. I don't know if he's going to, and if he doesn't, how can I keep working there?"

"Girl, I don't know. This has got to go on my prayer list. Better yet, I'm gonna put it on my mama's prayer list. Her prayer closet is the truth."

Montana laughed. "Well, why don't you put yourself on the prayer list too? You're gonna lose Darrin with your runaway bride syndrome."

"He should've thought about that when he hooked up with that hoochie at the cooking school."

Montana shook her head and chuckled. She and Emoni had had this conversation before. Darrin went to Savannah to cooking school, and had cheated on Emoni while they were dating. Emoni said that she'd forgiven him, but every time he tried to set a wedding date, she changed the subject.

"But you're still wearing the ring."

"That's because one day I will marry him. He's just gotta wait until I'm ready."

"You better hope he doesn't wise up and leave you."

"Please. He knows what a gem I am. Service is about to start, so I'm going back to the best section in the choir."

"Sike, y'all altos are ghetto. Sopranos rock," Montana said.

Once service started, Montana got so caught up in praising

and worshiping God that she temporarily stopped focusing on her confusing situation with Quentin. She did make a brief prayer in which she asked for clarity, but after that, she left it in God's hands. If Quentin was going to be the prince of all her dreams, then a whole lot of things would have to change. First of all, his dating status needed to go from "in a relationship" to "single." She wasn't about to share.

After the choir sang, Bishop Prentiss got up and preached a message on preparation. He said that God was preparing each person for His purpose for their lives, and that if the lesson was missed, then the person might have to learn it again. Bishop Prentiss called it the refiner's fire.

Near the middle of the message, Montana's jaw dropped when she saw who was walking down the center aisle of the church. It was Rio. Montana hoped this wasn't the beginning of him stalking her and harassing her to get back together. Rio stared at her in the choir stand and even waved when he saw her looking back.

She prayed that there wasn't another lesson she needed to learn with Rio.

After service, Rio waited for Montana at the steps near the choir loft. He smiled at her as she descended. Montana couldn't force herself to smile back. She gave him a toothy grimace instead.

"Are you surprised to see me here?" Rio said, as he gave Montana a bear hug.

"I am very surprised that you were able to set foot in the sanctuary without bursting into flames."

"Wow. That is not how you're supposed to treat a guest. You're supposed to tell me about the love of the Lord and help me to salvation."

"Don't play with God, Rio. He will not be mocked."

Rio rolled his eyes. "When did you get to be such a holy roller? Good grief!"

Seemingly out of nowhere, Chloe was suddenly standing next to Rio.

"Well, hello! You're new here. Are you a friend of Montana's?" Chloe asked.

Rio laughed. "With a church this big, how can you tell if someone is new?"

Chloe gave Rio a look like what he said was absolutely ridiculous. On that, Montana had to agree. No matter how many people were in church, single women were always able to spot a new single man.

"Chloe, this is Rio Watkins, an old friend of mine."

"An old friend?" Rio scoffed. "I am more than an old friend. I'm the man she almost married."

"Really?" Chloe asked.

Montana laughed. "Really? I don't remember marriage ever being a part of our conversations, but okay."

"You never know what's on a man's mind, girl. He could've been about to buy you a ring." Chloe said.

Montana shook her head. "Rio, this is Chloe. She's my employer's . . ."

"Fiancée," Chloe said before Montana was able to finish her sentence.

"Well, it's nice to meet you, Chloe," Rio said. "I enjoyed your church service too."

A huge smile burst onto Chloe's face. "Are you doing anything after church? My future mother-in-law is having a brunch at the Chambers family's Buckhead mansion. You can get a chance to see where Montana works."

Montana gave Chloe a blank stare. There was no way she wanted Rio anywhere near that brunch.

"I love brunch!" Rio said. "The combination of my two favorite meals."

"Then you absolutely should come," Chloe said.

Montana said, "I don't really have permission to invite anyone. You wouldn't want to get me in trouble at work would you, Rio?"

"Chloe's inviting me."

Chloe said, "What are you worried about? They're raving about you like you're the child whisperer or something."

"They are?" Montana wondered who she meant by "they." Was Quentin raving about her too?

"Yes, you can do no wrong. So let your friend come to the brunch. It'll liven things up."

Montana thought about what Quentin might think if she brought a man to the brunch. "I don't think it's a good idea, so if he comes over, he's your guest."

"It's like that, Montana? I came all the way to your church to visit you, and this is how you treat me?"

"What would Jesus do?" Chloe asked.

Montana stormed out of the choir loft and out the double doors that led to the foyer. Emoni stopped her by grabbing Montana's arm before she opened the door to the outside.

"What's wrong, Montana? You look like you're about to go and beat somebody down."

"I'm just trying to get out of here. My ex showed up at church, and Chloe just invited him to Estelle's brunch. I've got to go and coordinate the children. They're going to sing today."

"Really? Quentin's okay with his kids singing in front of everybody?"

Montana shrugged, "I didn't think he'd mind. They sound incredible."

"Okay, well, then I'm looking forward to it. I remember their mother's voice. She was a legend at our church," Emoni said. "I'll see you over at Estelle's."

"You bringing Darrin?"

"Why? Are there going to be some eligible bachelors over there I should meet?" Emoni asked.

Montana frowned and shook her head at Emoni. "God is gonna get you for this."

"Oh, all right, I'll bring him."

Montana continued on into the parking lot and into her car. When she got behind the steering wheel, Montana realized she was shaking. She felt something in her spirit about Rio showing up at church like that, and even more anxiety about him coming to the Chambers home. Why was Chloe so intent on having him there? If she didn't know any better, Montana would think that the two of them had planned their little attack.

When she got back home, Montana used her key on the kitchen door. She didn't have a key to the big doors in front. The first thing Montana noticed was that Quentin was leaving.

"You're not staying for the brunch?" Montana asked.

Quentin shook his head. "That would be no. My mother's friends from church are coming over, and that is my cue to leave."

"But you can't leave! The children have a surprise for you."

"A surprise? What kind of surprise?"

"The kind you'll love, but you have to stay to find out what it is."

Quentin started for the door again. "Well, I'm going to have to miss out, then."

"Please, Quentin," Montana said, as she grabbed his hand and pulled him away from the door. "Don't go."

Quentin looked down at Montana, and she put on a real show with her big, sad, puppy-dog eyes. The look he returned was full of heat, so Montana looked away.

"I love the way you beg," Quentin said. "I will stay, but this surprise better be good."

Not long after Montana had convinced Quentin to stay, Ms. Levy let Chloe and Rio in the house. Chloe threw her arms around Quentin's neck in a hug as soon as he and Montana came into the sitting room, where Estelle's guests would congregate before the meal.

"Quentin, baby, I'm glad you decided to stay. I didn't expect you to be here; you never stay for these events."

"Obviously you didn't expect me to be here. You brought a date."

Chloe jokingly punched Quentin in the arm and laughed. "This isn't my date. This is Montana's date, silly."

Quentin's eyebrows shot all the way up. "Is this the surprise?"

"What? No! And he is not my date. Chloe invited him."

Chloe gave Montana a scolding look. "Aren't you going to introduce Quentin to your boyfriend?"

"Quentin, this is my ex-boyfriend, Rio. He visited church today and managed to wrangle an invitation to brunch out of Chloe."

Quentin extended his hand. "Nice to meet you, Rio. Make yourself at home."

"I will, I will. So what do y'all have Montana doing here? Is she the help?"

Quentin replied, "She's not 'the' help, but she's a big help. I don't know what we ever did before her."

Chloe said, "You were doing a good job raising your children, honey."

Montana excused herself from the group because she couldn't stand how Rio was staring her down. He made her feel like she had a film of slime on her body. She wondered how she ever thought he was attractive. It was like the Holy Spirit revealed the man Rio truly was once she got saved.

Upstairs, she checked on the girls to see if they were ready to sing the song they had prepared. They were all in Deirdre's bedroom, wearing their clothes from church and looking very pretty. The twins, however, seemed nervous.

"What if Daddy doesn't like this," Morgan asked. "Will he fire you?"

It hadn't occurred to Montana that he might ask her to leave after this. "I don't think that's going to happen. I think God wants me to be here."

Deirdre said, "If God took our mother away, why would He let you stay?"

Montana sat down on the edge of Deirdre's bed and tapped the empty spot next to her so that Deirdre could sit down. Deirdre plopped down and folded her arms across her chest in a huff.

Montana beckoned for the other three girls to come too, and they gathered around. Danielle sat on Montana's lap even though she was too big for that.

"Look, I know how much it hurts to lose your mom. I lost mine when I was in high school. And I know this doesn't make sense, but sometimes you have to trust that God is going to make everything okay."

"Did your mother have cancer?" Danielle asked. "Why doesn't God just get rid of cancer?"

"My mother had a heart attack. No one expected it, and I didn't get to say good-bye."

Madison gasped. "That's awful. I'm so sorry, Ms. Montana."

"I miss my mother still. Every day. But do you know what I learned when she went to heaven?"

"What?" Deirdre asked. "That life isn't fair and that no matter what you do, bad stuff is still gonna happen to you?"

"No. I learned that everyone in your life is temporary, except God. He's the only one who stays forever."

The girls were quiet. Then Danielle said, "So Daddy's gonna die too?"

"Someday," Montana said. "Hopefully when he's an old, old man."

Danielle laid her head on Montana's shoulder. "If Daddy fires you, can you still come and hang out with us?"

Montana laughed out loud. "Let's stop with all this sad talk. We've got a song to sing and a crowd to wow. Help me carry my keyboard downstairs so we can get our applause."

All of Estelle's guests had arrived since Montana left the room, so she and the girls quickly set up the keyboard right outside the sitting room. The girls stood in a line, and Montana stepped into the room with the company. She noticed how uncomfortable Quentin looked and felt sorry for him.

Montana ran up and gave Emoni a hug. "Didn't I just see you?" Emoni asked.

"Yeah, but now you're a guest in my home," Montana said with a wink. "I had to greet you."

Darrin, Emoni's fiancé said, "Thanks for the invitation, Montana, but when do we get to eat? Bishop Prentiss preached kind of long this morning, and I'm hungry."

Montana shook her head. "It's almost ready, greedy."

"Y'all could've let me cater this thing. Then we'd already be getting our grub on," Darrin said.

"Mrs. Chambers and Chloe are throwing a huge masquerade ball in a couple of months. Maybe they'll want you to cater that."

Emoni said, "Hook my man up with that gig."

"Today she's claiming me, Montana."

Montana laughed at the two of them. Darrin had so much love in his eyes when he looked at Emoni, but she made him work so hard for her reciprocity. Montana knew that if she had a man look at her that way, he wouldn't have to work as hard for her love. She'd take adoration any day over that lustful gaze that Rio gave her.

"We have a surprise, everyone!" Montana announced. "The Chambers girls would like to bless you with a song. They'll be singing 'The Shepherd Song.' "

Quentin's head snapped up from looking at the floor. Montana smiled at him, but he didn't smile back. He did stand to his feet and shoved his hands in his pockets. Chloe stood to her feet too and locked her arm through his.

Montana went back to the girls and gave them a reassuring head nod. Then she sat down at the keyboard and played the introduction to the song. The girls looked at their father and froze. Danielle was the most terrified. She clutched her necklace and trembled.

Montana cleared her throat loudly to get the girls' attention. Then she mouthed the words "eyes on me." The girls nodded and stared at Montana as she played the introduction a second time.

This time, the girls opened their mouths and sang in unison. Their voices echoed from the high ceilings and sounded rich and full enough to be an entire choir. When Deirdre got to the solo part of the song, she came alive. She hit every riff and run that Montana had taught her and delivered it with a power that Montana hadn't had at her age. Deirdre was destined to sing. Her voice was too big of a gift not to.

The second time the girls sang the chorus part of the song was where they sang the harmonies Montana had taught them. They were all pitch perfect—their three-part harmony was flawless. Deirdre sang ad libs that had everyone in the room in awe. One of the guests had gone into worship.

It tickled Montana that Rio seemed completely out of place. That's exactly what he got for forcing his way into her church world.

Chloe held on to Quentin's arm for dear life, but his expression had changed from mild irritation to slack-jawed wonder. There was also a bit of pride there too as the girls finished the song and everyone in the room cheered.

The girls cared about no one's applause but their father's. They ran up to him and pushed Chloe out of the way. Montana followed closely behind them.

"What did you think, Daddy?" Danielle said, searching her father's face with her eyes.

Quentin said, "You all were incredible. I didn't know you could sing like that."

"Neither did we," Madison said.

Morgan chimed in, "Yeah, Montana taught us."

Quentin tipped Deirdre's chin upward and smiled at his daughter. "You sound like your mother."

"It's a shame these babies aren't singing in church. They sound like angels," one of the guests said, spoiling the family moment.

Quentin pressed his lips into a thin line and blinked rapidly. "Excuse me, everyone. Enjoy the brunch."

Montana and Chloe said simultaneously, "Don't leave."

Chloe gave Montana a look that could kill a room full of folk. As Chloe tried to follow Quentin, she actually scampered behind him. But Quentin's huge strides soon left her chasing him. It must've dawned on her that everyone was looking at her chase Quentin across the living room, and she stopped, turned, and smoothed her dress.

"Let's give Quentin some space," Chloe said thoughtfully.

Estelle said, "I think we should give my beautiful granddaughters a round of applause, and let's also acknowledge their wonderful teacher, Montana. Thank you for bringing music back into this home. It should've never left."

The girls took a bow, and then Montana bowed as well. The only person not smiling at them was Chloe.

"Is anyone else hungry?" Estelle asked. "Brother Lundy, can you bless the food?"

While Brother Lundy prayed over the food, Montana glanced up to see what Chloe was doing. She didn't expect to make eye contact with Chloe, who was already staring at her.

The look in Chloe's eyes was pure hatred. It sent a chill through Montana to the core of her being. It was the look of a newly formed enemy. Montana could almost imagine Chloe belting out a war cry. And although she didn't know for sure, Montana would venture a guess that a spar with Chloe wouldn't be fair.

Chloe looked like someone who fought dirty.

CHAPTER 23

After the brunch was over, Rio pulled Montana toward the front door. "Montana, can I please just talk to you?"

"No, Rio! Just go!"

"I sat through that long church service and that boring brunch just to get a few minutes of your time, and you can't do a brother just that one courtesy?"

Montana rolled her eyes and acquiesced. She had the feeling that Rio wouldn't just go quietly, and a few of the church members were still there.

"Let's walk up a ways," Montana said once they were outside. "I don't want anyone to hear us."

Rio followed Montana up the path to a cluster of peach trees. He gave her the smile that had charmed her right out of her underwear before. Now it had no effect on her, at least not a positive one. It made her skin crawl. She wanted him gone as quickly as possible.

Montana spun on one heel and put one hand on her hip. "What do you want to talk about, Rio?"

"You don't have to sound so irritated. I thought women loved for men to pursue them."

"Not when they have been delivered from the man."

"Delivered? Why you always talking about me like I'm the devil?"

" 'Cause you act like the devil. He's your daddy."

Rio laughed. "I remember when you called me daddy."

"The only reason I agreed to talk to you is because I want to ask you to please leave me alone. Don't show up at my church anymore, or here either.

"You're banning me from church?"

"I'm asking you not to come to my church. There are a gang of churches in Atlanta. If you're trying to meet Jesus, which I highly doubt, then you can visit one of them."

"How can I get you back if you don't want me around?"

Montana let out a huge sigh. "Seriously, Rio? It's not like you can't pull any woman you want. Why are you so insistent on having me?"

"Because you're the only woman to walk away from me. I'm a winner. I never lose. I want you back, girl."

"Why? So you can walk away from me? Will that make you feel better?"

Rio shook his head. "You think I'm just talking crap, and I can understand why you would, but I really want you back."

"Why can't you just move on? I have."

"With who? Your new boss?" Rio's voice escalated, and Montana looked around to see if anyone had heard him.

"No, Rio. I mean I've moved on from us. I am in love with Jesus right now. I'm saved, set apart, and celibate."

Rio laughed. "That's too many *s* words. Rewind that back."

"Celibate starts with a *c*. Please, just let me be. Don't make this hard."

Rio put on a sad face and sighed. "Okay, Montana. I hear you. I saw you that night, going on a date with that lame-looking dude, and I guess I started reminiscing. I didn't realize what a good thing you were until you were gone. I wish I could go back in time and change things."

Surprisingly, Rio actually sounded sincere. But there was no way Montana intended to find out. If he really had learned something from their relationship, it would be something he could use with the next woman.

Rio extended his arms. "Since this is the last time I'll probably get to be this close to you, can I have just one hug? A goodbye hug."

Montana looked around to see if anyone was in the vicinity who might misinterpret her hug with Rio. Since the coast appeared to be clear, she took three steps forward and gave Rio a very chaste hug. Just when she was ready to untangle herself from his arms, Rio pulled Montana in tightly and squeezed her behind.

She knew he hadn't changed! The devil's baby brother!

Montana slapped him away and stormed back toward the house.

"See you soon, Montana!" Rio said. "I think I just found my new church home!"

Montana balled her hands into fists and would've yelled at the top of her lungs if Estelle hadn't still had company. It would completely vex her spirit if Rio decided to join Freedom of Life.

Montana grabbed a bottle of water from the brunch setup and went to the most peaceful place in the mansion, the peach sitting room that looked out onto the lake. Unfortunately, the room was already occupied. Quentin stood by the window, staring out at the lake.

Montana turned to leave quietly, but Quentin noticed her presence. He said, "You can stay if you want. I was just about to leave."

"Are you okay, Quentin?"

He looked the opposite of okay. He'd obviously been shedding a few tears—his eyes were watery, and his face was tear-streaked.

He nodded. "I'm fine. "

"Want some company?" Montana asked.

Quentin said, "No. I said I was fine."

Montana felt a sinking feeling in the pit of her stomach. "All right. I'm sorry I disturbed you."

Montana turned to leave, and Quentin said, "What did you think? That I would have a breakthrough or something? That I'd hear their beautiful voices and let music back into my heart?"

"Yes. I actually did."

"Well, you're wrong. You know nothing about me, Montana. I don't have a heart anymore. Your God ripped it out of my chest and left a hole there."

"No. You're wrong. Your heart was broken, but it's still there."

Quentin grimaced. "You don't need to worry about the status of my heart. We hired you to take care of the children."

"Yes, Mr. Chambers. I'm sorry."

Quentin grunted and then turned to stare out the window again. Montana ran out of the room. She wanted to go and hide. Her plan had backfired, and now maybe she and Quentin weren't even friends.

On her way out of the room, Montana ran into Chloe, the last person she wanted to see.

"Was Quentin in there?" Chloe asked.

Montana nodded. She was on the verge of tears and hoped Chloe wouldn't want to hold a conversation.

"He's mad at you, isn't he?" Chloe asked.

Again, Montana nodded. "I think so. He didn't say it, but I think he is."

Chloe shook her head. "That's exactly what you get."

"What are you talking about?"

"You think I can't see what you're doing?"

"What am I doing, Chloe?"

Chloe walked in a circle around Montana. "You think you can come in here with all your singing and all your what-would-Jesus-do, sickening sweetness and that Quentin would fall for you just like the meat off a perfectly smoked rib."

"I'm not trying to get Quentin to fall for me," Montana said. "But I do want to see his heart mended."

Chloe stopped walking and got in Montana's face. "You don't need to be concerned with his heart. They hired you to pick up the children from school and drop them off at dance practice. You're not here for his heart."

"Quentin is my friend."

"He is your employer. Don't get it twisted. You start thinking he's your friend and I'll have to see to your firing."

Montana stood tall and looked Chloe in the eye. "What are you afraid of? You scared if he heals, then he won't need you as a crutch anymore?"

"A crutch? I'm no crutch to him, but I'm in his system. You don't have a chance, honey. You should stop before things turn ugly."

"I'm not afraid of you."

"You're stupid not to be, nanny. Don't get in my way."

"*You* shouldn't get in God's way."

Chloe threw her head back and laughed. "I hope you and the kids don't think this little singing display is going to change anything."

Montana swallowed. She wanted the exact opposite to happen. She wanted their singing to change everything.

"Let me go and fix my man. I know exactly what he needs."

Chloe left Montana standing there as she strode into the room with Quentin. She walked with purpose. Like a woman who knew her man.

Montana whispered a prayer. "Lord, please heal Quentin's heart . . . and please don't let him fire me."

Quentin would have that breakthrough he talked about. Montana was sure of it. God was bigger than all of Quentin's pain. Quentin just had to open his eyes.

CHAPTER 24

Quentin squeezed a key in the palm of his hand. Everyone in the house was asleep, so it was quiet. It was the perfect time to face his biggest giant. Montana had started this with the song. It was such a perfect song for the girls—exactly something Chandra would've had them sing. Seeing his daughters look to Montana for direction and hearing them hit those harmonies had almost been too much. He'd almost embarrassed himself by breaking down in front of all of his mother's friends.

Quentin missed Chandra like crazy.

He tiptoed downstairs so as not to wake anyone. He needed to be alone if he was going to do this. If he was going to open the floodgates, there didn't need to be any witnesses.

His cell phone buzzed in his pocket, and Quentin didn't even take it out. He knew who was texting him. Chloe didn't know how to leave well enough alone. She kept trying to talk to him about his feelings. He obviously didn't want to talk to her about his feelings, but she insisted on trying to reach out.

Quentin traveled down a long hallway and stood in front of a closed and locked door. It was a door that had been locked for five years. No one had come into this room after Chandra had been buried, and Quentin had had the lock installed to make sure of that.

He flipped the key over and over in his hand, trying to decide if he should go through with it or instead go back upstairs to his bedroom. He could still hide from the giant and leave it lurking in the shadows.

Quentin didn't feel like much of a lion. He felt like a frightened cub in the jaws of a bear. He was glad no one could read his thoughts, because he would come across like a real chump.

Quentin took a deep breath and inserted the key in the lock. He thought, *There's no turning back now,* as he shifted it in the lock. The lock had never been turned since it was installed, so it stuck a bit. After a bit of jiggling, it gave way, and Quentin slowly turned the knob.

He pushed the door open and coughed a little from the dust that rose into the air. Maybe he should've had the room cleaned, at least, but Quentin never imagined that the door would be opened again.

Quentin closed the door behind him and switched on the light. The soft illumination revealed a beautiful, albeit dusty, white grand piano. The stool had a red velvet seat cushion and there were velvet covers on the foot pedals.

Also in the room were music stands and a table scattered with sheet music, some of it practice music for the choir and some of it composed by Quentin.

Quentin swallowed hard as the first tears stung his eyes. He shook off the emotion and crossed the room. He stood in front of the piano and wiped away some of the dust with his sleeve. Then he sat down on the stool, lifted the cover, and stared at the piano keys.

A knot formed in Quentin's throat as he closed his eyes and remembered the last time he had been in the room with Chandra.

"Play Beethoven, Quentin!" Chandra said, as she spun in a little circle, her long straight hair flying like a fan around her face.

Quentin laughed out loud. "I want you to sing with me! You can't sing Beethoven."

"I can make up words," Chandra said. "I am a songwriter, you know!"

"You're the best, but I want to practice something for church."

Chandra pouted playfully. "Oh, okay. Play Andrae Crouch, then. I love singing his songs."

Quentin had smiled and cracked his knuckles. He started to play "We Are Not Ashamed," and Chandra began to sing. Her rich alto voice wrapped around the notes like they were created especially for her voice to sing.

Quentin sang and played along with the memory unfolding in his mind. Tears streamed down his face as he watched Chandra dance with his mind's eye. And then, at the end of the song, the memory faded. Chandra's image disappeared, and Quentin opened his eyes.

Quentin had not talked to God since he'd asked Him to save Chandra's life. He felt that they didn't have anything else to talk about. But tonight the pain was so fresh and so raw, Quentin couldn't help but cry out to God.

"How long is this going to hurt?" Quentin asked through his sobs.

Quentin heard one word in his spirit. *Always.*

Quentin slammed the piano cover shut. Was God mocking him now? After five years, he decided to talk to God, and He would just remind him of his pain? What kind of . . .

Then Quentin heard more. *But I am bigger than the pain. Rest in me.*

Quentin sat quietly waiting to see if there was more, because he had no idea how to rest. He barely knew how to survive.

When he was sure there was nothing further, Quentin opened the piano cover again. He let his fingers rest on the keys and imagined his children singing with their mother.

Quentin played and played for hours. Songs from memory, songs he made up, songs Chandra had liked to sing . . . songs she'd never heard. Quentin let the music fill the room, until he felt full himself.

And when he was finished, he felt like something had been restored. Maybe not completely, but for the first time in five years, he didn't feel like he had one foot in the grave. Not at all. He felt one hundred percent alive.

CHAPTER 25

A knock on her door woke Montana from her sleep. She squinted to focus her eyes and glanced at the clock on her nightstand. It was five in the morning. She thought, *Somebody better be on fire or in need of a tetanus shot, because it's too early for this.*

Montana scrambled out of her bed and mumbled, "Hold on," while she grabbed her robe and slippers.

Once she was decent, Montana opened the door, expecting to see Danielle or the twins. She was surprised that it was Quentin. Her hand immediately went to the bird's-nest-like hair on the top her head and tried to smooth it down.

"Hey, Quentin. Is everything all right?"

It was obvious to Montana that everything was absolutely not all right with Quentin. His eyes were puffy as though he had been crying, but he was fully dressed in his workout gear.

"Yeah. Everything is good. You want to go running with me?"

Montana cleared her throat. "Um . . . we don't have to wait for the sun?"

"No. Not if you stay close to me. I know the path. And the early-morning air is really invigorating."

Even with his puffy eyes, Quentin was very hard to resist in his snug, muscle-hugging workout shirt. Who wouldn't want to go running in the dark with this tall glass of fineness? She wondered if this meant he'd forgiven her for the song.

"Can I get like ten minutes to shower and throw on some workout clothes?"

"You can have fifteen," Quentin said. "You also need to brush your teeth and comb your hair."

Montana covered her mouth and slammed the door to her room in Quentin's face. "Okay!" she said from behind the door.

Montana dashed into the bathroom and took a very quick shower, her excitement growing with every moment. Maybe she and Quentin would be friends again. She was growing weary of trying to avoid him in the house. A whole week had gone by without him saying a word to her.

She picked out a very cute pink and green outfit that she bought to wear with her new running shoes. Then, before putting it on, Montana drowned herself in the fragrance that Quentin had enjoyed before.

When she emerged from her bedroom, Quentin was leaning on the wall, with his arms folded across his chest.

"Look at you!" he said. "It's almost like you're a different person."

"Ha, ha. Let's go running."

Quentin looked her up and down, and his eyes stopped on her feet. He kneeled in front of her and Montana's heart fluttered. What was he about to do?

"Quentin?"

He held up one finger and pulled at her shoelaces. "That's what I thought. Your shoes are tied too tightly. It's going to make you uncomfortable. May I?"

"Oh, uh, sure. Go ahead."

Quentin retied Montana's shoes and popped up from the floor when he was done. "Okay. You're ready now."

Montana followed Quentin outside to his running path. It was right before dawn, so it wasn't as dark as Montana thought it would be. The sky had a purple-pink glow as the sun began its morning ascent.

"Stay close to me," Quentin said. "See if you can keep up. I'll start out slow."

In the beginning, Montana was able to match Quentin's speed, but because his legs were so long, Quentin began to outpace her. Montana adjusted her speed to keep up but soon got winded.

When she could go no farther without a break, Montana grabbed hold of a tree and took some deep breaths. Quentin didn't realize she wasn't behind him at first. Then he stopped and turned around.

Montana wanted to call out to him, but she couldn't catch her breath. She waved instead. Quentin came running back to where she was standing.

"You okay?" Quentin asked.

Montana nodded. "I think so. I just need . . . to catch my breath."

How was Quentin not even winded? He had barely broken a sweat, and they'd been running for about twenty minutes.

"You're in great shape, Quentin. I can't keep up with you," Montana admitted.

Quentin nodded. "You will be in great shape soon. You have to keep at it. Rest for a few minutes. I'll loop around and come back for you."

"I'm gonna be in great shape soon? Really?" Montana asked jokingly.

"This is the first of many morning runs, Montana. I've never had a running buddy before. It's gonna be fun."

Montana watched him run off and had to avert her eyes before her mind wandered too long over his incredible physique. This whole running buddy thing might not be a good idea. Quentin was way too attractive to be Montana's running partner. She'd need to go to the altar every Sunday, to ask for forgiveness.

When Quentin returned to the spot, Montana was leaning on the tree and breathing easily.

"You ready to go now?" he asked.

Montana smiled. She really wanted to go inside, eat some

breakfast, and have some coffee. She took a swig from her water bottle and nodded.

"Good. This time, I'll go easier on you. Don't try to match my pace. I forgot that you are a tiny little thing, and your strides are a lot shorter than mine."

Montana was tickled at being called a "tiny little thing." It sounded so endearing that she wanted him to say it again.

They took off running again—or jogging, really. Montana felt her heart rate rise, and she remembered to breathe so that she didn't tire out too quickly.

Quentin stopped suddenly and turned around. "Can I ask you a question?"

"S-sure," Montana was happy for the break.

"Is that guy who came to the brunch really your boyfriend? Chloe said you two were thinking of marriage at some point."

Montana narrowed her eyes. That Chloe was such a hater. "No, he is not my boyfriend. He is my ex, and he was not my date at the brunch. That was all Chloe."

Quentin laughed. "Chloe is a mess."

"I don't think she truly likes me."

"You don't say," Quentin roared with laughter. "She doesn't want us to be friends."

"Why would she have a problem with it? You two are getting married. I'm the nanny."

Quentin took a few steps so that he was standing closer to Montana. "We're not getting married. I've never asked her to be my wife."

"Well, I guess after five years a woman would assume . . ."

"That her man might never ask her for her hand in marriage," Quentin said completing Montana's sentence.

"So if you're not going to marry her, why do you string her along?" Montana felt a little girl power coming over her. She wasn't anywhere close to being friends with Chloe, but she was not a fan of guys dogging women out.

Quentin looked away from Montana's demanding gaze when he answered. "I have always been up front with Chloe about the nature of our relationship."

"Really?"

"I have physical needs, Montana . . ."

"That God intended to be provided for in a marriage. If you ask me, Chloe is crazy for letting you get what you need and not getting what she needs."

"She gets what she needs too," Quentin said.

Montana shook her head. He was starting to annoy her. "She needs to be a wife. She needs the security of marriage."

"Are you Chloe's agent?" Quentin asked.

"No. I'm just saying that I would never stand for an arrangement like that."

"And I wouldn't ask you to."

Montana cocked her head to one side. "Quentin, what is this conversation about?"

"I'm not sure. I just wanted to know about your friend. Your ex, I mean."

"But why? Why do you care? You have Chloe, and we're friends, so . . ."

Quentin cleared his throat. "I'm ending things with Chloe. It's time."

"And you needed to know if I was available before you did that?" Montana asked, her voice going to another octave of annoyance.

Quentin shook his head and took Montana's hand. "I've been trying to figure out how to break it off for a while now. I-I've never had the motivation before."

"And now?" Montana asked, her voice barely above a whisper.

"And now . . . Montana, you have been the first woman who has made me reconsider love again, since my wife died."

"Quentin . . ."

"Montana, I am attracted to you in more than a physical way. There's something spiritual. I sat up all last night talking to God and finding music again. But I must be honest about something."

"What's that?"

"I am still grieving my first wife. I think I might always feel some pain about losing her."

Montana stared into Quentin's eyes, looking for a sign of anything insincere. "Quentin, you should ask God to help heal your heart before you move on to another relationship. You're hurting. I don't think you're ready . . . and I won't put my heart on the line, even though I am really tempted to say yes to what I think you're trying to ask me."

"I'm trying to ask you to be more than my friend," Quentin said. "After I break things off with Chloe."

"Why don't you handle one thing at a time? First, do what you need to do with Chloe, and then . . . heal. Then, maybe, down the road we can talk."

Quentin let Montana's hand go. There was a confused expression on his face. He probably hadn't expected her reaction. He was rich and handsome. He was probably expecting Montana to just say yes.

"Would you be with me? After all of that?" Quentin asked.

Montana shrugged. "I don't know. I'd be interested in finding out, though."

Quentin smiled. "You're right, Montana. I do have some things to take care of before I can even think about pursuing a woman like you. I just wanted you to know how I felt."

"You don't know what I'm like yet," Montana said.

"I have an idea," Quentin said.

She shook her head. "No, you don't. First thing, you'll have to chase me."

Montana took off running toward the house. She felt so exhilarated at Quentin's revelations that she could've run five miles without a break. Quentin wanted to be her prince, but he was a broken prince. With a girlfriend that he needed to break up with, and a heart that needed mending.

It wasn't a perfect situation, but Montana didn't need perfection. She had her own skeletons and wondered what Quentin would think if he knew about her past. Would he still think she was so incredible if he knew? Montana planned to show Quentin only the new and improved, spirit-filled Cinderella. She'd leave that old woman in the past, where she belonged.

CHAPTER 26

Chloe stared across the restaurant table at Quentin. Something was wrong, she could tell. He wouldn't make eye contact, and he'd said only two words to her since he'd picked her up. She'd asked him to breakfast just to see what he was thinking.

"So the masquerade ball planning is coming along well. We're meeting with a caterer tomorrow."

Quentin nodded. "You and my mother?"

"Yes, and Montana too. She's been my assistant, and we have similar tastes. It helps me to battle against your mother."

Quentin shifted in his seat at the mention of Montana. Chloe didn't miss the movement.

"That should be good, then," Quentin said.

"Yes, the potential caterer goes to church with us. He's the bishop's future son-in-law."

"Darrin's a great chef. I've enjoyed his food before. And he actually cooked for us when Chandra died. We ate gourmet food for weeks."

Why did Quentin bring up his dead wife? She was the last thing Chloe wanted to talk about. They'd always managed to avoid having conversations about her before, and Chloe didn't want to start now.

"Well, he's a great boyfriend too. He put a big rock on Emoni's finger, and I think they'll be getting married soon."

"Good for them. They've been dating a long time."

"Emoni has been punishing him because he cheated on her, but I think she's noticed the buzzards circling."

This made Quentin smile. "Buzzards?"

"Yes, those desperate single women who don't want to work on a relationship. They want to swoop in on one that is struggling, just to capitalize on all the work the other woman has already put in. A good woman always improves a man."

"Really? What have you done to improve me?"

Chloe scoffed. "What do you mean what have I done to improve you? I've done a lot, Quentin. I can't believe you!"

Quentin leaned back in his chair and folded his arms. "Okay, tell me what you've done."

"Well, for one, since we've been together you've enjoyed life more. You're more refined. You are more of a gentleman."

Quentin nodded slowly. "Does it bother you that I don't go to church?"

Where was this coming from? That nanny was going to ruin everything!

"Why are you asking all of these questions?" Chloe asked, trying to stall so that she could think of an acceptable answer.

"I'm just curious. You go to church every week. Doesn't it bother you that I'm not there with you?"

Actually, it didn't bother her at all, but she was sure that wasn't the answer that Quentin was looking for. Chloe went to church mostly for the social aspects. Their church was the pulse of the upper-class community. It was how she found out who was seeing whom and what charity dinners and golf classics she needed to twist Quentin's arm into attending. If she got a word every now and then from Bishop Prentiss, then that was all good.

"Well, Quentin, I understand your reasons for not being there. I support you. When you're ready, you'll come back."

"What if I'm never ready? What if I don't come back? That wouldn't bother you?"

Chloe sat her fork down on the table. "Quentin, the truth is that I love being with you. It wouldn't matter to me if you never set foot in a church again, as long as I have you to come home to."

"So my soul's salvation means nothing?"

Chloe burst into laughter. "Oh, what do you want me to say, honey? We have sex every time we get the chance. Aren't we already going to hell?"

Quentin locked his jaw and frowned. "I suppose we should get right then, huh?"

"Does that mean we're going to get married?" Chloe asked, with a giggle in her voice. She hoped to turn their lunch date back into positive territory.

"Nope. But it means we won't be sleeping together anymore."

Chloe dropped her fork along with her jaw. Maybe the nanny wasn't the problem at all. She couldn't have Quentin having a "come to Jesus" moment, not when she was so close to the prize.

"Okay, Quentin. I'm fine with that. But next time you wake up in the middle of the night, drenched in sweat, your body pulsating with need . . ."

"I'll pray really, really hard."

"You won't last seventy-two hours."

"Yes, I will. I'm not going to live a life of sin anymore. And sleeping with you isn't the only thing I'm giving up."

Chloe's eyebrows shot up. "What else are you giving up."

"Doesn't the Bible say that it is easier for a camel to go through the eye of a needle than for a rich man to enter the kingdom of God?"

"Maybe it does. I'm not familiar with that verse, though. What does that have to do with you? You care about your family's legacy, that much I do know."

"You think I care about this money? You're wrong. I'm about to turn it all over to my children."

"Well, of course. After you die, your children will inherit from you."

Quentin shook his head. "Not after I die. Today. Right now. I'm giving this up to go and live at Transitions. My mother will make sure the children are taken care of, but I have to discover my true purpose."

"What? Are you serious?"

"Yes. I believe that my ministry is at Transitions."

"Your ministry? So now the cancer patients are ministry? Don't you need money to run the foundation?"

Quentin said, "Mother will continue to fund the foundation. I will take a small salary from the budget and live in the house."

"So you're just going to leave your kids?"

"They're almost grown, and they have a nanny. I will spend the weekends with them, but I need to be at Transitions during the week."

Chloe's eyes darted from side to side. She was in panic mode. She didn't want a man who was in ministry with a vow of poverty. She wanted the fabulous life of a socialite.

"I know you were expecting to live a lavish socialite's life, but I'd still love to have your hand in marriage. You can be my ministry partner, and maybe you can get a job to keep you busy since I don't want any more children."

"A job?"

"Yes. You can work at the foundation if you want. As long as we have each other, who needs the mansion and everything that comes with it?"

Chloe jumped to her feet. "I do! I need the mansion! I need jewels, vacations, shopping sprees, and all of that! Am I being pranked? Where are the cameras?"

"No, this is real, babe. Will you marry me?"

Chloe plopped back down in her seat at the table. Suddenly she felt hot, so she fanned herself with the cloth napkin. Beads of sweat glistened on her forehead.

"Quentin . . . I need some time to think."

"What do you need to think about? We've been together almost five years. You stepped in right after Chandra died."

"I did."

"And don't you think we should be married by now?"

Here was her chance to finally have Quentin! But she wanted the rich Quentin. Not a salaried Quentin.

Chloe reached across the table and took his hand. "Of course, I hoped that we would, but I understand that you needed time to finish grieving your first wife."

Quentin snatched his hand away. "How long are you willing to wait?"

"As long as it takes to get my prize."

"Is the prize me . . . or my money?" Quentin asked, sure that he already knew the answer to that question.

"You and your money are a package deal. I'd be a liar if I said I didn't want this life."

"And now that I've decided to give it all up?"

"Stop speaking foolishly. Have your foundation, live there if you want, but that doesn't mean you have to give up your wealth. That's the most ridiculous thing I've ever heard."

"Are you even in love with me, Chloe? I'm being serious."

"Would I have worked this hard for five years if I didn't love you? We deserve this life."

Quentin sighed. "Falling in love shouldn't be hard work. It should be effortless."

Chloe clutched the single strand of pearls around her neck. "What are you trying to say to me, Quentin?"

"I talked to God about us. Asked Him for guidance."

"Really? What did He say?"

"He didn't say anything. But my questions . . . well, they confirmed what I've been feeling for a long time now."

"Quentin . . ."

"I can't see a future with you, Chloe. I'm sorry. Now you're free to find someone who can make you happy."

Chloe jumped up from her seat, reached across the table, and slapped Quentin in the face with all her might. Quentin smarted from the pain and clenched his jaw in anger.

"That's it? I'm sorry? That's all you have to say?" Chloe yelled. "I spent the last five years of my life being nice to those little brats of yours and kissing your mother's bougie behind, and all you can say is 'sorry'?"

Quentin stood to his feet so that he was staring down at Chloe. "This doesn't have to get ugly. Let's end it on a high note."

"You will be screaming all kinds of high notes when I get through with you."

"Are you threatening me, Chloe?"

"I'm promising you that this is not over. You owe me, Quentin."

He laughed. "What? Do you want a check? You want me to give you a condo like that dead white man you sent to an early grave?"

Chloe scoffed. "I thought you didn't want this to get ugly."

"Don't make a scene, Chloe. I've arranged for a car service to come and take you home. Good-bye, Chloe."

"See you soon."

Chloe's farewell was a promise and a threat. She watched Quentin stride out of their favorite restaurant. A restaurant she couldn't afford to dine in without Quentin paying the bill. She kicked herself for having been so complacent for so long.

Chloe swore that it wasn't over with Quentin. She'd be back in her rightful place as soon as she did what she should've done from the first time she laid eyes on Montana. Get that scheming man stealer out of her man's house.

CHAPTER 27

All five of the Chambers children sat in the family room looking at each other. They'd gotten a text from their father to gather there, but none of them knew why.

"What's this about?" Reese asked Deirdre.

She shrugged. "Who knows? Daddy has been acting really weird lately."

Madison said. "I thought I was the only one who noticed that. Daddy just hugged me for no reason yesterday. I thought he was about to cry or something."

"Right. And he came outside while I was shooting hoops, giving me all this advice and stuff. It was crazy," Reese said.

Danielle said, "Well, I like Daddy like this. I think he should stay like this."

"As long as he doesn't start trying to hang with us all the time," Morgan said.

Quentin walked into the family room. "As long as who doesn't try to hang out with you?"

All of the kids looked at each other, but no one replied.

"Today is family day," Quentin said.

"All day?" Deirdre asked.

"Yes, all day. What do y'all want to do?" Quentin asked.

"Can we play?" Danielle asked. "Outside, I mean."

Both the twins and Deirdre moaned. "No one wants to play tag with you, Danielle."

Danielle puffed her cheeks with air and blew it out in an angry huff. "No one ever wants to do what I want to do."

Quentin clapped his hands. "You know what, Danielle? We are playing tag. And we're having a water-gun fight."

"Uh, I just got my hair done," Deirdre said.

Quentin shrugged, "Since you're on punishment, you won't be needing to look cute for anyone, right?"

Deirdre frowned while her siblings laughed at her. Quentin laughed too. He was glad the kids were finally warming up. He'd felt like a stranger for a moment.

"Everybody go change and meet me out back in ten minutes. Get your super-soakers ready, so we can go to war!"

Danielle seemed the most excited as all of the children took off running. Quentin was as stoked as they were. It had been a while since they'd spent time together. Maybe it was time for a family vacation.

Quentin had thought of inviting Montana to join them for their day of fun, but then he changed his mind. First of all, he'd just broken up with Chloe, so it was probably too soon. Second, he wanted to follow what Montana had told him. He wanted to face his grief head on before pursuing her. Not only did it make sense, but he wanted her to know that he was serious about getting his life back.

On Quentin's way back downstairs to meet with the children, he did run into Montana in the hallway. She looked at his camouflage wear and chuckled.

"What are you about to do?" Montana asked.

"Destroy these kids with my water gun."

Montana burst into laughter. "I hope they know what they're in for."

"If they don't, they're going to find out."

"So I'm off for the rest of the afternoon, then?" Montana asked.

Quentin nodded. "Yes. You can go and do whatever women do on the weekend. You need money? You want a pedicure? Want to go shopping?"

"As much as I would love to say yes to all of that, I don't really feel right taking your money. Not right now. Not while Chloe thinks you're still her fiancée."

"She doesn't think that anymore. We broke up this morning."

"You did?" Montana asked, her voice full of excitement. "You did."

She repeated the phrase, making it sound more solemn, but Quentin knew that her excited response showed her true feelings.

"Yeah."

"Are you okay?"

Quentin nodded. "I'm better than okay."

"Well, good."

Montana sashayed past Quentin on the stairs in a snug, knee-length jean skirt. Having the object of his affection under his roof was probably going to be a problem that Quentin hadn't considered.

"Oh, Quentin," Montana turned around on the stairs. "I forgot to ask you if you wanted to come to church tomorrow. I have a solo."

"I'd love to," Quentin replied.

"All right, have fun with the kids. I'll see you later," Montana said.

"Okay. See you later."

Quentin felt the butterflies again when Montana waved at him with one finger. She was wearing shiny lip gloss, but there was no other makeup on her face. She didn't need it.

Quentin stared after Montana for a few moments after she left. Until he felt something wet on the back of his head.

"You coming or what?" Reese asked from downstairs.

Reese had shot him with his water gun, while Deirdre watched. They were snickering as he walked down the stairs.

"Daddy, do you want Montana to be your girlfriend?" Deirdre asked.

"What? No," Quentin said.

"Good, because I really like Chloe mentoring me," Deirdre said.

Quentin raised his eyebrows. He hadn't thought about this. Chloe had only recently taken an interest in Deirdre, and he doubted that she'd keep it up now that they'd broken up.

"Deirdre, Chloe and I broke up. I don't think it'll be a good idea for you to keep spending time with her."

Deirdre burst into tears. "Daddy, this isn't fair! She's the only one who even tries to understand me!"

Quentin was at a loss. He hadn't seen Deirdre attached to any woman since Chandra died. He guessed it would be okay to let them continue a friendship, as long as Chloe knew that it didn't mean they were getting back together.

"You can continue seeing Chloe. It just has to be away from here."

Deirdre ran up the stairs and hugged Quentin tightly. "Thank you, Daddy! We were supposed to go shopping this afternoon. Can I still go?"

"Are you sure she still wants to go?"

"Why wouldn't she? She broke up with you and not me."

Quentin almost corrected Deirdre. Chloe hadn't broken up with him. It was the other way around, but at the end of the day it equaled the same thing. They weren't together. And since they weren't an item anymore, there was one more thing Quentin needed to do. Call his accountant and cancel Chloe's credit cards.

CHAPTER 28

Montana sank her feet into the bubbly water in the tub beneath the massage chair at the nail salon. She and Emoni were getting pedicures for church the next day since Montana had the afternoon off. The water felt great on Montana's feet. She'd been running with Quentin every other day, and her dogs could use some tender loving care.

"So what is so important that you dragged me away from my man on a Saturday afternoon?" Emoni asked.

Montana laughed. "I definitely don't want to drag you away from Darrin. I hope you're gonna marry him sometime this century, so please don't let me be in the way of that."

"We set a date."

"What? You did? Oh, congratulations. When?"

"Next summer. June twentieth. You want to be my maid of honor?"

Montana clapped her hands and blew Emoni air kisses. They couldn't turn and hug since both had their feet submerged.

"Of course I do. I can't wait. You're going to be beautiful."

"Enough about that. What's going on with you and Quentin?"

Montana's face broke into a wistful smile when she thought about Quentin. "He broke up with Chloe."

"Shut up!" Emoni said. "When?"

"He said this morning. I don't know what happens next, though. It's not like he's gonna break up with her one day and be my man the next day."

"Oh, and I guarantee Chloe isn't going down without a fight. She's been in his face since Chandra died. You know Quentin is her retirement plan."

"But if Quentin wants to break up with her, what can she do? She has no choice in the matter. It's not like she can force him to be with her."

Emoni shrugged. "How are you gonna keep living there if you start dating Quentin?"

"There is a guest house in back. I'm gonna ask if I can move in there, because we definitely won't be able to coexist under the same roof."

"See . . . you're gonna have your black prince."

"I'm not sure. I have some conditions before that can even take place."

"Conditions?"

"He needs to be healed, Emoni. I don't want him broken, and he is definitely broken. He's not over his wife."

Emoni nodded. "I will pray for him. I'm serious. Quentin has to give this over to God."

"I know. I invited him to church tomorrow. I hope Bishop preaches something good that speaks right to Quentin's heart."

Emoni whipped out her phone. She started texting.

"Who are you texting?" Montana asked.

"My dad. He loves Quentin and wants him back at church. He'll preach something especially for him."

"Do you want the deluxe pedicure?" asked the young pretty girl who was about to work on Montana's feet.

"No, just the regular today."

"Splurge a little!" Emoni said. "Get the deluxe!"

"Girl, I can't afford the deluxe. Everybody ain't balling like you."

Emoni laughed. "Give her the deluxe. I'll make up the difference."

"You know, Quentin actually offered to pay for my pedicure today. He wanted to give me money."

"And you didn't take it? What's wrong with you?"

"It didn't feel right. I think Quentin doesn't know how to woo a woman without money. He started right out spending money on me."

Emoni laughed. "That's what rich men do. They spend money on women."

"Yeah, well, he's gonna have to do more than buy me. He did something so sweet the other day, and I don't even think he realized it."

"What?"

"We were about to go running, and he noticed that my shoes were tied too tightly. He got down and retied my shoes for me."

Emoni laughed. "Awww . . . how sweet."

"Oh, shut up! I'm serious. It made me think that he would take care of me, and not just financially. He pays attention. Like he noticed my feet were hurting and bought the shoes in the first place."

"So he is a great guy. We knew that already."

"I just want to know how he ended up with Chloe."

Emoni laughed. "You don't know this story. She showed up at the funeral with her boobs hanging all out and drenched in perfume. She's been stalking him ever since. She used to be with this old billionaire before Quentin."

"Old? How old?"

"Old enough that he died on her?"

"Literally on her?"

Emoni howled with laughter. "No, not on her like that! He had an aneurysm or something. He was in his seventies."

"His seventies? Ewwww . . . Could you imagine?"

"No ma'am, I could not imagine. That is disgusting. But she came up with a house, car, and cash, so maybe it was worth it."

"His seventies, though? Ain't that much money in the world."

"Old men need love too," Emoni said. "And she was just the one to give it."

Montana leaned back in her seat and closed her eyes while the pretty girl rubbed all of the pain and tension out of her feet, but it did nothing to ease the apprehension in her spirit. If Chloe was desperate enough to sleep with an elderly man for a buck, what twisted things would she do to hold on to Quentin?

CHAPTER 29

Chloe picked Deirdre up at their designated time for their "mentoring" session. Quentin must've been out, because Deirdre absolutely looked like she was going to meet a boy with that tiny jean skirt and face full of makeup.

Chloe shook her head as Deirdre got into the front seat of her car. "Did you put on enough perfume? The poor boy's gonna die from the fumes."

"You sound like a hater right now. Just because my daddy decided to break up with you doesn't mean you have to hate on me and my boo."

Chloe rolled her eyes. "The breakup between me and your father is temporary."

"That's what you say, but I just saw my daddy breaking his neck to watch Montana walk down the stairs. You need to work fast, because I think the warden is trying to be my stepmama."

"That may be what that broke nanny wants, but it's not going to happen."

Deidre smacked her lips and applied another layer of lip gloss to her already too-shiny lips. "Anyway. I needed to get an Oscar for the performance I did for my father. I cried and everything, all because I didn't want to be separated from my mentor."

"As if those tears had anything to do with me. You just want to keep hanging out with your hood boyfriend. How long are you and the thug going to be in the movie theater?"

"The movie is two and a half hours long with the previews, and we probably want to get something to eat afterward."

"I'll be back in three and a half hours. And then, tomorrow night, I may need you to do something for me."

"What?"

"I'll give you further instructions."

Deirdre laughed. "Who do you think you are, Don Corleone or somebody? You can't just tell me to wait for instructions. Ain't nobody got time for that."

"You don't tell me what you have time for. I don't have time to be your taxi service, but I'm getting you to this boyfriend of yours."

"I can find another way to be with Moe. You're just making it convenient."

"Keep it up and you're going to have to exercise your options."

Chloe pulled in front of the movie theater, and Deirdre opened the door. "Chloe, you need me more than I need you. It just so happens that I don't want my dad with Montana either. She's too goody-goody, and I'm not trying to be singing in the youth choir at church."

"I'll let you know what I need later on."

Deirdre stepped out of the car. "No, Chloe. I'll let you know what I need."

Chloe rolled her eyes as Deirdre slammed her car door way too hard. The girl was taking advantage of the situation, but Chloe did need her. With her and Quentin broken up, she wouldn't have access to their home anymore, and all the things she needed were inside the Chambers mansion.

After dropping Deirdre off at the movie theater, Chloe stopped at her favorite boutique. After all she'd been through today, she deserved a new dress.

As soon as Chloe stepped through the boutique's doors, she knew she'd made a mistake. Lichelle was there, and she was the last person Chloe wanted to see. Chloe didn't want to gossip about everyone in their circle. Chloe wasn't even sure she'd still be in the circle after breaking up with Quentin.

Lichelle waved at Chloe as she walked inside. "Get my homegirl a glass of champagne," she said.

"I sure need it," Chloe replied.

Chloe sat down next to Lichelle, and they hugged. "What's wrong with you?" Lichelle asked.

"Everything," Chloe said.

Chloe refused to break down in tears to give the boutique salesgirl something to talk about to her other clients.

Lichelle whispered, "Quentin?"

"Yes," Chloe whispered back. "We broke up this morning, but I think it's only temporary."

"That low-down . . ."

Chloe held a finger to her lips. "Shhh. I've got a plan. Well, it's a piece of a plan so far, but it's coming together pretty quickly."

Since the salesgirl was staring at Chloe and Lichelle and probably trying to read their lips, Chloe motioned for her to come over.

The salesgirl handed Chloe a glass of champagne. "How can I help you?"

"Can you wrap this handbag up for me? You already have card information on file for me."

"Yes, Ms. Chloe."

Chloe sipped her champagne and sighed. The shock of Quentin's breaking up with her was just starting to fade, and reality was setting in. She hoped she could get rid of Montana quickly. She didn't want to spend months trying to get Quentin back.

The salesgirl came back to them and she had a smirk on her face. "Your card was declined, ma'am."

Chloe frowned and Lichelle gasped. Quentin was heartless. They had just broken up this morning and he'd already canceled her credit card? This was more dire than she'd thought.

Even though Chloe couldn't really afford the five-thousand-dollar purse without Quentin footing the bill, she still whipped out one of her own credit cards. She wouldn't have this girl spreading around town that she wasn't even able to buy a purse.

"Oh, I'm sorry. I meant to update my information last time I was here."

The girl smirked again and took Chloe's card. She turned on one heel and marched away.

"Did y'all get into a fight?" Lichelle whispered as soon as the girl was out of eavesdropping range. "He didn't have to cancel the card. Y'all didn't even get to have make-up sex."

Chloe decided not to tell Lichelle that Quentin promised to never sleep with her again. That would be too juicy for her not to share.

"I still have a few things up my sleeve," Chloe said. "It ain't over till the fat nanny sings."

"Doesn't she sing every Sunday at that church you go to?"

"Oh, shut up, Lichelle."

CHAPTER 30

Deirdre felt butterflies in her stomach as Moe slid his arm around her shoulders while they walked to the food court after the movie. She was sure he was going to try and kiss her, and she was ready. It would be her first kiss. Her first kiss from her first love.

"What you want to eat, babe?" Moe asked.

"I'm not really that hungry. I just want something to drink."

Deirdre was being truthful. After eating popcorn and candy in the movie, she was full, and she felt too nervous to eat anything else.

"Well, we don't have to eat. We can go shopping for your prom dress."

Deirdre clapped her hands and squealed. "You decided to go to your prom?"

"Yeah. I know it's last minute. I hope you don't mind."

"I don't mind. What is prom anyway, but a new dress and new shoes? I've got plenty of dresses and shoes."

"So you're gonna be my date for prom, after prom, and after-after prom?" Moe asked.

Deirdre stopped walking and cocked her head to one side. "What is after-after prom?"

Moe laughed out loud. "That's when we go back to the hotel and do what we do."

"Oh."

Deirdre didn't know if she was ready for after-after prom, especially since it was taking place inside a hotel room with Moe. She thought about what her grandmother would say. Then she thought about what her father would say. They would both be mortified at what she was considering.

But at least Moe was up front about it and hadn't tried to trick her. The choice was still hers.

"It's okay if you don't want to," Moe said. "I can ask someone else to go with me."

"No. No! I'll go. I just wasn't sure what you meant. I'm down."

"Cool. You think your father will let us drive one of his fly cars to the prom?"

Deidre's jaw dropped. Her father couldn't know that she was going at all! How in the world would she be able to borrow one of his cars?

Moe burst into laughter. "I'm joking! You should see your face!"

"Stop playing! You know my daddy isn't going to let you drive one of his cars. I'll be lucky to get out of the house."

"We need to fix that. Your father is in the way of our love."

Moe took Deirdre's hand, squeezed it in his, and continued, "I'm staying in Atlanta for college, so you don't have to worry about losing me after we get together."

A smile spread over Deirdre's face. Her friends would be so jealous that she was dating a college freshman. She could imagine herself at step shows and frat parties. She wouldn't care if she had to go to that ridiculous all-girls school if she could hang out on the college campus on the weekend.

"So what color are we wearing?"

"Money green, baby. What else?"

Then it happened. Moe wrapped Deirdre in a hug and

kissed her deeply on the mouth. Deirdre trembled, and Moe smiled.

"I remember when I saw you at the mall. All my boys said you'd never holla at me, but they were wrong."

Deirdre beamed up at him. "They didn't know you had that good game."

Moe popped his collar. "I do, don't I."

"Yeah, baby, you do."

Deidre thought quickly. Prom night would require an all-night escape. She'd have to be a little bit sweeter to Chloe when she picked her up later. Maybe even be a little apologetic. It looked like Deirdre and her mentor were going to have a slumber party.

CHAPTER 31

Chloe tried to stay in the shadows of the strip club she'd selected for her meeting with Rio. She had no idea if he'd reply to her Facebook message asking for a meeting. She had no idea what she'd say if he said yes. She'd chosen the strip club to avoid any nosy members from Freedom of Life. If she ran into one of them up in there, then they certainly wouldn't mention it.

Her plan was to meet with Rio and find out the real scoop on the way-too-perfect Montana. There was no way she was as good as she seemed. Every saint had a past, and Rio was part of Montana's.

Rio finally arrived and slid into the booth across from Chloe. "Hey, Chloe. What's going on? Is this about Montana? Is she okay?"

Chloe rolled her eyes. Why was everyone so concerned about little Ms. Nanny's well-being?

"She's fine. In fact, she's doing so well that she's stolen my man."

Rio looked confused. "No, she said she wasn't interested in him. So you don't know what you're talking about."

"Are you trying to get her back?" Chloe asked.

"Maybe. But I was just going to keep showing up at church until she got weak and came running back to me."

"Are you stupid? Quentin is almost a billionaire. You can't compete with him by showing up at church!"

"I ain't thinking 'bout his money."

Chloe shook her head. "Well, you should. Most girls find it impossible to resist rich men."

"You don't know Montana."

"Right. But you do. You and Montana were together a long time, right?"

Rio nodded. "Yeah. What does that have to do with anything?"

"Did she ever send you a sexy photograph?"

Rio laughed out loud. "Just about every day."

Chloe grinned. She knew Montana was a freak. "Did you save any of them, by chance?"

Rio whipped out his phone and flicked through his gallery until he found the picture he wanted. Then he held the phone out to Chloe.

"What about this one?"

Chloe's grin changed to a huge smile when she saw the picture. Montana was wearing some very sexy lingerie as she sat in a chair turned backward. Chloe's plan materialized in her mind. She knew exactly what she was going to do to get her man back.

"That's perfect, Rio."

"So what do you want me to do with the picture?" he asked.

"Text it to me. I'll take it from there."

Rio sat back in his seat. "Should I be worried?"

"No. You just get ready to get your little girlfriend back."

"You're pretty sure of yourself."

Chloe took a sip from the glass of water in front of her. "Trust me. This isn't my first rodeo."

Although her plan was downright diabolical, Chloe did not feel bad about what was going to happen to Montana. If the girl was bold enough to move in on her man, then she was woman enough to deal with the consequences. It was simply cause and effect.

CHAPTER 32

Quentin stood in the mirror and appraised his "going back to church" outfit. He'd thought about going casual. Freedom of Life was a church where a person would feel comfortable wearing jeans and flip-flops if that's what he wanted to wear. Bishop Prentiss never made anyone feel inferior if they didn't have on a designer suit or dress, so Quentin knew that his three-piece black suit was not imperative.

He chose the suit, however, because Montana had invited him to hear her sing. He had heard her singing in the house, but it was quiet praise and worship. He'd never heard her truly sing, and his mother said that Montana's voice was phenomenal.

"You look nice, son," Estelle said from Quentin's doorway.

"Thank you, Mother. I think I might be a little formal, though."

Estelle walked into his room and touched Quentin's back. "Well, there's nothing wrong with formal. I think sometimes folks get lazy when it comes to church. In my day, we always gave our best to God."

Quentin smiled at his mother. She had never gone along with the "come as you are" revolution in the modern church. Every time she saw a pair of flip-flops in the sanctuary she gritted her teeth. She would never hurt anyone's feelings about it, but if they cared to ask, she would certainly give her opinion on the topic.

"Come on, let's all ride together in the Escalade," Estelle said.

"Reese told me he was leaving early. I guess a friend of his wants to come to church today," Quentin said.

Estelle nodded. "Well, then that's perfect. Montana can ride with us too."

Quentin wondered if he should ask Montana to ride in the car with them. He wondered how it would look to the Freedom of Life members, but then he decided that he didn't care about that at all.

Quentin and Estelle went downstairs and met with the rest of the family in the foyer. Ms. Levy went to her own church in Lithonia. Her family had been founding members of Big Miller Grove Missionary Baptist Church, and she had no intention of changing her membership, no matter how much action was taking place at Freedom of Life.

Quentin's pesky butterflies started acting up big-time when he saw Montana. She was wearing a pink dress with puffy sleeves and a modestly plunged neckline. It looked like she'd straightened her curly hair, which was parted on one side with a flipped bang over her eye. The look was very flattering on her. Quentin wished that she was already his, because surely half the single men in the congregation were going to try to get her number after service.

"You all look really nice," Quentin said to everyone. He didn't want to single out Montana with the kids there.

Madison said, "Daddy, doesn't Ms. Montana look incredible? She's hot, right?"

Quentin closed his eyes and grinned. "She does look incredible," he agreed.

"And hot too, right?" Morgan asked.

Montana said, "Girls . . ."

Deirdre sucked her teeth. "Y'all are sooo corny."

"Thank you! Are we all riding in one car, or do I need to drive?"

Danielle said, "Ms. Montana, your car is not that cute. Let's ride in Daddy's truck."

"My car gets me from point A to point B, thank you very much. And it's paid for," Montana said.

Estelle said, "Yes, but you look gorgeous today, honey. It's the perfect time to ride in style."

Once Estelle said something in their home, it was settled. Montana would ride to church as a member of the Chambers family. The thought of that being a permanent situation made Quentin's heart leap.

At the car, Quentin opened the doors for all six of his favorite ladies. He mused that it would've been nice for Reese to be there, just to close some of the doors.

When they got to church, many heads turned, and Quentin could only guess the reasons. Some of them were probably shocked to see him at church after all these years. Those who were aware of his relationship with Chloe probably wondered what was going on with Montana stepping out of his car instead.

Danielle linked arms with Montana and walked toward the church. No matter what happened, Quentin knew he had to make Montana a permanent fixture in their lives.

"Where do you want to sit?" Estelle whispered. "I'm singing today, so I'll be in the choir loft."

Quentin considered his choices. He could sit in the back of the sanctuary, but it was huge and he wanted to be able to see Montana's face when she sang. If he sat in the front, where his mother usually sat, people were going to be staring and whispering the entire service. He decided that he cared more about Montana's invitation than the chatter.

"I'll go up front. Might as well."

Estelle chuckled. "Get ready to be bombarded with hugs and greetings. Whether you realize it or not, people miss you and want you back."

"One Sunday at a time, Mother. This doesn't mean I'm back."

Estelle nodded. "It means you've taken the first step."

Estelle left Quentin with the children and ascended the choir loft with Montana. Quentin sat at the end of the aisle, which almost immediately he found to be a mistake.

"Well, look at what we got here. Is it Easter? Surely the dead have been resurrected."

It was Sister Ophelia, one of the nurses and chief gossip ambassador of Freedom of Life. She stood in front of Quentin, with her hands on her hips, looking like a sanctified superhero. Her special power was being able to throw a sheet over a woman if she showed even a glimpse of skin. She didn't seem to realize her poor choice of words, as she chuckled at her own joke.

"Sister Ophelia," Quentin said, as he stood to hug her. "Long time no see."

"Yes, it has been a long time. I would've seen you if I ever got an invite to one of those fancy brunches your mother throws at that big old house. But I guess those are just for the inner circle."

Quentin closed his eyes and laughed. Ophelia was hilarious. She was determined to be included in the high-society affairs, and Estelle was as equally determined not to include her. Every now and then, though, Estelle and First Lady Prentiss had no choice but to break bread with Ophelia, because one of the pastor's daughters was married to her grandson.

"Sister Ophelia, you know I don't go to their little parties."

Ophelia patted Quentin on the cheek. The hand smelled like mothballs and peppermint.

"I know, baby. You always were the approachable one of the family. How you been?"

"I'm making it," Quentin said truthfully.

"Where's that barracuda of yours? She's usually not here this early. Guess it takes extra time to put all that Jezebel makeup on."

Quentin burst into laughter. "You mean Chloe?"

"Yes, your fiancée."

Quentin shook his head. Why did everyone want to insist that Chloe was his fiancée? She was not wearing a ring, and no engagement announcements had been sent.

"She's not my fiancée, Sister Ophelia."

Ophelia furrowed her eyebrows and pulled Quentin by his lapel close to her face. "So what is she? A booty call? Let me take you on up to the altar right now. God is faithful and just to forgive all your sins. Even illicit relations."

Ophelia pulled Quentin out of the aisle, but he resisted. "Sister Ophelia, I think I can take myself to the altar if need be. I thank you for your concern."

"Quentin!"

He would know that shrill voice anywhere. Quentin had hoped that Chloe would be tardy, as was her custom. That day, of all days, she decided to show up on time.

"Here she is now," Ophelia said. "Y'all can go to the altar together. There's room at the cross for both of y'all."

"Hello, Ophelia," Chloe said.

Ophelia's eyes swept Chloe from top to bottom. "Did you get a new haircut?"

"Yes, I did."

Ophelia nodded. "It kinda makes you look like Dorothy Dandridge."

"Why, thank you, Sister Ophelia."

"It shows off the angles of your face," Ophelia continued. "Your strong jawline is especially noticeable. Like if Dorothy Dandridge had a brother. Dorothy Mandridge!"

Ophelia burst into laughter at her own joke. Quentin closed his eyes and shook his head. Sister Ophelia hadn't changed a bit.

Chloe glared at Ophelia. "I think I just heard one of the ministers ask for a cough drop."

Ophelia zipped open her fanny pack and pulled out a package of cough drops. "Which one was it?"

Chloe shrugged. "I think it was all of them. You probably need to go and find out."

Ophelia rushed off at breakneck speed. No one was going to be able to tell her she wasn't on her job. The salvation of the sinners apparently had to wait.

Chloe cocked her head to one side as she smoothed Quentin's lapel. "So you're back at church."

Quentin's lips became a thin line. He didn't want to talk to Chloe this morning.

"It was a spur-of-the-moment decision."

"So you break up with me and find Jesus again, all in one weekend."

"Chloe . . ."

"I'm not going to make a scene here, Quentin. It's the house of the Lord."

Chloe walked calmly up the center aisle smiling and waving to those who stopped her. She didn't let on that anything was amiss with them as she made her way to the rear of the sanctuary.

Quentin noticed changes in the order of service. Instead of the choir opening service with a song, as they had done when he was the minister of music, a group of six singers stood up and sang praise and worship songs. Montana was one of them, and she was really good. Quentin found himself clapping and almost stood to his feet, but he didn't want anyone to stare at him.

He had to ease himself back into the worship experience. Twice, the musician on the keyboard played a wrong chord. It was barely noticeable, but Quentin couldn't help but hear it. He had always been a perfectionist with his music, and he couldn't turn his ears off. The tenor in the praise team was a little flat too, but overall the congregation was roused into uproarious worship.

Quentin remembered when he was a part of that. When he could lead the congregation into a frenzied worship by playing to match their energy. When he had been on the keyboard, it was like he was tapped into the very pulse of the congregation. When they got high, he'd take it there, and when they were ready for the quieter sounds of worship, Quentin met them exactly where they were. Quentin hadn't realized how much he missed it.

But every moment of the worship reminded him that Chandra was not there. She had been his partner in every way when it came to the music. When his playing hit the frenzied pace, her singing complemented that.

After the praise and worship team finished, the welcome

committee, greeters, deacons, and all the other church auxiliaries did their morning routines. When they asked the visitors to stand, Quentin almost did so as a joke, but then he thought better of it, because a hugging brigade was sent to the visitor, and he was not trying to hug anyone else.

Next the choir was introduced, and Montana took her place in front of the microphone reserved for the soloist. She smiled out at the congregation as the introduction for her song started.

"Have you ever been through something you felt like nobody could understand?" Montana asked the audience. "Not your mother, not your father, not your pastor? Have you ever experienced a trial that you could only talk to God about? In those times when we struggle, and we think that no one can empathize with our pain, that's when we stand on God's Word, remember what He said, and encourage ourselves."

When Montana sang the first few notes of Donald Lawrence's song "Encourage Yourself," Quentin could tell that her voice wasn't just good. She had an anointed voice. It rose and fell in time to the music and to match the lyrics. The choir sounded like her backup singers, because Montana moved the congregation like a solo artist. She went from one side of the pulpit to the other, making eye contact with members. When she got to the vamp part of the song, the choir sang "I'm encouraged" over and over, but Montana's ad libs were a sermon all by themselves. Quentin had no idea there was so much power inside that petite package. He was in awe of the God in Montana.

"Daddy, you're crying." Deirdre handed Quentin a tissue, and he quickly wiped his face. The last thing he wanted anyone to think was that he was soft or that he was sitting in service crying over his first wife. He was touched by the sheer beauty and the Holy Spirit that was evident when Montana sang that song. It took everything in him to stay in his seat and not go and push the keyboard player out of the way. He wanted to play while Montana sang.

As Montana and the choir continued, Quentin stood to his feet. He didn't seem out of place, because about half the congregation was standing too. He couldn't stay seated when that type of praise was going forth. He had to be a part of it.

When the song was over, Quentin, along with the rest of the congregation, gave the choir and Montana a huge round of applause. Montana smiled at Quentin, and he smiled back. Quentin was so caught up in the presence of God that he didn't care if Chloe paid him any attention.

Finally, Bishop Prentiss took the stage. Quentin made eye contact with him, and they exchanged smiles before Quentin took his seat. Bishop Prentiss had always been a second father to Quentin, and Bishop was one of the few people that Quentin still talked to from church. Of course, the conversation always turned to when Quentin was coming back, so their discussions weren't as frequent as Bishop would probably like them to be.

"I've been talking to God about this message for a few weeks," Bishop Prentiss said. "He's been giving me so much to share with you on one passage that I might just have to split it up. I might finish it in Bible study. Y'all do remember that little middle-of-the-week service, right?"

The congregation chuckled at Bishop Prentiss's joke. It was no secret that their church was packed every Sunday morning, but it was always just a faithful few for the midweek Bible study. Quentin wasn't surprised that it hadn't changed in that regard.

"But I want y'all to open your Bibles to the book of Job," Bishop said. "It's in the middle of your Bible, right before Psalms. Go to chapter thirteen and verse fifteen. It is one of my favorite verses, because the message there illustrates our lives as Christians."

Quentin opened the Bible application on his phone and clicked to the verse. He stared down at the words and felt a knot form in his throat. The verse read, "Though He slay me; yet will I trust in Him: but I will maintain mine own ways before Him."

Bishop Prentiss said, "Y'all know who Job was referring to in this Scripture, right? Who is doing the slaying? Or who has Job perceived to be the slayer? Job is talking about God in this verse. Job was a man who had lost nearly everything. If anyone had been slain, it was Job."

Quentin empathized with Job. He, like Job, had lost much. And Quentin, like Job, had blamed God for all his losses. Quentin definitely viewed God as the slayer in his situation. Unlike Job, though, Quentin was having a difficult time with the "yet will I trust in him" part of the verse. It was almost impossible for Quentin to trust God again. He'd trusted him to be a healer, and he hadn't healed Chandra. He'd trusted him to work miracles, and no miracles had gone forth. Quentin was still trying to understand how to trust God.

Quentin listened to Bishop Prentiss explain the mind-set of Job.

Bishop said, "Job was a man who had lost nearly everything. In the Scripture he refers to himself as being slain, and he perceives God to be the slayer. He has lost children, wealth, and health. He feels tried, tested, with the instructor being his heavenly father. Yet after reflecting back over his loss, Job realizes that he has no other choice but to trust God. Without his faith in God, Job would perish from grief and lack of understanding. His trust in God is what allowed him to have a life after his loss. He trusted in God for restoration, even though on the surface it looked as if none was possible."

Quentin's jaw tightened as he listened to the words from the pulpit. How was it fair that God allowed these things to happen when He could stop them? All his life Quentin had heard the Scripture "By His stripes we are healed." Why was it only in certain situations that the power came into play? Had he not prayed hard enough? Had he and Chandra not served God with all their hearts? There were many "amens" and "hallelujahs" going up from the congregation, but none of them came from Quentin. He was unable to join the chorus of believers.

Bishop continued. "Sometimes we think that God should just enfold us in bubble wrap and shield us from every danger, hurt, or trauma. We want our lives to be sheltered and covered at all times. But I ask of you, how would you know that God was a provider unless you were ever in need? How would you know that God was a waymaker if you were never in a bind? How would you know that He could heal you if you've never been sick? The trials in our lives help us to understand how much we need Him. Our lives, our purpose, our joy, and our pain are designed to do one thing—bring us into a reconciled and divine relationship with Him."

Now the claps and shouts were echoing from the walls and the ceilings. The congregation was on fire, some dancing in the aisles, some clapping and shouting with joy.

"If you trust God," Bishop said, "in the midst of your trials, I promise He will sustain you, He will restore you. He will mend you where you're broken. His love will fill every place of lack."

The message touched Quentin in a way that no one would understand. For once, he didn't feel guilty for blaming Chandra's death on God. Job had done the same thing, but he had also chosen to trust God for the future. That day, Quentin decided to trust God that there was more for him after this pain. He looked into the choir loft and gazed at Montana. Was she a part of his future? Was she a part of what was promised if he trusted God?

Quentin knew that he, like Job, had no other choice but to trust God. If he remained where he was, stuck in a dead-end relationship with Chloe and sinning every chance he got, he'd never have that reconciliation with God. Trusting meant that the future was in God's hands and that hopefully restoration was there too.

After service was over, Montana and Estelle descended the choir loft and came to stand with Quentin while he was bombarded by church members and well-wishers. Many of Quentin's old choir members hugged him and begged him to return. He just smiled and accepted their greetings.

Quentin extended his arms to hug Montana, but she gave him a crazy facial expression. He ignored the face and pulled her into the hug.

"You did really great on your solo! Thank you for inviting me today. I needed to be here."

"I'm glad you came, Quentin."

"Quentin Chambers!" Bishop Prentiss walked up to Quentin with his arms outstretched. "Why didn't you tell me you were coming? I could've put you on the program to play a solo."

Quentin chuckled. "Bishop, that's exactly why I didn't tell you."

Quentin hugged the man he once called his spiritual father.

"Are we going to see you again?" Bishop Prentiss asked.

"I'm not sure. Montana invited me today. I came to hear her sing."

"You know we can let Montana sing a solo every week," Bishop Prentiss said, "if it'll get you back in the house."

Quentin smiled. "Now that's a plan that might actually work."

"I'm sure these ladies want to have brunch or something, am I right?" Bishop Prentiss asked.

All of the girls voiced their agreement, and Montana stood with a serene smile on her face. Quentin hoped she felt like part of the family. That's how he wanted her to feel.

"Hope to see you soon, Quentin," Bishop Prentiss said, before patting Quentin on the back and moving to another group of members who wanted his attention.

"Dad."

Quentin turned around to face Reese, who was standing behind him. There was a girl with him. She was pretty, but a little chubby in the face.

"Is this your friend?" Quentin asked.

"Yes. I . . . uh . . . wanted you to meet her. Dad, this is Mariah. Mariah, this is my dad, Quentin Chambers."

"How do you do?" Mariah asked.

This made Quentin smile. Reese had obviously coached her. The girl looked a little rough around the edges, and definitely not someone who was raised to say "How do you do?"

Reese said, "Mariah, this is my grandmother, Mrs. Chambers, and my sisters Danielle, Madison, and Morgan. You already met Deirdre."

"Mmm-hmm!" Deirdre said. "What's up, Mariah?"

Mariah looked at Reese and he nodded. Mariah looked back at Deirdre. "Hey, Deirdre."

"Hello, young lady," Estelle said. Quentin knew her facial expression. She didn't approve of the girl, but she wouldn't be rude enough to treat her badly.

"And the lady in the pink is my sisters' nanny, Ms. Montana."

Montana walked up and hugged Mariah, the way she greeted everyone. "Hi, honey. Welcome to Freedom of Life."

"Dad, do you mind if Mariah goes to brunch with us? We are going to brunch, aren't we?"

"Yes. Where would you like to go? Since you're bringing a guest, you pick the place."

"Mariah likes Paschal's, so how about there?"

"That works," Quentin said. "Let's roll out."

Quentin noticed the serious look on Reese's face as they walked out of the church. He tapped his son on the shoulder and let the rest of the family continue on while they stayed back.

"Everything all right?" Quentin asked Reese in a low voice.

Reese shook his head. "No."

"What's going on, son?"

"Mariah is pregnant."

Quentin exhaled. "Is it yours?"

"Yeah."

Quentin figured that Mariah was his girlfriend based on the enthusiasm of his response. He exhaled again. The last thing Reese needed was to be a baby's father.

"What am I gonna do, Dad?"

"Let's talk about it later. First we eat."

Quentin wrapped his arm around Reese's shoulders and squeezed. It was a man-to-man hug. It was a good thing he'd decided to accept Montana's invitation to church. Because he was going to need a whole lot of prayer to fix this situation.

CHAPTER 33

Deirdre stood at the top of the staircase reading a text message from Chloe. She'd asked for a favor. In exchange for the favor, Chloe would make sure Deirdre was able to get out of the house all night long for Moe's prom. And the after-after prom.

She clutched the phone and thought about the task for a moment. All she had to do was get Montana's phone for a few minutes. She was to retrieve a picture off a Web site link that Chloe was going to send her, and then she was going to text her father the picture, and she was supposed to address it to a guy named Rio to make it look like a mistake.

Deirdre didn't like the plan.

She knew that Chloe was desperately trying to get her father back, but as much as she hated to admit it, Montana was growing on Deirdre too. Montana was nice to her little sisters, and her dad really seemed to like her. Maybe she should stop helping Chloe. If her father wasn't so unreasonable, then maybe she could do that. But Deirdre knew her father would never let her anywhere near Moe, let alone go to his after-after prom.

So, yes, she would help Chloe this one last time. And then she was on her own. If she wanted to get her father back, she'd have to find someone else to do her bidding.

Deirdre put her game face on and bounced down the stairs. Her grandmother and Montana were seated at the informal dining table in the kitchen, and it smelled great.

"Is it dinnertime?" Deirdre asked. "It smells great in here."

Estelle smiled at Deirdre. "We're having a food tasting for the masquerade ball. Sit down and join us. Since Chloe is no longer coordinating this shindig, I need your opinion."

Deirdre spied Montana's phone on the shelf over the microwave and nodded. "I hope this food is as good as it smells."

Deirdre made herself a plateful of salad and sat down. She was anxious to get this phone swiping thing over with, but she had to do it at the perfect time.

"Did you have homework?" Estelle asked. "I know it's almost the end of the school year, but it seems like you should still be busy."

"I don't have any homework. I did it at school."

"Are you happy it's almost summertime?" Montana asked.

"Yep. Are you happy? You'll get to spend more time running with my dad since you don't have to take anyone to school."

Estelle shook her head. "You need to stay out of grown-folk business."

"I'm almost grown. And I'm trying to hold a conversation with the nanny. Is that all right?"

Montana chuckled. "The nanny? How about just Montana?"

"Okay then, Montana."

"And to answer your question, yes, I am glad the school year is almost over."

"That wasn't the whole question."

"Oh, the other part of the question wasn't your business."

"Right."

Deirdre wasn't sure, but she thought that maybe Montana was trying to check her on the sly.

"That salad was fantastic," Estelle said. "I can't wait to taste the rest of the meal. Darrin is a really good cook."

Montana nodded. "He really is. I'm surprised Emoni isn't huge, what with all the food he cooks for her."

"She's a very lucky girl. Darrin's a hard worker, and he comes from money."

"Darrin is wealthy? I didn't know that about him."

"Yes. The Bainbridges are lovely people. We met them when they visited last year."

"Emoni is lucky, then. Darrin is the whole package."

Estelle smiled. "Well, maybe she'll just have to rub some of her blessings off on you."

Deirdre rolled her eyes. This conversation was completely boring. She had to focus on getting the phone. She saw the perfect opportunity when the caterer's staff burst in with the main course.

"I'm full from the salad," Deirdre said.

"Okay, honey. We've got a lot more food to try. You're welcome to stay in here if you want."

"I'm good."

While the waiters hustled and bustled in with plates, trays, and serving carts, Deirdre slid behind them and swiftly slipped Montana's phone in her hoodie pocket without anyone seeing what she did. She hurried out of the kitchen and back upstairs to her bedroom, while her grandmother and Montana finished devouring all that food.

Once in her room, Deirdre opened up the Web link that Chloe had sent her from Montana's phone. When Deirdre saw the picture, her mouth dropped open. Chloe was dirty! She wondered if the picture was Photoshopped, because Montana was looking like a straight video hoochie.

Deirdre hesitated again. Of course, Chloe was trying to break them up, but this was drastic, not to mention her father had looked kind of happy at church. Especially when he was listening to Montana singing.

Deirdre's phone buzzed with a text. It was a picture of Moe in his tux, at the tuxedo shop. He looked so fly that all the girls were going to be jealous when they saw them together. She just had to go to prom with him.

Before she changed her mind, Deirdre downloaded the picture onto Montana's phone. She wrote the text exactly the way Chloe had told her to write it. **Hey Rio. Thinking of you . . . Can't wait until you . . . well I won't say. It wouldn't be ladylike. xoxo.**

Then she sent it to her father.

Finally, she took a picture of the sent text message with her phone and texted it to Chloe to prove that she'd done it. Once she was sure it was sent, she deleted the text from Montana's phone and Chloe's text with the link from her phone.

The job was almost complete.

Deirdre waited at the top of the stairs until she heard her grandmother and Montana go into the office with the caterer to talk business. She made a dash into the kitchen and slid the phone back onto the countertop.

Deirdre felt a little twinge of guilt at the pit of her stomach. But maybe it would backfire on Chloe. As long as she could keep her date with Moe, it would be worth the risk.

CHAPTER 34

Chloe smiled when she looked at the picture text sent from Deirdre's phone. Chloe had worried Deirdre would chicken out and not do it, but the girl had really come through. She deserved to go to prom with that thug if she wanted to, although Chloe had no idea what she saw in that boy. He was a hot one, but that was about it.

Chloe looked at the clock and sighed. She had been waiting to see her attorney, Doris Lindman, for an hour. Doris was popular and expensive. Chloe was going to have to put down a ten-thousand-dollar retainer for her work on the project Chloe had in mind.

"Ms. Lindman will see you now," the receptionist finally said, after another twenty minutes had gone by.

Chloe walked into the familiar office and gave Doris a big sisterly hug. Doris had hardly changed in five years. She was a petite powerhouse of a woman, and although her blunt-cut, shoulder-length bob now contained more silver than black, her face was still very youthful.

Chloe and Doris had been friends throughout her ordeal with Walter's children after he died. Of course, she hadn't won that time, but she had at least been able to keep her property. Walter's children were trying to claim that she was a con artist who had tricked their father into giving her gifts at the end of his life.

Now she needed Doris again. After Quentin had embarrassed her by bringing Montana to church as though they were a family, she knew it was over. And she was going to be destitute in a few months. She didn't like that idea one bit.

"So why are you here, Chloe? Last I heard, you had that widower wrapped around your little finger and sniffing behind you like a lovesick puppy."

Chloe gave a dry laugh. "You know if I'm here that means there's trouble in paradise."

"Oh no! Don't tell me he's called things off."

"Yes. After five years, Doris. Can you believe this? He had the audacity to cancel my credit cards the same day."

Doris tapped her chin as she walked back around her desk and sat down. Chloe continued talking.

"I wasted five good years, shoot, probably my last five good years, taking care of his needs, and then he does this to me."

"Was there another woman involved, or did he just call it off?"

Chloe frowned deeply. "He's falling for the nanny, I think. His mother just hired a nanny . . ."

Chloe's eyes widened as the truth hit her like a bag full of bricks. She bet that Estelle had planned this all along. She knew Montana from church and decided that she'd be the perfect wife for her son and mother to those kids. Oh, now she was even more determined that Quentin wasn't going to get away with this.

"And? Then what happened?" Doris asked.

"And then Quentin started treating me badly. She was hardly there a couple of weeks before she was cooking for him and leaving flowers in his office."

"Smart girl."

"Tell me about it. She's not as sweet as she seems. But tell me, after five years, do I have any recourse?"

Doris's lips became a thin line while she pondered the question. "How long had Quentin been giving you spending money?"

"For the past three years."

"Have you attended society events together as a couple?"

"Yes, of course. Multiple events."

Doris was silent for a long moment. "Had he ever proposed marriage? Do you have a ring?"

"No, I don't have an engagement ring from Quentin, but I have lots of other jewelry."

Doris put on her reading glasses and started clicking on her computer.

"Hmmm . . ." Doris said. "Not exactly what I'm looking for."

After a few more minutes of searching, Doris took off her glasses and turned to Chloe.

"Well, there isn't much precedent for a thing like this. Most of the time, this type of lawsuit is settled out of court. Have you tried to reason with Quentin? Maybe if you let him know how much you sacrificed for your affair, he'll agree that a settlement is in order."

Chloe laughed out loud. "He'd rather eat a bag of nails. It's funny. He claims he doesn't care about his money, but as soon as I bring a lawsuit against him he's going to treat me like I'm his sworn enemy."

"So we may be successful if we can prove that Quentin's actions showed he had every intention of marrying you until this nanny came along. The amount of money he spent on you will be important. And anything—letters, e-mails, texts—in which he declared his love. We'll sue him for promissory estoppel."

"What's that?"

"It's a law doctrine that lets you punish someone for breaking their promises."

"That's exactly what Quentin's done, but I don't know if I have any letters."

Chloe sighed. Quentin wasn't very sentimental with her. She had expensive gifts, but no notes with sweet words written inside.

"Do you think he really cares about the nanny?" Doris asked.

"I don't know. Maybe. He's even going back to church now."

Doris nodded. "Very good. I'll write the filing to assassinate her character a bit. Make it seem like she pursued the job just to destroy your relationship and land him for herself."

"It'll be public record."

"Yes, indeed,"

Doris said. "This will be an interesting case."

"Do you think we'll win?"

"No, but we will make it uncomfortable enough for Quentin that he'll give you a fortune to disappear."

Chloe felt tears form in her eyes. She absolutely wanted to be financially stable, so having the money would be great. But her society position would be ruined after this. No man would want to touch her with a ten-foot pole.

"I have to win, Doris. Quentin will be the last rich man in Atlanta I'll be able to seduce."

Doris laughed. "Maybe in Atlanta. But there are lots of rich men all over the country. The world. I know a sheik who would love to make your acquaintance."

Chloe smiled, but it was a sad and weak smile. How quickly she had gone from being the next Mrs. Chambers to Quentin Chambers's ex. If Quentin was able to throw her away so quickly, had he ever loved her at all? She hoped the text message would break them up. If she couldn't have Quentin, then she wouldn't rest until Montana didn't have him either.

No matter what Doris said, Chloe wasn't suing for a broken promise. Chloe was suing Quentin Chambers for a broken heart.

CHAPTER 35

Quentin paced back and forth across the carpeted floor in his office. He picked up the phone, looked at the text, and put it back down. He'd looked at it a hundred times, and he still couldn't believe it.

He was out with the guys at happy hour when he got the picture message of a scantily clad Montana. She looked incredible in the picture, and his first thought was that she was sending it to him—which confused the heck out of him. Why would she invite him to church and then send a lingerie picture the next day?

Then he'd read the photo's caption. She'd meant to send it to her ex-boyfriend Rio? He couldn't wrap his brain around the fact that the girl who was singing "Encourage Yourself" was also the vixen who was on his phone. Was she really that stereotypical freaky church girl?

Quentin picked up the phone and looked at the photo again. He shook his head and put the phone back down.

Quentin had never been fooled by a woman before, not to these proportions. He knew what Chloe was all about. He was rich; she wanted a rich man. She'd had a rich man before him. There was no secret agenda—it was pretty obvious. Because he knew what she wanted from day one, Quentin always knew that their relationship was a temporary one.

But this revelation about Montana had caught him totally off guard. She'd become his friend, invited him back to church, connected with his children. Maybe she had the same goal as Chloe—land a rich man. They just had different methods.

Maybe that's why Montana was so annoyed that Chloe had invited Rio to the brunch. She knew that she was still messing around with him, so perhaps she was afraid her secret would get out.

It bothered Quentin that he didn't really have anyone he could talk to about this. His homeboys thought he was stupid to think of remarrying anyone, so they'd tell him to see where it would lead with Montana, because she looked like a goddess in the photo.

There was a knock on his office door, and Quentin quickly closed out the text. "Come in," he said.

It was Montana. She was wearing a pair of jeans and a baby T-shirt, but Quentin could only imagine her in the lingerie from the picture.

"Hey, Quentin. Can I talk to you for a second?"

"Sure. What's going on?"

"Well, I'm not sure if I'm going to attend the masquerade ball."

Somehow he'd been expecting her to say something totally different. He said, "What? Why not?"

"Well, Chloe made it seem like it's going to be a high-society affair. And I just don't want to be embarrassed."

"Chloe isn't going to be there."

"I know, but Atlanta's elite will be there. I'm not sure I will fit in."

"Mother is inviting the church members."

"Okay, I'll just come out and say it. I don't really have anything to wear."

Quentin said, "I still think you should come to the ball. You've worked hard with my mother and with Chloe. You should at least get to enjoy it."

Before he saw that photo addressed to Rio, Quentin would've whipped out a credit card with a quickness and let Montana go bonkers buying whatever she wanted. Dress, shoes, jewelry.

On the defense now, Quentin tried to figure out Montana's angle. Was she trying to seem like she wasn't a gold digger? Why would she come in here with this whole sob story of not having a dress? It felt like she was fishing, but she was using the wrong bait, because Quentin couldn't figure out what she was trying to do.

"Well, I think you should do whatever you feel is best. I won't be offended if you don't go to the ball. My mother might be, but I won't."

"So it won't affect our friendship?"

Quentin shook his head. "Not one bit."

Now the picture on his phone was a different matter. It absolutely would affect their friendship, but he just didn't know how.

"Is there something bothering you, Quentin?" Montana asked.

"Nope."

"You sure?"

"Okay, well then, let me know if there's anything you need. The kids are either asleep or doing homework, so I think I'm going to go read."

Or put on some skimpy lingerie and take more bathroom shots. Quentin couldn't keep that thought from crossing his mind.

Montana paused for a moment more and then left Quentin's office with a confused look on her face that made Quentin want to burst into laughter. Why was she confused?

Quentin didn't get much time to think about Montana and her motives because Reese poked his head inside the office.

"Dad, can I talk to you?"

Quentin nodded and Reese came in. He didn't sit but stood with his hands clasped in front of him. The pose made Quentin flash back to when his son was a little boy, dressed in his Easter clothes and ready for his close-up. But he was almost a man now. Even though he was only eighteen, he was about to be a father.

"What can I do for you, son? You look like you've got a lot on your mind."

"Mariah's mother is going to kick her out when she finds out. Can she stay here?"

Quentin considered his son's request. Of course, the girl couldn't stay under their roof. It wouldn't be proper. But he also wasn't going to let the mother of his first grandchild wander from pillar to post without a place to lay her head.

"How about we rent her a really nice apartment. Is she eighteen yet?"

Reese nodded. "Yes, but I don't want her staying by herself. And I don't think she wants to live alone. She needs people around her."

"She can't live here as your baby's mother, Reese. Are you saying you want to marry her?"

Reese swallowed. "I would marry her."

"Do you love her, though?" Quentin asked.

"Sometimes I think I do. But we'll fight about something stupid, and then I'm not sure. How do you know when you're in love with someone?"

Quentin shook his head. "I knew I was in love with your mother after we had our first argument. Having her angry with me made me realize that I always wanted to see her smile. But I don't know how to tell someone else if they're in love."

"I wish I had the answers too," Reese said.

"I will support you if you want to marry Mariah. Your grandmother will hate it, but she'll get over it."

Without warning, Reese hugged Quentin as he had when he was a little boy. Quentin could feel Reese's body shake with sobs. He wished he could change the situation for him, but he couldn't. His son had already made some grown man choices that he had to live with.

"Thanks, Dad," Reese said when he was finally composed. "I think I will marry her. I'm going to get her a ring."

"Son, we need to sit down with Mariah's parents and talk about college and everything else. Do her parents know?"

Reese shook his head. "Her mom thinks something is up, and her dad isn't around."

"Well, you're not in this alone. I'll go with you to talk to Mariah's mother."

"Thanks, Dad."

"I've got your back Reese. Don't ever forget that."

Reese gave Quentin an unblinking gaze, making Quentin wonder if Reese *had* forgotten that he had his back. The thought of this made Quentin's heart hurt, but the fear that he might lose Reese and his daughters forever was devastating. Quentin vowed in his heart to change his parenting. With or without Montana, his children needed him.

CHAPTER 36

It was a quiet Friday evening, and Quentin sat in his office feeling anxious about the weekend. He picked up a new vase of fresh flowers that Montana had left on his desk. The scent of the blossoms filled his office, just as his head was filled with thoughts of Montana.

He had been praying all week, ever since he got that photo of Montana, and asking God what he should do. Everything in him said to ask her about it, but what if her answer was that she really was seeing Rio?

Quentin's phone buzzed with a text message. **Docs say Alex won't make it through the night. Better get here.**

A knot formed in Quentin's throat. He knew Alex was terminal when she'd moved into Transitions, but she was his friend, and now she was going to be gone. He kept losing the people who were close to him.

He stood up from the desk and sighed. Although they were in the same house, he called Montana's cell phone instead of going to her room, which was on the other side of the mansion.

"Quentin, is there something wrong?" Montana asked.

"Yes. Alex is probably going to die tonight. Will you ride with me to Transitions? Maybe you can pray with her again, and some of her family may be there too."

"Yes, absolutely. Let me throw on some clothes really quickly."

"Meet me downstairs in ten minutes."

Quentin disconnected the phone. Even though he wasn't sure about Montana being his replacement wife anytime soon, he knew that she had a way of calming those who were suffering. He'd seen it firsthand when he'd taken her to Transitions.

Montana was already waiting downstairs when Quentin got there. She was wearing jeans and a T-shirt, and her hair was pulled back into a ponytail. Even with her face bare of makeup and in plain clothes, Montana was still exceptionally beautiful. Her naturally pink lips didn't need any gloss, and those eyelashes didn't require mascara. Quentin felt his heart sting with the knowledge that she wasn't as sweet as she seemed.

"You ready?" Quentin asked. Montana nodded.

It wasn't a fun night, but Quentin chose the Aston Martin to drive anyway, because he knew Montana liked it. Since it was windy, he kept the top up on the car.

Quentin hadn't anticipated how much tension there would be in the car during the drive to Transitions. Obviously, Montana knew there was something wrong too.

"Quentin, what's wrong?" Montana asked.

"My friend is dying."

"Yes, of course. I'm sorry. Stupid question."

Quentin knew she didn't mean just tonight. He'd been cool to her for the entire week. He'd gone running without her several times, and she'd said nothing about it.

Quentin thought about the text message again. It was to Rio. It was actually starting to annoy him that she was hiding this huge thing and acting like he was the problem.

"Montana, you could've told me you were seeing someone. I would've understood. Heck, I was still tangled with Chloe and trying to see myself untangled. Why did you lie to me?"

Quentin blurted out the words and waited for Montana's reaction. Either she was an Oscar-worthy actress or she was genuinely confused.

"I'm not seeing anyone, Quentin."

"So you're just gonna keep lying about it? I thought we were friends. You could've just said you weren't interested in me."

Chloe dropped her forehead into the palm of her hand as if she was trying to make her brain work. "Quentin, I have no idea what you're talking about. Why do you think I'm seeing someone? What gave you that idea?"

Quentin pulled the car over on the side of the road. He took out his cell phone, scrolled to the message, and shoved the phone in Montana's face.

Montana's jaw dropped and her eyes bulged out of her head when she saw the picture. "W-where did you get this?"

"You made a mistake and sent it to me, I guess. The text says it's for your man, Rio."

Montana shook her head in disbelief. "But how?"

"Are you saying that it's not you in the picture? Did someone Photoshop your head onto that body? If so, they picked a great body."

"This picture is at least two years old, Quentin, and I didn't send this."

Quentin pointed at the phone. "The text came from your number!"

"I can see that, and I am still telling you I didn't send this. Someone has either hacked into my phone or my computer or something."

Quentin could hear the panic in Montana's voice. It sounded sincere. But was she panicking because she was telling the truth or because she'd been caught, and now he knew the woman she truly was?

"Why would anyone want to do that to you?"

"Come on, Quentin. I know at least one person who'd want to do that to me."

Quentin burst into laughter. "Who, Chloe? This isn't even her style! She's not a tech guru."

Montana looked back down at the picture. "Quentin, you can tell this is picture is old. Look at my hair. I've only been wearing my curly style for two years. Look at how short my hair is in the picture compared to now."

Quentin snatched the phone. He looked at the picture again. Admittedly, he hadn't paid too much attention to her hairstyle. There were too many other details in the picture to distract him.

He must've gazed at the picture for too long, because Montana snatched the phone away from him.

"So you think that Chloe did this?" Quentin asked. "What about Rio?"

Montana gripped the phone in her fist. "I don't think he would want another man to see me like this."

"And I don't think that Chloe would fight that dirty."

Montana gazed at Quentin with tears in her eyes. "Do you . . . do you believe me?"

"I want to, but honestly, I'm not sure what I believe."

"Wow. So do you still want a relationship with me?"

Quentin paused for a long and pregnant moment before he replied. "Even if the picture is old . . . I didn't think you were this type of girl. I guess I have a different view of you now."

"I'm not proud of who I used to be, Quentin. I was this girl. I didn't know God at the time. I was lost. I wish that when you walk up and give your life to Christ, everything you did before would just disappear. But it doesn't. Sometimes it lingers, and apparently can come back to bite you."

"I understand. We all have a past."

"We do, but I want you to know that this is my past. Not my present. No matter what you believe, I didn't send you this text."

Quentin couldn't ignore the tears in Montana's eyes as she spoke. He wanted to believe her, but even if he did, her image was still tarnished in his eyes.

"I believe you, and we're still . . . friends. But let's get to Alex, okay? We can talk more about it later."

Montana swallowed and nodded. "Quentin, why did you keep the text?"

"Are you kidding? Do you see yourself in that picture? I am still a man, Montana."

Montana pursed her lips and rolled her eyes. Then she made a big production out of deleting the text message.

"Now it's gone. You won't be able to lust after me anymore."

Quentin laughed. "It's gone from the phone, but it's always gonna be right here."

Quentin tapped the side of his head and laughed at his joke, although Montana didn't join him.

But now Quentin was curious. He'd said he didn't think Chloe would play that dirty. But would she? Quentin still wasn't sure he believed Chloe had anything to do with the picture getting to his phone. But if she did, then that meant she was still intent on getting him back. And if she was still trying to get him back, then what other tricks did she have planned?

CHAPTER 37

Nurse Charlene was standing on the porch when Quentin and Montana pulled up to Transitions. The anxious look on her face let Quentin know that things with Alex were bad and that the doctor's prediction probably would come to pass.

Montana whispered under her breath, and Quentin guessed that she was praying. From thc look on Charlene's face, the prayers were needed.

"How is she?" Quentin askcd, as they walked up the front steps.

"Almost there. Her family is with her now saying good-bye."

Quentin nodded and motioned for Montana to follow him inside. In silence, they ascended the stairs to Alex's room.

Slowly, they entered the room, which was filled with family and friends of Alex. She'd already written her last wishes. She didn't want a funeral. The friends who'd loved her had celebrated her while she was alive. She simply wanted to be buried next to her mother, who had also succumbed to cancer many years before.

Alex's eyes were closed, and her breathing was slow and labored. She appeared to be sleeping. Her lips were dry and chapped, and one of the nurses periodically wet them with a dropper filled with water. Alex was past the point of being thirsty, hungry, or afraid. She was ready to transition.

Quentin whispered, "Will you please pray?"

"Dear God, we thank you for Alex's life. Lord, we thank you for the love she has shown and the gifts she has shared. As you open your loving arms to receive her spirit, we pray for peace in accepting her transition, oh God. Show us that this life on earth is only preparation for our true place with you. Grant us serenity, and let our hearts not be too heavy. Lord, we know that Alex is going to a place where pain, crying, medicines, and cancer do not exist. Her body is going to eternal rest, but her spirit is transitioning to its next phase in eternal life. Lord, wrap us in your arms too, and give us peace that surpasses understanding. Make us to know that there is no sorrow that your love cannot heal. We ask these things in the name of Jesus. Amen."

When Montana started to pray out loud, Quentin was shocked. He'd thought she would whisper a prayer to Alex, as she'd done before. Then he understood exactly what she was doing. The ones who needed the prayer were in the room. Alex was ready to leave this world for the next, and her family and friends who would be left behind needed more prayer than she did.

There wasn't a dry eye in the room when Montana finished the prayer. Alex stirred a bit and started to moan and speak in a low, scratchy voice. No one could make out the words.

"What is she saying?" asked a young lady sitting next to the bed. Quentin knew her. She was Alex's niece.

"I'm not sure, but my wife did the same thing," Quentin shared.

Montana touched his arm. "We're not supposed to understand this. She's talking to God now."

Everyone was silent as Alex's voice rose and the sounds became a little bit more excited. Quentin hoped she wasn't in pain, but she didn't seem to be. There was a faint smile on her face in between the words and sounds.

Finally, the sounds stopped, and one last quiet breath came from Alex's body. After experiencing many transitions since his wife had died, Quentin was familiar with the eerie feeling that hung in the room for a brief moment after death. It was how he always knew the deceased was truly gone without the doctor saying anything.

Quentin glanced over at the clock. It was eleven minutes after eleven. Someone had told him once that 1111 was the number of angels. Now, for Quentin, it would be a time to remember his friend.

There were a few quiet sobs from Alex's aunt, and everyone had tears trickling down their faces. It was over. Alex had transitioned to her heavenly home.

Quentin and Montana stepped out of the room to allow the family quiet time with Alex's body. In a few moments, the crew that Quentin had on standby would come and remove her and take her to a local funeral home to prepare her for burial.

Then the whole process would start over with a new Transitions resident.

Montana followed Quentin downstairs and outside. They leaned on his car and didn't speak for a while. Quentin cried a little and then composed himself. Montana held one of his hands in both of hers and gently rubbed it. It was a small gesture, but Quentin felt his insides warm at her touch.

"When I first heard about your foundation," Montana said, breaking the silence, "I wanted to know more about you. I wanted to understand why a man who had lost so much would surround himself with death and dying."

"I ask myself that all the time, and I can't figure it out. Let me know what you come up with."

Montana said, "Thank you for inviting me to come here. Not just tonight. I mean, period."

"You know, I've never brought Chloe down here. Never even thought about it."

"Why not?"

"Honestly, I didn't think she'd know how to act. I thought she might embarrass me."

Montana didn't respond to this. Quentin knew it sounded crazy, but it was the truth. Chloe would never understand this place, and would probably be uneasy around the residents. She could stay in Atlanta counting his money and thinking of ways to spend it.

"Thank you for being here," Quentin said. "I'm sorry about the text message. God definitely used you tonight. I wish there had been someone like you around when Chandra died. I could've used a prayer warrior like you."

"I-I'm not perfect, Quentin. I am a prayer warrior, but I've got some battle wounds. That text message came from the part of my life that's stitched up and scarred over. It's not pretty."

Quentin stroked the side of Montana's face as tears fell from her eyes. Now it was his turn to comfort her.

"You're perfect enough for me."

Quentin leaned down and planted a soft kiss on Montana's lips. He felt her arms wrap around his neck, and he lifted her from the ground just a little. She tasted exactly as he'd imagined. Sweet, like honey.

When they separated, Montana stared into his eyes as if she was trying to see through him to the depths of his heart. He didn't know what she'd see if it was exposed, but he wanted her to look for it anyway. If he had any heart left, then it was hers.

CHAPTER 38

Montana stomped angrily around the living room of Emoni's apartment while she told the story of the text message. Emoni sat with rapt attention and shook her head angrily. Montana couldn't remember ever being this furious.

The only thing that was keeping her from going totally ballistic was Quentin's kiss. He'd kissed her and held her as though she belonged to him. But what if it was only because he was sad about losing Alex?

"And you think Chloe did it?" Emoni asked, when Montana finally sat down on the sofa next to her.

"Yes, although I have no idea how she did."

Emoni shrugged. "So it's settled. She did it. Let's move on. Did Quentin like the picture?"

"Of course he liked the picture! I'm hot! Why wouldn't he like the picture? The problem is that this heffa made it seem like I was sending it to Rio but put in Quentin's number by mistake."

"Yeah, like their names are anything alike," Emoni said. "Quentin believed that?"

"He doesn't know what to believe. But he was thinking I was some kind of Mary Poppins or somebody. I think he believes me, but I don't want that hanging over my head. He used to think I was Mary Poppins, now he thinks I'm a freak."

"I don't know any men that want to marry Mary Poppins."

"Emoni!"

"Just saying."

Montana shook her head sadly. "This is a nightmare. I was one step away from the romance of my life, and now he thinks I'm some video vixen."

"Again, that doesn't have to be a bad thing."

"I have to convince him that Chloe did this."

Emoni bit her bottom lip. "He broke up with Chloe already. He knows she's a villain. I think when he really ponders it, he'll let it go. But if he doesn't, will Rio tell the truth?"

"Are you kidding? Rio wants me back! He's definitely not going to help me fix things with my rich boss that I'm totally falling for. And he kissed me, Emoni. It was the best first kiss ever."

"Wait, he kissed you? Oh wow. So he really is feeling you?"

"Yes, I think so. But what if everything sinks in and he decides I'm not the type of woman he wants as an example for his children. I mean who wants a woman who sends freak pictures to be their daughters' stepmother?"

"You do have a dilemma."

Montana sucked her teeth. "Thank you, Captain Obvious."

Emoni burst into laughter. "You have been hanging around those teenagers for too long."

"I know. I love those kids, girl! I didn't think I would be so attached to them so quickly, but I can't imagine life now without them."

"Awww . . . look at God!"

"Shut up!"

"Well, let me know what you need me to do. You need me to go with you to jump Chloe? You know she can't fight."

Now Montana laughed. "Um, I don't know. I think she got a little bit of street in her."

"Well, there are two of us, and one of her old-man-looking self."

Montana dropped her jaw. "See, you are wrong for that. You need to repent."

"Tell me you didn't think it the first time you saw her."

"She just has strong features. Mrs. Chambers said she has a strong jawline."

Emoni clutched her stomach laughing. "A man's jawline."

"Stop it! God is going to get you."

"You are always warning me about getting a smite from the Lord. He knows I like to laugh."

Montana shook her head. "Well, I need you to stop laughing and start praying. I don't want to lose this relationship with Quentin. He is so incredible. You should see him with those terminally ill cancer patients. I have never seen a man look so sexy when he cries."

"Oh, yeah, you are totally far gone. I guess we need to fix this thing in a hurry, huh?"

Montana nodded. "I just can't see myself going on a date with Trent after this."

"Why you gotta play Trent out? So he's not rich, and he's a bit vertically challenged."

"He's small, Emoni."

"He's smallish. And he has a huge spirit. You ain't about to talk trash about my friend."

"I'm sorry. I didn't mean to. Trent's a sweetheart, but he's not Quentin."

"Okay, Operation Catch Chloe is in full effect, and it's on the prayer list. Let me know if you want me to drive the getaway car."

Emoni squeezed Montana's hand and continued. "It's gonna work out. Trust me. When I saw Quentin in church, I knew that you were meant to be in his life. Mrs. Chambers probably hired you for just that reason."

"You think so?"

"That is a smart woman, okay. She can't stand Chloe, just like we can't!"

Montana considered Mrs. Chambers a potential ally. It would be wonderful if she already was one. Most women thought the best way to a man's heart was through his stomach, but Montana knew the truth. The best way to win a man like Quentin's heart was through his mama.

CHAPTER 39

Whenever Tippen, Quentin's attorney, came to his office early in the morning, there was something amiss. Tippen was young and successful, so he entertained to the wee hours of the morning with whomever was his flavor of the week. Early mornings weren't his thing.

But this morning he sat in front of Quentin's desk, with red eyes, probably from the previous night's exploits, and puffy bags under his eyes. His hair was a little mushed on the side, but Quentin tried to ignore it. Tippen was usually dressed impeccably. When Quentin took him around the sistas, they said, "He could get it," even though he was white.

So Quentin knew there was a problem.

"What's going on, Tip?"

"She's suing you, man."

Quentin cocked his head to one side. "Who's suing me?"

"Chloe. She filed a civil lawsuit against you for promissory estoppel. She's asking for twenty million dollars."

"What?"

Tippen sighed and reached into his briefcase. He pulled out a stack of pages. "See for yourself."

As Quentin scanned the pages, he felt himself get more and more furious with every word. In the lawsuit, Chloe was alleging that he had made promises of gainful employment to her as a director at Transitions, and that he took the position and gave it to Ms. Levy. She also said that the credit card he'd given her for expenses and shopping was proof that he was becoming financially responsible for her in preparation for marriage. He really felt his blood start to simmer when he read how Montana had manipulated him to make him fire Chloe from the foundation. A flat-out lie.

Quentin spoke three words. "Can she win?"

"She could," Tippen said, as he cracked his neck in one direction and then the other. I've seen cases like this, but most of the couples were engaged with wedding dates and rings purchased. Basically she has proof that you were her sugar daddy."

"I wasn't her sugar daddy. We were in a relationship. It didn't work out. I shouldn't have to pay her."

"I agree. That's why I'm your lawyer. But the fact that she mentioned Montana in her lawsuit bothers me. What does she have to do with it?"

"She needs to leave Montana out of it. Montana just happened to show up right at the end of a very long relationship that was never going anywhere."

"Well, you could settle with her. I bet she'd disappear for a few million, and you could make her sign a confidentiality agreement. Then she wouldn't be able to say anything else about you and Montana."

Quentin pounded a fist on his desk. "If I let her win, women all over Atlanta will be trying to sue their sponsors."

"Not really," Tippen said. "Most of their sponsors know enough to send them packing with a hefty amount of cash. Apparently, you left Chloe high and dry. In the allegations, she said that you canceled her credit cards the same day you broke up. That's kind of cold, man."

"She wasn't my wife! We weren't committed on that level. Since when do boyfriends have to pay alimony?"

"When the boyfriend is worth almost a billion dollars a payday is always part of the equation."

"I won't do it. I'm not paying her anything."

"Whatever you decide, I'm here for you, man. Let me know how you want to proceed."

Quentin's chest rose and fell with deep, angry breaths. He never thought Chloe would go to these lengths to keep from having to take a job. In his mind, she was the lowest of the low. And he wouldn't give her a penny.

But he did know who he was taking on a shopping spree. Montana needed a dress for the masquerade ball.

CHAPTER 40

Montana relaxed in her bedroom after dropping all of the children off at school. She tried to read a novel, but she couldn't concentrate. Her mind kept drifting to the kiss she and Quentin shared, and how it had made her feel. She wondered what would come next.

Chloe was out of the picture—at least Montana thought she was—so there should be nothing holding her and Quentin back, except that photo. Quentin said he believed her, but she wanted Chloe to admit she'd done it. And that was something that would probably never happen.

A knock on her bedroom door pulled her from her thoughts. She knew it wasn't one of the children, so she hoped it was Quentin.

It was.

"Montana, do you have anything pressing to do this morning?"

"No. I was just reading. Do you need anything?"

"No, but you do. I can't let you take on the planning of this ball, alongside my mother, and not be able to enjoy the fruits of your labor."

"It'll be fine. I'll watch from the top of the stairs with the children."

"No, you won't. You're going shopping for a dress."

"I am?"

"No, we're going shopping for a dress."

Montana was hesitant. Did this mean she was stepping into Chloe's place? Was she going to be the next woman Quentin splurged on but never married? She wouldn't wait around five years.

"Quentin, I don't know if I should accept any gifts from you. I wouldn't want to think we were going in one direction and then get my heart broken."

Quentin nodded slowly. "You're thinking of Chloe, aren't you?"

"I'm thinking of me."

"Montana, I want you in a way that I never thought I'd want someone ever again. Having you here makes Chandra's memories only sweet and not bitter. Chloe never did that for me. I think Chloe may be the reason I grieved for so long."

"But what if I can't live up to Chandra's memory either? I don't want to forever be compared to the perfect wife."

"She wasn't without flaws. None of us are, especially not me."

"If you want me to go to the ball, I'll go, but I will wear something I already have. One of my church ensembles."

Quentin dropped his shoulders. "Why won't you let me do this?"

"Because I want you to know that your money isn't the best thing about you. And that it's not the reason I like you."

"I know that the money isn't important to you. That makes me want to spend it on you even more."

"Well, spend it on breakfast, then. I really want a waffle from Waffle House."

Quentin laughed. "I haven't eaten there since college."

"Well, let's go. There's a pecan waffle calling my name right next to a pile of greasy bacon."

"Oh, I see you're trying to run for two hours," Quentin said.

There was another tap on the door. It was the rapid triple knock that was Ms. Levy's signature.

"Well, what do we have here?" Ms. Levy asked, as she stepped into the room and saw Quentin.

"Quentin was just here for a visit."

"In your bedroom? Quentin, you know better than that. That's not proper."

Quentin dropped his head with false repentance. "You're so right, Ms. Levy. I'm horrible."

Then Ms. Levy smiled. "It's about time you handled your business, though. Your mother and I wondered what took you so long."

"What? You've been waiting on me to fall for Montana?"

"It was like putting a piece of chocolate birthday cake in front of a toddler. At some point, the cake is . . . well, I don't think I like where my analogy is headed. It isn't proper either."

Quentin and Montana burst into laughter.

"Ms. Levy," Quentin said.

Ms. Levy slapped Quentin on the arm and smiled. Montana could tell she'd been beautiful in her youth; she was still beautiful from the inside out.

"Listen here, boy, I served plenty of cake in my day."

"I bet you did," Quentin said, still laughing.

"But I didn't come in here to school you two on that. I came to tell Montana that Danielle's dance class will go a little late today, because they are preparing for a recital. I just got an e-mail."

"Okay. Thank you, Ms. Levy. I'll know what to expect, then."

Ms. Levy nodded and headed for the door. Then she turned around and winked at Quentin and Montana.

"You know the best part of the cake is the frosting," she said, as she left the room.

Quentin looked at Montana with a confused face. "What does that mean?"

"I have no idea, but I'm almost one hundred percent sure it wasn't proper."

"Was Ms. Levy a freak?" Quentin asked, before bursting into laughter.

Montana joined him. "Who said it was past tense?"

Quentin scrunched his face into a frown, and then he doubled over, holding his midsection from laughing so hard.

Montana gazed at him and smiled. He looked so happy. This was the Quentin she wanted to be around. This is the man she would've fallen for if he hadn't had two nickels to rub together.

This was her prince.

CHAPTER 41

Estelle was beyond furious. Quentin's lawyer had informed her about the lawsuit, but not before a few of her society friends had already heard. The news of the filing had gone around fast, just as Chloe had intended.

More than anything, Estelle blamed herself. Chloe's gold-digging ways should've been dealt with long ago. But she'd left it alone, because her son was a grown man and she didn't want to interfere with his love life.

Estelle invited Chloe for lunch, not because she wanted the girl's company, but because she wanted to know how much it would take to get her to drop the ridiculous lawsuit. She knew her son. He'd never agree to a settlement, even if Tippen told him it was the best option.

But Estelle was the matriarch of the family. And in the best interest of the Chambers's good name, this strumpet needed to be dealt with. Estelle wanted no other roadblocks to Quentin and Montana becoming a couple.

Her son was smiling again, the way he had when Chandra was alive. The two of them had always been like children, laughing at some joke or playing some prank. Quentin had lost that youthful spark when Chandra died.

But it was back now. Estelle had watched Quentin chase his

children around outside with water guns. And she'd felt her heart swell with love for her only son.

Estelle purposely arrived at the lunch twenty minutes late. She wanted Chloe to sit there and wonder if she'd ever show up. She wanted Chloe to feel as uncomfortable as she was making the family feel.

Chloe perked up when she finally saw Estelle. Chloe had to know what this meeting was truly about. She wasn't stupid. She and Doris had played exactly the right cards.

Estelle sat in the seat that was being held out by the waiter.

"Ma'am, can I get you anything to drink?"

Estelle nodded. "I'll have coffee. Thank you."

Estelle stared at Chloe. Chloe stared back. She didn't seem intimidated, but Estelle guessed that her confidence was an act.

"You've really made a splash in the society news circuit of late," Estelle said.

Chloe shrugged. "That wasn't my intention."

"What was your intention? You have to know that your case will never win in court. You'll come across as that woman that men love to hate. That term that I despise, but fits best here—a gold digger."

"So what does that make your son? Did he think he could exchange gifts and money for sex for all of those years and not have to compensate me in the end? I am not a prostitute."

"But yet you're asking for money in exchange for your five years of service. As far as I know, you only served my son in one way."

"He promised me that I could run Transitions Kids, and then he took it from me. I never wanted to just get a check. I've always worked for mine."

"Yes, Chloe. You've put in hard labor indeed."

Chloe frowned. "Did you ask me here just to insult me?"

"That would've been a fun afternoon, but no," Estelle said, "I didn't invite you here for that."

"Well, let's get to it. I have to meet my lawyer soon. We have to discuss our strategy."

Estelle shook her head and chuckled. "You want money. I've got it. I'm offering you two million to end this right now."

Chloe laughed out loud. "Two million? Quentin offered me a job and promised me his hand in marriage! Do you think I'll accept two million when you all are worth so much more. Try again."

"Quentin never offered to marry you. He would've continued bedding you for the next ten years if I hadn't brought Montana to our home. She is a woman who will get a ring from Quentin."

Chloe narrowed her eyes. "I knew you planned to have that nanny steal Quentin from me."

"You never had him, honey. You laid claim to his private parts, but never his heart. Two point five million."

"You can't buy me out of this, Estelle. I'm going to win the full amount."

"It'll be a cold day in hell before my family gives you twenty million dollars for services rendered."

Chloe stood from the table. "Well, Estelle, you better get your mink coat and snow boots ready, because it's about to get a little chilly in your final resting place."

"If I'm going to hell, then you're leading the way," Estelle said.

"Maybe so," Chloe said, "but I'm going there in a pair of Jimmy Choos."

Estelle fumed as Chloe stormed out of the restaurant with her head held high. She had underestimated Chloe, but no more. It was time for Estelle to pull out the big guns. She was about to call her private investigator. And her prayer group.

CHAPTER 42

Montana prayed silently as she sat at a table in the coffee shop where she'd first met Rio. She'd asked him to meet her after she read the contents of Chloe's lawsuit against Quentin. Montana wanted to punch Chloe in the face for putting her name in it. She hadn't encouraged Quentin to break up with Chloe. Obviously, he wasn't in love with her. And since when was dating someone considered a contract?

When Rio walked into the coffee shop, Montana took in a deep breath and then exhaled. She had no idea what was going to happen once she talked to Rio, but she needed to know why he'd helped Chloe.

"I knew you'd call me," Rio said, as he handed her a cup of coffee. "Your favorite."

Montana took a sip and set the cup down as Rio sat in front of her. "It's good, but it's not my favorite anymore. I drink chai now."

"You do? You've changed, haven't you?"

Montana nodded. "But you haven't. You're still the same, Rio. Still selfish, still competitive, still always having to win."

"Whoa! I thought this was a friendly meeting. I was hoping for a reconciliation here. Why are you insulting me?"

Montana stared directly into Rio's face. "Why did you give Chloe that picture? What were you trying to do? Get me fired?"

"What makes you think I gave it to her?"

"Oh, come on, Rio. You are the only man who has pictures of me like that. I never sent those to anyone but you."

Rio cracked his knuckles and stared back at Montana. "Chloe said it would help me get you back. I didn't know her plan, but I know I want you in my life."

"See, I don't understand why you're so hell-bent on getting me back now! I begged you to come to church with me. You were the only man I wanted!"

"Besides that pastor, Kumal Prentiss."

Montana shook her head. "Don't you see that it wasn't about Bishop Prentiss? I had fallen in love with Jesus, and I wanted you to have the same thing! You made me choose. You did that."

"So what if I said I wanted to change now and go to church with you? Would you stop pretending like you don't still love me?"

"It's not about going to church. It's never been about that. Going to church is not a condition of being with me. Loving God is the condition."

"That's not the condition. I've done some checking around on your employer. He used to be a church guy. Not so much anymore. He's a sinner just like me. What do you think he and Chloe have been doing all these years?"

Montana frowned. "I know about Quentin and Chloe."

"Okay, then you are full of crap. You're just like the next chick who wants a rich guy. You don't care whether he loves God or not. You just want a happily ever after. You think life is a romance novel."

"You're wrong."

"And you know what else?" Rio said. "That's why I gave Chloe that picture. I was hoping it would bring you back to your senses. I was thinking it would make you remember what we had. Maybe it wasn't perfect, but it was a hell of a lot better than some fictional, fairy-tale bull you made up in your head."

"I haven't made up anything in my head."

"Yeah, well, Quentin Chambers isn't Prince Charming. All

you have to do is ask Chloe about that. I felt sorry for her, and I don't regret helping her."

"Rio, if you ever cared anything about me, would you please just tell Quentin the truth?

"Why would I do that? Why would I help you get with him?"

"Because, Rio, I just don't want to be with you anymore."

"That's what you think now. But when you finally see the truth, you'll be looking for me. See, I accepted you for who you were."

"But you've never accepted me for who I am right now. A child of God."

Montana got up from the table and walked out of the coffee shop. She hoped to never see Rio's face again. There was a time when she wondered if she'd ever be able to live without him. But now she knew that she hadn't come alive until she'd left him behind.

Still, the things he said about Quentin struck a nerve. Had she excused his indiscretions with Chloe because she'd romanticized him? Deep down, was she really any different from Chloe?

The questions scared her. She couldn't have one standard when it came to Rio and another when it came to Quentin. Even though she thought it hadn't accomplished anything, Montana was glad she'd met with Rio. It made her even more determined to not embark on a relationship with Quentin until he was right with God.

CHAPTER 43

Quentin read the notes Tippen had compiled for his response to Chloe's court filing. Tippen had hit all of the major points Quentin wanted covered. He had never once told Chloe he loved her. Chloe had volunteered to become a part of his organization; it wasn't a job offer. He didn't pay her living expenses; he gave her gifts. As a boyfriend.

Seeing his relationship with Chloe spelled out on paper, in black and white, bothered Quentin. He'd never intended for any of this to happen. He'd never intended for five years to go by without falling in love with Chloe.

Quentin heard a soft knock on his office door and was drawn from his thoughts.

"Come in," Quentin said.

Montana stepped inside the office but stayed near the door. "Quentin, can I ask a favor?"

"Yes, of course. Whatever you need."

"Do you mind if I move into the guest house? I can still care for the children from there."

Quentin nodded but looked confused. "Is there something wrong?"

"No, not really. I just don't feel comfortable living under the same roof with you after you kissed me."

"Well, I don't want you to feel uncomfortable."

Quentin put the papers down on his desk and crossed the room. He tried to hug Montana, but she resisted.

"I thought you said there was nothing wrong."

"Quentin, let's slow down with the affection, okay?"

"Okay. Why?"

Montana looked at his face and frowned. "Chloe's lawsuit. I don't like the things she's saying about me."

"We both know they're not true."

"Yes, but what about everyone else? People from my church are able to read that court filing. She makes it seem like I came here and seduced you. What if people feel sorry for her? What if they make me a villain?"

"Who cares what other people think?"

"Maybe I shouldn't, but I do. I'm not a man stealer."

Quentin took Montana by both hands and pulled her over to his desk. He sat down on the edge and squeezed her hands tightly.

"How could you steal my heart from Chloe? She never had it."

"It just doesn't feel right."

Quentin let go of her hands. "What would you like me to do? I can't erase the past five years. I can't. And I never meant for any of this to happen. I didn't go into my relationship with Chloe thinking we'd end up this way."

"What did you expect?"

Quentin eased up off the desk and paced the floor. "Do you know what happens when a person breaks a bone and it's not set properly?"

"It doesn't heal correctly."

"Right. Sometimes it ends up twisted and deformed. Sometimes you can lose the use of a limb."

Montana shook her head. "What does this have to do with us?"

"When I met Chloe, I was broken. I tried to heal myself with sex and fun. I looked healed, but inside I was still twisted."

"So now what?"

Quentin stopped pacing and stood in front of Montana. He needed her to see how serious he was about this.

"Now I want to *really* be healed. I want to be there for my kids. My son needs me."

"Deirdre needs you too, Quentin."

He furrowed his eyebrows. "I don't know what to do with Deirdre. We're like oil and water these days."

"All of the children need you to be whole."

"I know. Breaking up with Chloe is one of the steps to getting me there. When a bone doesn't heal properly, you have to re-break it and start the healing process all over again."

Montana nodded in agreement. "I don't want to hinder the healing. I'm not as strong as I seem, Quentin. I need to not be under the same roof with you."

"As long as it's not because of Chloe. I'll have someone clean the guest house tomorrow and move your things there."

"Thank you, Quentin."

Montana started to leave Quentin's office, but then she turned and said, "You know, Quentin, God can heal things a lot more quickly than you think. You should ask Him to help you."

"I have. I'm waiting for Him to show up."

"Maybe He's waiting for you."

Montana left, and Quentin sat back down and read the court filing again. He sighed and put the papers down. This whole lawsuit needed to be over as soon as possible. If it went on too long, it could ruin his chances with Montana. He couldn't lose her; he wouldn't lose her.

Then the answer came to him all at once. God had told Quentin to rest. Even though he was in the middle of a battle, that's what Quentin was going to do. Lay down his weapons and rest.

He already felt victorious.

CHAPTER 44

Deirdre was furious! It was prom night, and Chloe wasn't answering her phone—it was going straight to voice mail. She needed a ride to Moe's house, and there was no one she could ask except Chloe. She wanted to kick herself for not getting her driver's license.

Plus, Chloe was her cover story for the evening. She was going to be on punishment for life if she stayed out all night long with Moe. She might not even get to go to her own prom.

Deirdre felt panic setting in. If she stood Moe up for his prom, he was absolutely going to break up with her. She was sure of that. Not going to the prom wasn't an option.

She dialed Chloe's phone again, and again it went straight to voice mail. How could she not keep her part of the bargain?

Deirdre typed a furious text. Where r u? Prom?

After several minutes with no reply, it sunk in that Chloe wasn't going to help her with this. She was going to have to sneak out. If only she was off her father's draconian punishment, she could've just spent the night at her best friend Kae's house. Chloe was her only cover story.

It annoyed Deirdre that she had to hide her boyfriend. At least she wasn't pregnant like Reese's little hood chick. She should be able to walk out the front door and go to prom with her boyfriend and take pictures and the whole nine yards.

Then she remembered who her father was. *That* wasn't going to happen.

Finally, Deirdre broke down and called Moe. "Can you come and get me?" she asked.

"I thought your mentor was bringing you."

"Yeah, well there was a change of plans. Can you meet me here? At our spot, in fifteen minutes?"

Moe said, "Of course. Anything for my little rich girl."

"Okay. See you later."

She disconnected the phone, and there was another knock on her door. "Go away!" she said.

"Deirdre, it's me. Open the door." It was her father, the last person she wanted to speak to.

She put her bags inside her closet and opened the door.

Quentin came in and sat on the edge of her bed. "Look, Chloe isn't going to be able to mentor you anymore. I don't think it's a good idea."

"You don't get to choose my friends, Daddy. That's not fair."

"I do get to choose your friends. Until you're grown and out on your own, I get to choose."

Deirdre burst into tears. "You just hate me, that's all. And now that you like Montana, you're going to hate me even more because I look like Mommy. Well, guess what? I don't want a new mother. Montana can leave me alone."

Quentin sighed and stood to his feet. "You know I don't hate you, and Montana just wants to be your friend too. I promise she'll be a better friend than Chloe ever could be."

"Daddy, can I just be alone right now? I don't want to talk anymore."

"Yes, but remember that we all love you, Deirdre. Everyone in this house loves you."

Deirdre shook her head and plopped down on her bed. "Okay, Daddy."

Deirdre waited until she heard her father's footsteps go all the way down the stairs, and then she opened her door and waited until she heard his office door close. He'd be in there for hours now, and because she'd just thrown a mini-tantrum he wouldn't come looking for her. So this was the time to make her escape.

Deirdre tiptoed to her closet and quietly picked up her garment bag and her overnight bag. She hurried out of her room, holding her shoes in her hand. She'd put them on outside.

She went out the side entrance that no one ever used except Ms. Levy for deliveries. That exit put her closer to the path and would conceal her as she walked away from the house.

When she got to the edge of the property, she looked at the clock on her phone and waited. She didn't need anyone seeing her standing there. No one from inside the house would be able to spot her from a window, but if anyone drove up, she was pretty exposed. Her heart raced. She was too close now to give up.

Finally, she saw the car Moe said he was driving for prom. It was a silver, drop-top Benz. Chloe would be impressed that she was riding in it.

Deirdre didn't even wait for Moe to get out and open the door for her; she was that anxious to leave. She jumped in on the passenger side and threw her bags in the back seat.

"You can get dressed in our hotel room," Moe said.

"Okay. Where are we staying?"

Moe cleared his throat as if there was about to be a big announcement. "We have a two-bedroom suite at the Embassy Suites. They even have a free breakfast buffet."

Deirdre's countenance fell. "The Embassy Suites?"

"Nice, right? And the breakfast is not that continental stuff. This is the real deal, with a waffle maker and everything. First class for my first-class chick."

Deirdre had never stayed in an Embassy Suites. She was thinking he was going to take her to the W or the Ritz Carlton in downtown Atlanta. It was prom weekend, after all. Wasn't he supposed to go all out?

Even though Deirdre did not appreciate the hotel selection, she was extremely appreciative of Moe's look. His shoulder-length hair flowed free with so much body he looked like an Herbal Essences model.

When they got to the hotel, Deirdre was even more unimpressed. It was clean and decent, but it wasn't anywhere close to what she was used to. But she tried to make the best of it and took an hour to get beautiful.

When Deirdre emerged from the bathroom in her metallic green, skin-tight Herve Leger gown and silver Louboutin sling-back heels, Moe jumped to his feet and stared at her in awe.

"Dang, baby. You are looking right."

"Thank you."

He laughed. "Can we just skip prom and get to the after-after prom."

Deirdre shook her head and offered Moe a bottle of water from her bag. "You sound a little thirsty. Indeed, you sound parched."

Moe burst into laughter, but Deirdre was actually nervous about that part of the evening. She kept putting it out of her mind that Moe wanted to take her virginity. A part of her wanted to make an excuse to try and get out of it.

"Okay, you're right. Let's go and enjoy the prom. It's gonna be fun."

"Well, I'm ready, so let's go."

On the way out of the hotel, Deirdre and Moe got so many compliments from the other hotel guests that she knew they were looking good. They probably could've posed for a teen magazine.

When they got to the prom, Deirdre was disappointed yet again. First the Embassy Suites, and now prom in the high school gymnasium? She knew that his school was in the hood, but really? The gym?

The first smell that hit Deirdre's nose was stale gym sneakers, and that was followed up by dirty socks. Trying to overpower the gym's native funk was the aroma of somebody's version of a soul-food feast. There was a huge buffet set up on one side of the gym, with paper plates and plastic forks and knives wrapped in little sections of paper towel.

It was like a family reunion from the hood.

Deirdre couldn't believe she wore Herve Leger to this thing.

Moe took Deirdre around and introduced her to all of his friends. The boys gave him mad props for having a girl as fly as she was on his arm. The girls gave nothing but mean glares. It didn't bother Deirdre. She was used to haters. She smiled at them anyway.

"Hey, babe, I'm gonna take some pictures with my homeboys. I'll be right back."

Deirdre started to object, but then she changed her mind. She didn't want to seem needy, but she sure didn't want to be left with the dates of his friends.

One of the girls boldly walked up to Deirdre. "Is that Malaysian?"

"Is what Malaysian? My dress? No. It's Herve Leger."

The girl burst out laughing. "Your sew-in. Is that Malaysian or Virgin Remy? What brand is it? Bohyme?"

Deirdre had absolutely no idea what this girl was talking about. It was almost like she was speaking another language.

"Your hair?" the girl asked again when Deirdre didn't reply. "What kind of weave you got?"

"Oh, I don't have a weave. I'm sorry. I didn't know what you were talking about."

The girl signaled for all of her friends to come over. They surrounded Deirdre like a little gang.

"This look like her real hair?" the girl asked.

Another girl said, "That ain't real."

Deirdre shrugged. She didn't have to convince them of anything. She didn't care if they thought her hair was fake. She didn't care about them at all.

"And I know them ain't no real red bottoms," the ring leader said.

Deirdre only smiled. She had nothing to prove.

Finally, Moe and his boys came back from their impromptu photo shoot. Moe broke through the circle of girls and put his arm around Deirdre's waist. The ring leader of the girls sucked her teeth.

"What's your problem, Katina?" Moe asked.

"You know what my problem is. How you gonna bring this fake ho to prom when your baby mama is sitting at the house with y'all newborn son."

Moe held up a hand to stop her noise. "Not. My. Kid. I keep telling y'all Boosy was pregnant when I started kicking it with her. Plus, have you seen it? Ain't no way that chocolate baby is mine. How two light-skinned people have a chocolate baby?"

"That's yo baby, Moe. She said you was the only one she's ever been with."

"Whatever. Come on, Deirdre. Let's go dance. Let these birds keep clucking."

When they got to the dance floor, Deirdre snatched her arm away from Moe. She hoped he didn't think she was going to let this baby mama stuff slide.

"You sure Boosy's baby isn't yours?" Deirdre asked.

He nodded. "Yes. Her stomach was already poking out when I met her. I just thought she was a little chubby. I wrapped it up when I got with her."

Deirdre narrowed her eyes into slits. "Why should I believe you?"

"Because I wouldn't lie about a kid. If it was mine, I'd claim it, on everything."

Deirdre cocked her head to one side and wondered if she should believe him. Moe pulled her close and into his arms. Deirdre felt her resolve go by the wayside as she felt Moe rub little circles on the small of her back.

"Don't you want to dance with me? It's prom night. You can be mad about Boosy later."

Deirdre nodded and she and Moe got out on the dance floor and jammed to hip hop and R & B cuts. At least everyone on the dance floor was there to party. No hating at all.

Then, out of nowhere, there was a ruckus on the other side of the dance floor. It got chaotic really quickly as people started running off the floor. Moe grabbed Deirdre's hand and was pulling her toward the exit when someone ran up behind him and hit him in the back of the head with a stick.

Deirdre screamed but couldn't stay where she was because

she was about to get trampled, so she moved with the crowd. Sirens blared in the distance, and security guards swarmed the area.

Deirdre frantically searched the crowd for Moe. When she didn't see him, she went into panic mode. What if he was unconscious? She tried to go back inside the gymnasium, but the security guards stopped her in her tracks.

She felt her heart drop when the paramedics brought Moe out on a stretcher. He had an oxygen mask on his face, and his hair hung down limply.

She ran a few steps after the ambulance and wondered what to do. She didn't have the keys to the car Moe was driving, and she didn't even know how to drive, so the keys wouldn't have helped.

Deirdre hated to do it, but she pulled out her cell phone. She was going to have to call someone to come and get her.

First she called her best friend, Kae.

"Kae, can you come and get me? I'm at Moe's prom and drama popped off. He's in an ambulance on the way to the hospital."

Kae giggled. "You're where? I'm at . . . oh wait . . . whose house are we over?"

Someone yelled in the background, and Kae started cracking up again. Deirdre groaned. Why would she pick this night to get drunk and party?

"I don't know if I can drive, Dee. Somebody hid my keys from me. I'm pretty smashed."

"Ugh! Bye, Kae."

Then an SUV pulled up next to the curb where she was standing and the window rolled down. It was Katina and the pack of mean girls.

"Hey, that's messed up what happened to Moe. You want us to drive you to the hospital?"

Even though the girls were mean before, they seemed friendly now. And since she didn't have many other options, Deirdre jumped in their truck.

"I can't believe they messed our prom up like that!" Katina said.

Another girl said, "Well, I'm not graduating anyway, so it doesn't really matter. I can go again next year."

"That don't even make no sense. That's your third prom, Renee."

"Oh well! Maybe Boosy can go with me since she had to miss it this year."

An eerie silence fell over the car, and Deirdre was suddenly uncomfortable.

"Those are some nice shoes you got on," Katina said to Deirdre.

"Thanks."

"Take them off."

Deirdre grimaced. "Take them off for what?"

" 'Cause I want them," Katina said in a calm and measured voice.

"I'm not giving you my shoes."

The girl sitting next to Deirdre in the back seat pulled out a straight-razor blade. She said, "You will if you trying to stay pretty."

Deirdre reached for the door handle, but Katina hit the lock. Deirdre swallowed and sized up the girls. She'd never been in a fight in her life. She wouldn't have a chance.

She reached down and took off her shoes. She'd buy more next week. No reason to get sliced up for them.

"I like her dress too," the girl sitting next to Deirdre said.

Katina nodded. "Switch. Give her yours."

Deirdre rolled her eyes. She regretted getting in the car with this gutter trash. She unzipped her dress down the side and gave it to the girl. She was way too fat for the dress and was going to look like a stuffed sausage in it if she could even zip it up.

The girl handed Deirdre her gaudy spandex and sparkly mess of a dress, and Deirdre quickly pulled it over her head. Katina pulled into a gas station parking lot.

"Get out," Katina said.

"But I don't know where this is!" Deirdre complained.

"Aww . . . use the GPS on your cellie. Better yet, gimme that phone. Somebody give her a dollar so she can use the pay phone over there."

Deirdre shook her head. The pay phone didn't even look like it worked. But at this point all she wanted to do was get out of the SUV.

When Katina finally released the locks, Deirdre jumped out of the truck and started running. She could hear the girls laughing in the background. But she didn't care. She'd probably never see those birds again.

Deirdre was barefoot in an ill-fitting dress and racking her brain for who she could call. She couldn't remember any of her friend's numbers. They were in her phone, and she didn't know them by heart. She knew her father's number, Reese's, her grandmother's, the twins', and Montana's. She shook her head and sighed. The only one she could call and not lose her life was Montana.

She got change from inside the store, where the clerk looked at her like she was a drug addict or prostitute.

"Obviously, I was just robbed!" Deirdre said, when the girl took the dollar from her with a turned-up nose.

The girl shrugged. "Then you probably should call the police."

"I just want to go home."

Deirdre sighed and dialed Montana's number, hoping she would answer the phone so late. It was almost midnight.

"H-hello?" Montana said in a sleepy voice.

"Hi, Ms. Montana. It's me, Deirdre."

"Where are you calling from? Aren't you here? Are you okay?"

Deirdre burst into tears from the onslaught of questions. "Please come and get me! Some girls robbed me and took my clothes, and my purse and phone. My boyfriend is at the hospital. Please!"

Montana gasped. "Oh, honey. I'm on my way."

"Hurry!"

"Putting on my shoes right now. What is the address?"

Deirdre read Montana the address from the side of the building. As she looked away, she also saw a man leering at her from the gas station store.

"Montana, I'm scared."

"I'm getting in the car now. Just stay on the phone with me."

It seemed to take forever for Montana to get to the seedy part of Atlanta where Deirdre had been left. When Deirdre finally saw Montana's car turn into the gas station parking lot, she dropped the phone and ran to the car, making sure to avoid broken glass and other trash on the ground.

Deirdre exhaled as she slammed and locked the passenger-side door. She had never been more relieved in her life.

"Are you okay?" Montana asked. "Nothing else happened to you, did it?"

"No. They were just some jealous girls. They were staring at me the whole time we were in the prom."

"Prom? This happened to you at someone's prom?" Montana asked.

Deirdre nodded. "Yeah, my boyfriend Moe's prom was tonight. All I wanted was to be his date and have a good time. They had to start fighting and mess everything up. Can we go to the hospital and see if Moe is okay?"

"Are you sure you want to go dressed like that?"

"I don't care about that. I just want to make sure he's okay. He was on a stretcher, Montana! I couldn't even tell if he was breathing or not."

"Okay, okay. Calm down. Which hospital did they take him to?"

"I don't know."

"The closest is Atlanta General. Let's see if that's where the ambulance took him."

Deirdre felt herself calm down a little, but not completely, because she still didn't know if Moe was okay.

"Are you going to tell my daddy about this?" Deirdre asked, although she thought she already knew the answer.

"He is very worried about you. When he noticed you were gone from your room, he tried to call you. He was just about to call the police when you called me. So your father is already involved."

Deirdre bit her lip and shook her head. She was going to be on punishment until she was grown.

"Then why didn't he come and get me?"

"I asked him to stay home. I think you should try to talk to him," Montana said. "He might be more understanding than you think."

"He understands Reese, Not me. Reese got a girl pregnant, and I haven't even had sex, but I'm on lockdown."

Deirdre thought it was okay to leave out her plans for after prom since it obviously wasn't happening tonight.

"He wants to understand you too, but he's a man," Montana said with a soft chuckle. "They don't always get us girls."

They pulled into the emergency entrance of Atlanta General Hospital. There were hardly any parking spots, because they were filled with shiny, fancy prom automobiles. Katina's SUV was nowhere in sight. Montana handed Deirdre a pair of flip-flops from her back seat.

"Are these the only shoes you have in here?" Deirdre asked.

"Yeah. Sorry."

Inside the hospital, the lobby was standing room only. It seemed like everyone from the prom was there. Deirdre spotted the group of guys that Moe took pictures with and ran up to them.

"Did y'all hear anything about Moe?"

One of Moe's friends looked at her and laughed. "Looks like somebody got jacked."

"Moe. Is he okay?" Deirdre asked, ignoring the ridicule.

"Yeah, he cool," another one of the friends said. "He just got a concussion. His mama and his baby mama are in his room now."

"He said that girl Boosy isn't his baby's mother," Deirdre said, feeling herself getting real irritated.

"Not Boosy," the first guy said. "His other baby mama, Natasha. They got a little girl. I think she's about two."

Deirdre's eyes widened. Moe had a two-year-old? She remembered seeing his grandmother with a little girl at church, but she had no idea it was Moe's baby. And Moe had conveniently neglected to mention his child. Was he planning on making her baby mama number two? Or three?

Deirdre shook her head and turned to Montana. "Let's go. I don't care what happens to him."

"She mad, y'all!" Moe's friend said.

Deirdre didn't allow one tear to spill until they were outside the hospital, but once the night air hit her face, the floodgates opened. How could she have been so stupid? She had been dating Moe for months, and she knew absolutely nothing about him.

Montana pulled Deirdre into an embrace. "It's okay. Let's just go home."

After a few minutes of driving without conversation, Deirdre said, "Thank you for coming to get me."

"Of course," Montana said. "I'm your nanny, remember?"

This made Deirdre smile. She thought she didn't need a nanny, but after the night's events, she realized that maybe she did.

"You really like my dad, don't you?" Deirdre asked.

Montana smiled, but didn't answer right away. After a very long pause, she said, "I do like him a lot. I don't know if that's professional, but you're almost grown. You're not stupid."

"He likes you too. I've never seen him look at Chloe the way he looks at you."

Deirdre noticed Montana frown at the mention of Chloe's name. Of course, Montana couldn't stand Chloe. Chloe had done some low-down stuff to Montana—with Deirdre's help. Suddenly, Deirdre felt remorseful.

"I'm sorry for how I've treated you, Montana."

Montana patted Deirdre's hand. "I forgive you. Actually, I forgave you a long time ago."

"Thank you. Can you go with me when I see my dad tonight? I want to live to see another day."

Montana laughed. "I will. And maybe I can help reason with him."

"I sure hope so."

Montana squeezed Deirdre's hand again, and Deirdre smiled. It felt good to have an ally, someone without any agenda who wanted to help her. She never imagined having a mother again, had never let herself hope for one. She said a silent prayer. *Lord, please don't take Montana away from us.*

For the first time since her mother had died, Deirdre felt herself in a very vulnerable place. She found herself wishing again.

CHAPTER 45

Quentin and Tippen had both worn navy blue suits for their arbitration meeting with Chloe and her lawyer, Doris Lindman. Their coordination wasn't on purpose, but Quentin hoped that it meant they were in accord.

Quentin wanted everything to go quickly today. He had other matters to attend to—namely, Deirdre and her escape to the hood. He'd barely gotten any sleep the entire weekend. He planned to talk to her when she got home from school, with Montana as the mediator. It would be his second arbitration meeting of the day.

"I still don't know if this is the best thing to do," Tippen whispered, as they approached the conference room.

Quentin nodded. "I know."

They walked into the conference room, where Doris and Chloe were already seated, along with the Honorable Judge Killian. She used to be a family court judge and was a neutral party agreed upon by both Tippen and Doris.

"Good morning," Quentin said, as he took his seat.

Chloe said nothing, and Doris grimaced. They seemed ready for battle. Quentin wondered why they had ever agreed to the arbitration. Neither one of them looked ready to bend or budge.

"Good morning, Mr. Chambers and Attorney Carey. Since we're all here, let's go ahead and get started. I've read Ms. Brooks's complaint and Mr. Chambers's response, but I will listen if you'd like to state your main points again. Ms. Brooks, you can go first."

Chloe looked directly at Quentin and narrowed her eyes. "Quentin strung me along for almost five years. He gave me a monthly stipend on a credit card, he paraded me around Atlanta on his arm, and everyone in our circle thought we would be married. Then he met another woman. His nanny. And the next thing I know, he's dumping me, telling me he doesn't love me. He canceled my credit cards and embarrassed me in front of everyone we know. I haven't had a job in five years. I haven't had to. Now I don't know what I'm going to do."

Chloe burst into tears, and her lawyer handed her a tissue. She blew her nose and continued.

"Now I'm going to be destitute. Quentin has made me a laughingstock."

Judge Killian waited to see if Chloe was done. "Is that all, Ms. Brooks?"

Chloe put one finger up, a signal to wait. "One more thing. I didn't want to do this. I would've stayed with him another five years if I had to. He pushed me to this."

Judge Killian raised her eyebrows. "Now are you done?"

Chloe took a deep breath and nodded. Quentin tilted his head to one side and gave Chloe what he hoped was a look of compassion. He hadn't meant to hurt her. If he could take the past five years and give them back to her, he would.

"Mr. Chambers, you may have your say now."

Quentin closed his eyes and cleared his throat. Chloe's nose flared, as if she was preparing herself to be angry at his rebuttal.

"She's right," Quentin said. "Give her what she asked for in her complaint."

Chloe's jaw dropped, and Doris clapped her hands together. Judge Killian looked confused.

"The entire twenty million?" Judge Killian asked. "We could've skipped this meeting today if you were so agreeable."

"Well, I prayed about it. And I did lean on Chloe during my time of grief. I did not fall in love with her, but that's not her fault. I don't want her to suffer."

Tippen shook his head. Perhaps he'd been hoping that in the eleventh hour Quentin would change his mind. Tippen had been furious when Quentin called him with his plan. He'd said Chloe didn't deserve anything more than she'd already spent.

"So that's it? After five years, you wire me some money and send me on my merry way?" Chloe asked.

"On one condition. That you stop trying to damage Montana's reputation. Leave her out of this. She hasn't done anything wrong."

Tears coursed down Chloe's cheeks. "Right. She's above reproach. So sweet, so anointed. So perfect."

Quentin sighed and looked at Judge Killian. This wasn't going anywhere positive. He'd agreed to Chloe's terms. Now it was time to wire the funds and go.

"I can buy a whole lot with twenty million, huh?" Chloe said. "I wonder if I can afford a heart transplant, since you broke mine."

"If you don't want the money, then what do you want?" Quentin asked.

In a small voice, Chloe said. "I want your heart."

Doris handed Chloe another tissue and placed one hand over hers. "I will give you the wire transfer information, Mr. Chambers," Doris said.

"I'm sorry, Chloe. I'm so sorry," Quentin said. "I hope you can find a way to forgive me."

Judge Killian said, "The agreement made here will be binding. Ms. Brooks, you will not have the ability to continue litigation against Mr. Chambers if you accept his offer. Do you accept his offer?"

Chloe nodded. "I accept his offer, but not his apology."

"That's good enough," Judge Killian said. "I will leave the payment details to the attorneys."

Quentin waited for the ladies to stand from the table before he stood to leave. Doris held Chloe's arm as she led her to the door.

"I will never forgive you, Quentin. For as long as I live, I will never forgive what you did to me."

"I admit what I did was wrong," Quentin said. "But you're not blameless, Chloe, while you insist on withholding your forgiveness."

"All I've ever done is be there for your selfish behind."

"Tell me, how did you know my wife again?" Quentin asked. "From Spelman? My mother's investigators said you dropped out of high school and went to a community college in Alabama."

Chloe turned to face Quentin. "That's a lie," she said.

"It's not. You never knew my wife. Take this twenty million, Chloe, and move on. Be happy."

Chloe shook her head and stormed angrily out of the conference room. Doris followed closely behind.

Tippen said, "Quentin, you could've used that information to prove that you were a mark from day one. Why didn't you?"

"Because I can afford it, and I truly am sorry I didn't fall in love with her."

"Well, if you're just throwing millions around, you can hook a brotha up," Tippen said. "I've been with you for a lot longer than five years."

Quentin chuckled. "Tip, man, you're family. But I'm fresh out of settlement money right now. Hit me up in another five years."

"I'll be past my prime by then," Tippen said.

Quentin shook his head and followed Tippen out of the conference room. He hoped that Chloe would change her mind. She was a wealthy woman now.

CHAPTER 46

Quentin could tell that Deirdre was nervous. No one had been invited into his music room since Chandra had died. Quentin sat at the piano and tapped a couple of keys. It needed tuning. He'd handle that later.

"Why did you want to talk to me in here?" Deirdre asked.

Quentin patted the piano bench and motioned for her to sit. "Because I don't want to talk right now. I want to sing."

"Why do you want to sing with me?"

"Because I have been neglecting your gift. You've managed to be incredible without my help, but you can be better."

"Am I on punishment, though?" Deirdre asked.

Quentin cleared his throat. "No shopping for the next three months. Now, let's talk about singing. I want us to do a duet for your brother's wedding."

"I can't believe he's marrying that hood rat."

"Your future sister-in-law is a very nice girl. Have you talked to her?"

Deirdre rolled her eyes. "You talked to her, but you wouldn't talk to Moe. You wouldn't even let me see Moe."

"Why do you keep trying to talk about that when I'm trying to sing?" Quentin tapped a few keys.

"Because, Daddy! You're not being fair. Moe . . ."

"Took you into a dangerous situation. He should've been man enough to come here and ask my permission to take you out. He wasn't. End of story. Let's warm up."

Deirdre groaned. "I don't feel like singing."

"We're going up the scale first. Sing 'today is a good day today.' "

Deirdre sang without much enthusiasm. Quentin said, "And up, today is a good day today."

Deirdre followed Quentin's lead and went up the scale and then back down to the lowest notes she could muster.

"So, what are we singing?" Deirdre asked when they finished the scales.

" 'Can't Take My Eyes Off of You,' the Dionne Warwick version," Quentin said.

Deirdre scrunched her nose. "Can't we sing some Beyoncé?"

"I don't think so."

"Okay, well, at least can we do the Lauryn Hill arrangement?"

Quentin mulled this over for a minute. "Okay, we can do it that way. Do you know it already?"

"Yeah, I do."

"So, let's sing. And one, and two, and one, two, three."

Quentin beamed at his daughter as they sang the lyrics to the classic song. He actually liked Lauryn's version. He sang the low parts and Deirdre sang the high parts. She could've done the whole thing by herself, but they harmonized perfectly.

When they were finished, they sat quietly for a moment, both blinking back tears. He hadn't sung a song with her since she was a little girl.

"Do you know how much I love you, Deirdre?"

"It doesn't always feel that way."

"I know it and I'm trying to change. I know I've got some making up to do."

"It feels like . . . sometimes it feels like we lost you and mom."

Quentin swallowed hard to hold back more tears. He knew that God didn't want his children to feel like orphans, and he was so glad that his heart was finally healing.

"I love you too, Daddy," Deirdre said. "I want to tell you something, but you have to promise me you won't be mad."

"Does it have something to do with Moe?" Quentin didn't think he could take any more revelations.

"No. It doesn't have anything to do with Moe. I don't even like him anymore. It's about Chloe."

Quentin pulled his eyebrows together tightly. "What about Chloe?"

"Promise you won't get mad, Daddy!"

"Whenever you ask me to promise not to get mad, it's because you're about to make me mad!"

Deirdre crossed her arms over her chest and sighed. "Never mind."

Quentin closed his eyes. He wanted Deirdre to open up. He wanted her to talk to him, and he definitely wanted to know what information she had about Chloe. "Okay. I won't be mad, Deirdre. I promise. Whatever you tell me, I won't get angry."

"Remember that picture you got of Montana in your text message?"

Quentin felt the nerve next to his eye twitching. "Yes. Why do you know about it?"

"Because Chloe asked me to help her. She asked me to send it. I didn't really care about Montana at the time, so I did what Chloe asked, but I'm so sorry I did it."

Quentin's mouth formed a little line. "You should be."

"You're not gonna tell her, are you?"

"No. She would be hurt, Deirdre. I won't let her know you had anything to do with that."

Deirdre jumped up and hugged Quentin. "Thank you, Daddy!"

"You're still grounded, though. Just so you know."

Deirdre sighed. "The story of my life."

CHAPTER 47

Montana, as usual, was running late for choir practice. There were some last-minute runs she needed to make for the masquerade ball, and she'd tried to cram everything into a few hours without thinking about Atlanta traffic.

Brother Odom hated when they were late, so she hoped that they were still on the praise and worship part. Sometimes, if a lot of people were running late, Brother Odom would drag that part out until the stragglers came in. He'd roll his eyes at every one of them as they tiptoed into the choir stand.

Montana ran into the sanctuary and up the middle aisle. She was fortunate. Brother Odom hadn't even started yet. He was standing at the organ talking to the musicians. Wait. Was that Quentin at the second organ? What in the world was he doing there?

Quentin waved at her as she ascended the stairs into the choir stand. Emoni abandoned the alto section and met her in the last row of sopranos.

"What's going on?" Montana whispered.

Emoni shrugged. "All I know is that Quentin came in and met with my dad this afternoon. They talked for hours, and he prayed with Quentin. You think he's back?"

"He must be. Why else would he be sitting at the organ?"

"Well, what do you think about that?"

Montana bit her bottom lip and gazed over at Quentin. He looked right at home at the organ. He caught her looking and gave her a smile. She looked away.

Brother Odom finished talking to the musicians and stepped up to his podium. "Praise the Lord this evening. I want y'all to give a hearty handclap of praise for our very own prodigal son, Quentin Chambers. He's joining the music ministry again. I think we'll test him out on the organ. What y'all think?"

Everyone who had been in the choir for many years laughed and clapped. They obviously knew how good he was. He'd led them all before Brother Odom was ever a member of Freedom of Life.

Brother Odom worked the choir hard that night. He took them through several songs that they already knew and started teaching another one. He directed the choir like he had something to prove. But Montana was sure Quentin wasn't there to steal Brother Odom's job.

After rehearsal was over, Montana tried to leave quickly. She didn't want to talk to Quentin in public. Not after Chloe's court filing. By now everyone had heard her accusations of treachery. Emoni said that no one believed it, but she wasn't sure.

Montana heard Quentin's voice as she tried to rush out of the sanctuary. "Montana! Wait up!"

Montana took a few more steps and decided to stop and wait for him. "Yes, how can I help you?"

"Are you okay with me being back on the music staff?" Quentin asked.

"Of course I want to see you back in church, Quentin. You belong here. I'm glad you're here," Montana replied.

"Then why are you running away without speaking?"

Montana said, "Because I see you every day. I already spoke to you today."

"Well, I'd like to speak to you again. Hi, Montana. I hope you're having a wonderful evening."

"I am. I will see you later."

Emoni walked up to Montana and Quentin. "Hey, do y'all want to go out to Houlihan's with us?"

"Sure!" Quentin said.

Montana shook her head. "I've got some things to handle back at home. Next time, okay?"

"Stop lying in the sanctuary," Emoni said. "You have nothing to do."

Montana's eyes widened. She couldn't wait to get Emoni back for betraying her. Obviously, she didn't want to go anywhere public with Quentin.

"Yeah, come on, Montana. My treat," Quentin said.

"Oh, all right," Montana said.

Emoni said, "Yay! Meet y'all there."

When Emoni was out of earshot, Montana said, "Quentin, you can't do this. You can't infiltrate my friend circle."

"They're my friends too."

"You barely know Emoni."

"I've known Emoni her entire life. In fact, you are infringing on my friend circle. I'm getting reconnected."

Quentin headed out of the sanctuary, but Montana stood still. He turned around and asked, "Are you coming?"

"You're not going to let me get away, are you?" Montana asked.

Quentin shook his head. "Not at all. Let's go. I'm hungry."

Montana followed Quentin out of the sanctuary. She watched him talk with Darrin and Trent before getting in his car.

When she'd seen Quentin sitting at the organ, Montana's heart had fluttered, but she was cautious. As much as she wanted to let herself fall in love with Quentin completely, playing the organ didn't mean he was right with God or healed.

Montana had to be sure. Then she realized that she had absolutely no idea how she'd be certain of Quentin's change. She'd have to trust him, and God.

Montana didn't have a problem trusting God; it was Quentin she wasn't so sure about.

CHAPTER 48

Montana wanted to strangle Emoni. They weren't having their usual post-choir-practice dinner outing. It was just Emoni, Darrin, Quentin, and herself. They were on a double date. She and Quentin hadn't even had a regular date yet, but they were going on a double.

Montana was glad she'd driven herself to the restaurant. It had given her time to think about what was going on without being in close proximity to Quentin. It was hard to think clearly with Quentin and all his pheromones wreaking havoc with her senses.

When she got to the restaurant, Emoni, Darrin, and Quentin were already waiting for their table.

"What took you so long?" Quentin asked. "Which way did you come?"

"I follow all traffic laws. That's why it took me the proper amount of time to get here," Montana said.

Emoni laughed. "Translation: Montana drives like a grandmother."

"You should've let me drive you," Quentin said. "Part of it is her car too. It's like a dinosaur."

Darrin said, "Depending on what dinosaur we're talking

about, that could be a good thing. Have you ever seen a pterodactyl swoop through the air?"

"When have *you* seen a pterodactyl?" Emoni asked. "And please don't tell me you saw it on *Jurassic Park.*"

Darrin shrugged. "Well, yeah. That's where I saw it, but they did a lot of research prior to filming that movie. It's pretty accurate based on the fossilized remains of dinosaurs. Don't hate."

Montana covered her mouth with her hand and giggled. She wondered how a conversation about the state of her car had turned into a debate session for Darrin and Emoni. They seemed to enjoy sparring as much as they enjoyed talking sweet to one another and holding hands.

The hostess showed them to the table, and a waitress was right there to take their drink orders. They'd chosen a booth, and Emoni and Darrin decided to sit on the same side. So that left Montana uncomfortably close to Quentin. She felt her mind go foggy.

"So I'm just going to come out and ask," Darrin said. "What are your intentions with our sister?"

Quentin chuckled. "Dang, bro. You could've given me a warning that you were about to ask me that."

Now Montana wanted to strangle Darrin *and* Emoni. First they set her up on a double date, and then they commence to interrogating Quentin. That was a complete and utter violation of some unwritten friend rule.

"It's an easy question," Emoni said. "Or it should be."

"Well, you all should be asking Montana what her intentions are. I've made it clear that I plan to pursue a relationship with her. I just had to get some things right first."

"And is everything right?" Emoni asked.

"Emoni!" Montana fussed.

Emoni shrugged. "I'm trying to help you out. You should be thanking me."

Quentin touched Montana's arm. "Things are right, Montana. I promise."

Montana nodded and quietly ate a piece of bread from the

basket on the table. She believed that things were right with him, but she wondered what people would think about them having a relationship so soon after he broke up with Chloe.

"Maybe we should just keep this on the low, until the Chloe stuff dies down," Montana said.

"Why?" Emoni asked. "Everybody understands that things don't work out sometimes. Most people are wondering why it even took so long for them to split up."

Darrin nodded. "And rich men getting sued by women is nothing new. Nobody cares about what Chloe did."

Darrin gave Quentin a fist bump across the table to emphasize his point.

Montana turned to look at Quentin, and he was grinning at her. He was enjoying this night out with her friends.

"I just want everyone to stop bringing my ex-girlfriend up in conversation. She wasn't a fiancée, she was a girlfriend. I've moved on."

Montana was convinced that Quentin had moved on, because he was pursuing her without restraint. It might not be a perfect situation, but Montana did feel that their coming together was the will of God. Just a little more chasing, and Montana felt that maybe she'd slow down just enough to be caught.

CHAPTER 49

Quentin followed Montana back home after they'd left the restaurant. He was glad that Emoni had invited him. He felt that it was her way of letting Montana know that she, and everyone else at church, would be fine with her dating him. And it seemed necessary, because Montana had, all of a sudden, gotten a case of cold feet.

Quentin jumped out of his car to walk Montana to the door of her cottage. She rewarded him with one of her smiles.

"Did you enjoy yourself?" Quentin asked.

Montana nodded. "I did. Did you and Emoni plan that whole thing?"

"No, but I think maybe she planned it. You're not mad at her, are you?"

"I'm not mad, but I don't know if I want everyone to know about us yet."

Quentin slid his hand in hers. "I know you don't. But no matter when it comes out that we're dating, it still won't change what Chloe said in her lawsuit."

"You thought you'd slip that in, huh? We're not officially dating yet, sir."

Quentin said, "Why aren't we?"

"I'm not sure," Montana said with a shrug.

"You know, I prayed about this before I went to Bishop Prentiss and asked if I could come back. I asked God to forgive me for what happened with Chloe. That's why I decided to give her the twenty million she asked for."

"You asked God to forgive you? Wait you gave her twenty million dollars?"

"I asked God to forgive me for my sin. Chloe was a part of that. I want to be a better father—well, a better man. I know I can't do that without God in my life."

"But you gave her twenty million dollars?" Montana said.

"It was worth it to be done with Chloe. I didn't want a long drawn out lawsuit. I want to be with you."

"You did all that so we could be together?" Montana asked.

Quentin smiled. "I am falling in love with you, Montana. The right kind of love. I don't want you to be my girlfriend or arm candy. I want you to be my wife. I know you're not ready yet, but do know that is my goal."

Quentin felt relieved that he'd gotten it all out. Montana had to know that this was different than what he'd had with Chloe. His love for Montana was pure and not sullied with sin. He wanted to keep it that way.

"Are you okay with that being my plan?" Quentin asked.

She answered him with a kiss that buckled his knees. Then she turned her key in the lock to the cottage door.

"Good night, Quentin."

"Good night."

With his lips still tingling from her kiss, Quentin jumped down the cottage steps and jogged to his car. He felt his heart beat out of his chest with love for her. He wasn't falling, he had fallen. There was no way he'd be able to date Montana for five years or even five months without making her his bride.

CHAPTER 50

It was the day of the masquerade ball, and the mansion was abuzz with activity. The florists had started arriving yesterday and were placing flowers everywhere. It smelled like a honeybee's amusement park with the sweet scents of the roses, lilies, and tulips.

Darrin had arrived early in the morning to start the meal preparation, so in addition to the flowers, the scents of slow-roasting meats filled the mansion. Montana's stomach growled in expectation, but she was so nervous that she couldn't eat anything if she tried.

Montana made her way to the kitchen, where Emoni and Trent were assisting Darrin. They were his kitchen staff, and they were probably free labor.

"Moni, babe, hand me that spatula," Darrin said.

Emoni rolled her eyes. "Did you forget to say please? Don't just be barking orders. Trent and I are volunteers."

Trent handed Darrin the spatula and said, "Here you go."

Emoni poked out her lips and rolled her eyes. "You are empowering him, Trent! You teach people how to treat you!"

Darrin looked up and saw Montana. He smiled and waved. "Montana, will you please remove your friend from my kitchen. She is messing up my cooking vibes with her fussing."

"Remove me?" Emoni said. "See this is exactly what I'm talking about. He is always bossing somebody and barking . . ."

Darrin crossed the space between them in two steps and silenced her with a kiss. "Hush! It is stressful in here, babe. I will be barking orders all day. If you don't want to hang, you don't have to. Go help Montana, please, and thank you. Love you."

"Do you have everything you need?" Montana asked.

Darrin nodded. "I do. This is going to be huge for me. I'm sure to have a bunch of clients after this. Thanks for pulling some strings for me."

"You're my brother! Of course!"

Montana pulled Emoni out of the kitchen and into the parlor and living areas that had been transformed into a ballroom equipped with tables with white tablecloths and chairs with big white linen bows on the back of each one. The floral centerpieces added color against the white and silver scheme.

Emoni burst into laughter. "Girl, thank you for rescuing me from that kitchen! All that steam was going to sweat out my roller set."

"So you were just gonna fuss until he kicked you out?"

"Um, yes. I couldn't seem like I wasn't supporting his dream."

Montana burst into laughter. "You are a real hot mess, do you know that?"

"Only lukewarm, baby. God is working on me."

"So what's up with your date?" Emoni asked.

Montana scrunched her nose into a frown. "What date?"

"I think it's the perfect time to come out with this. Chloe showed her behind to all of Atlanta. So why keep it a secret?"

"Because I don't want it to seem like I stole him from her."

"She gave him to you. You have nothing to feel guilty about."

Montana shook her head. "Oh no. I don't feel guilty. I'm just saying there's a better way to do this. We don't need to humiliate Chloe further."

"Why do we care about Chloe again? She's gone!" Emoni said.

"Do you have your dress for the party here, or do you need to go home and get dressed?"

"No, I have it here. I was hoping to be able to get dressed in your little cottage."

"Oh, not a problem. We might even get a chance to relax before this thing starts."

Estelle descended the spiral staircase with a smile on her face. She'd already had her hair done in a high, curly bun. She looked regal, and she wasn't even wearing her ball gown yet.

"How is everything progressing?" she asked Montana.

"Everything is perfect. It's going to be wonderful."

Estelle touched Montana's arm lightly as she approached the two young women. "Well, then, I want you to relax. Go and get beautiful. You've got to look flawless in that gown, honey."

"Oh, I'm wearing one of my dresses from church."

Estelle said, "I may have left something for you to wear in your cottage."

"Estelle, you didn't."

"I'm not sure what was done, actually. I think you're going to have to go and see," Estelle said with a laugh.

Montana and Emoni squealed like two teenagers on their way to their first concert. Montana hugged Estelle gently, making sure not to muss her hair.

"Thank you so much for whatever you've done, Estelle. And thank you for what you've already done."

Estelle said, "Only the best for my son."

Montana's eyes filled with tears. It meant so much to her that Estelle believed that she was a match for Quentin. A lot of women had to spend time convincing their man's mother that they're even worthy, but Estelle had been her advocate from day one.

Montana and Emoni dashed out of the main mansion to Montana's cottage. Montana stopped in her tracks when she walked through the front door. There were racks and racks of designer dresses, stacks of shoes, and a display case of jewelry in her living room.

"Are you Montana?" asked the petite British woman standing in the center of the room.

"I am! Is all of this for me?"

The woman smiled and handed Montana a note. "I'm supposed to give you this first."

Montana grinned from ear to ear as she opened the note. *Montana, I know this is really last minute, but I was wondering if you'd be my date for the evening. And please forgive me, but you can't go to a formal ball wearing one of your church dresses. I think you're beautiful in your church clothes, but I wouldn't want the society ladies to have anything negative to say about my date. Please let Serena dress you. I can't wait to see the results. Affectionately, Quentin.*

"What does it say?" Emoni asked.

Montana winked at her. "None of your business. I'm ready to pick a dress now."

"My name is Serena, and I will be your stylist for the evening. Quentin wasn't sure what you'd like, so he had me bring lots of options. Do you have something in mind?"

Montana fingered through one of the racks of dresses, unsure of what she should wear. The only time she'd ever worn a formal dress was at her prom.

"Do you have anything in a pale blue?" Montana asked.

Emoni said, "Yes! Pale blue and shimmery."

"Yep. Like Cinderella."

Serena smiled. "Yes, I have just the thing."

The dress Serena selected was a knee-length, pale blue halter dress with a crystal covered bodice. The skirt had mini pleats and flared. It was perfect.

"The only jewelry you need for this dress is a pair of diamond earrings and a diamond tennis bracelet. And of course glass slippers," Serena said.

Serena's idea of glass slippers were clear sling-back pumps covered in crystals. They completed the fairy-tale look.

Next was hair and makeup. An entire crew of stylists worked on Montana and Emoni, creating a fierce updo for Emoni and a headful of ringlets for Montana. The curls were pinned up on one side, giving Montana a very youthful look.

When she was completely dressed, Serena led Montana to a mirror. Montana yelled when she saw her reflection. She almost didn't recognize herself.

"You look incredible," Emoni said. "Who knew you cleaned up so well?"

"I know I didn't," Montana said.

Emoni said, "This looks so much better than your church dress."

They both laughed.

"You ready to go and get your prince now?" Emoni asked.

"It seems like he's insisting on it, huh?"

Quentin certainly didn't have a problem with letting his intentions be known. He was in pursuit of Montana and planned to claim her, at least for the evening. But as much as Montana loved the new dress, shoes, and jewelry, she wasn't impressed. Spending money was easy for Quentin. He'd have to do more than buy her things to win her heart.

CHAPTER 51

Quentin stood at the foot of the spiral staircase, fully dressed in his tuxedo and bow tie, and beheld the mansion transformed into a ballroom. With all of the drama that had gone on in the past couple of weeks, Quentin hadn't taken time out to remember what the event was all about. They were going to raise a boatload of money for the women at Transitions.

The auction area was full of unique and rare jewelry pieces and an art collection by a local painter who was featured at a New York City gallery. Of course, the rich bachelor auction was sure to rake in the dollars as well. It was going to be a great event.

Estelle walked up and kissed his cheek. "You look quite dapper, son. I wish your father was still alive to see you in a tux."

"He did, at my wedding, remember?"

"That's right. Well, you're older now, and more handsome. You look just like him."

"Thank you, Mother."

The guests had started to arrive, so Estelle turned on her hostess charm. She moved through the room, granting air kisses to her associates and real hugs and kisses to her dear friends. Estelle was never fake, and every one of the party's guests knew where they stood with her.

It was hard to tell who was who with the sea of masks floating through the front door. Quentin had opted not to wear a mask, but many of the men did. The masks gave the event a haunting feel that made Quentin apprehensive.

The party really became festive when the band started to play. They had opted for old-school R & B and jazz instead of classical or gospel, and many of the couples took to the dance floor even though dinner hadn't yet been served.

The social circles in Atlanta were quite small, and most everyone had heard about the demise of Quentin and Chloe's relationship. Quentin felt fortunate that no one, so far, had asked him where Chloe was. He planned to say to anyone who asked, "I don't think she's going to be able to make it." It was the truth without giving away any of the bad blood or embarrassing Chloe even further.

Emoni walked by and hugged Quentin. "Look at Lord Chambers, looking quite scrumptious. I might just have to ditch my boyfriend. Who's your date for the evening?"

Quentin laughed. "As much as I would love to have you on my arm, I've asked Montana. Plus, your man is kind of swollen in the biceps area, so I think I'm going to pass."

"Your loss. It would've been grand!"

"You are a nut. Where's Montana?"

"Well, she has to make an entrance. She looks spectacular. You better make her official real quickly, because if you don't, she is going to have a long line of suitors after tonight."

Quentin nodded. "I hear you. I plan to make that happen real soon."

"Don't snooze, playa."

"How did you get so hood, Emoni? Where did Bishop go wrong?"

Emoni punched Quentin in the arm. "Where did he go right, you mean? Don't make me beat you down and get your little tux all dusty."

And then Quentin saw Montana walk into the room. His breath caught in his throat at the sight of her in the pale blue dress. The sparkling shimmer of the fabric seemed to extend to her arms, face, and shoulders. She was aglow, and like the star that she was, she caused all activity in the room to cease. Dancers stopped dancing, chatters stopped chatting, and those who were eating appetizers stopped chewing as she captivated all with her presence.

From head to toe, there was not one flaw Quentin could find in Montana. He wanted to end the party right then and sweep her away somewhere, to Vegas, and make her his bride.

While everyone gazed at Montana, she seemed to have eyes only for Quentin. She beamed at him as she stood facing him. Who was Quentin kidding with not announcing Montana as his date? Anyone who looked at them would see that something was there. And that something was an attraction so deep it was almost like there was no one else in the room.

"Hi, Quentin. What do you think?" Montana asked.

"Uh . . . wow. I can't think! You look incredible."

Her smile grew. "Thank you."

"You're welcome. You can have every one of those dresses if you want. I'll plan a formal dinner every night of the week just to see you wearing them."

Montana slapped Quentin on the arm. "Stop trying to buy me stuff."

"No. I am not going to stop buying you stuff. You're just going to have to get used to it."

"They're about to serve dinner," Montana said. "I promised the members of Freedom of Life that I'd sit with them. Is that okay with you?"

Montana looked so breathtaking that he didn't want her out of his sight. "Of course it's okay. I want to sit where you're sitting."

Montana blushed and looked away from Quentin's intense gaze. Quentin was serious about what he'd said. He wasn't going to stop buying her things. He wasn't going to stop wooing her. He wasn't going to stop chasing her until she was caught.

Montana waved as she made her way to the tables reserved for their church members. Estelle had wanted them to have a high-society experience, just like they were millionaires too, so their table was near the center of the room. Bishop and First Lady Prentiss looked stunning in their attire, and Bishop Prentiss's assistant, Oscar, looked like he was having a good time for a change. Emoni and Darrin were perfect together.

The men at the table stood when Montana and Quentin approached. Montana waved for them to sit down, but they waited until she slid into the chair Quentin held out for her.

Tyler, Bishop Prentiss's oldest son and fellow bachelor in the auction, said, "So who does everyone think is going to get the highest bid in the auction tonight? Me or Quentin?"

Quentin laughed out loud. "I think it's more than obvious that you are going to lose, Tyler. It's all right, though. You can graciously defer to your host."

"Man, listen! Lots of women want to be a preacher's wife."

Darrin said, "Y'all should just be glad Emoni wouldn't let me be in the auction. Every woman wants a man who can cook."

"And why would you be in a bachelor auction?" Emoni asked. "This is how you get yourself in trouble."

Darrin laughed, "I wouldn't, sweetheart. I'm just teasing you."

Emoni frowned until Darrin kissed her cheek and her sour facial expression melted. Quentin couldn't wait until he and Montana had that rapport. He knew that they were at the beginning of their journey, but Quentin was convinced that he and Montana would be soul mates.

"Montana, honey, you look lovely," First Lady Prentiss said. "Estelle just raves about you all the time. She said she couldn't have done this ball without you."

"We worked really hard to pull this together. And it's for a wonderful cause."

Bishop Prentiss said, "A blessed cause. Quentin, Montana has been telling me so much about the work you do at Transitions, and Freedom of Life wants to be a help to you. You don't need to do it alone."

"Right, Quentin," Tyler said. "We've got ministry partners who would be glad to volunteer for shifts at Transitions."

"Freedom of Life wants to partner with you," Bishop Prentiss said. "It was Montana's idea, though. She saw the ministry there. You never stopped serving God, son. Your ministry was outside the church walls."

Quentin grinned at Montana. He wanted to kiss her right here at the table. She'd gone, on his behalf, to talk to Bishop Prentiss, because she saw a need. He needed help with Transitions. It was time for him to stop carrying that particular burden alone.

"Bishop Prentiss, I welcome your help," Quentin replied.

"Well, you've got it. We'll meet and talk about it next week."

Quentin squeezed Montana's hand under the table. He kept talking to God about Montana, and all he felt was confirmation that she was the one and that He didn't fail.

God didn't fail, but Quentin was all too aware of his own imperfections. He'd been blessed with a near-perfect woman in Chandra, a soul mate and a partner. Could he be blessed again? Would God favor him that much to give him a second woman of his dreams?

CHAPTER 52

Dinner had gone off without a misstep. Every course of the meal was scrumptious, and the guests couldn't stop buzzing about how talented a caterer Darrin was. Montana was excited for him, because there were holders of millions upon millions of dollars in the ballroom. He only had to connect with the right ones. Next up on the evening's agenda was the wealthy bachelor auction, the highlight of the night for a lot of the women in attendance. Montana knew quite a few of the ladies from Freedom of Life had pulled money from their savings accounts to land a date with one of the wealthy guys. Montana was happy she didn't have to bid for Quentin's attention, and she was happy to be the auctioneer. She'd taken over those duties when it became clear that Chloe was no longer going to be a part of the festivities.

Montana stood on the stage, ready to be the auctioneer. She looked around the stage area and didn't see what she was looking for. Her wireless microphone. Then she remembered. She'd left it in Quentin's office when she went to put away the invoices for the final flower deliveries.

Montana dashed off the stage to go and get it. This was one time she wished the house was smaller. It took her several minutes to get to Quentin's office from the ballroom. As she pushed the door open to grab the microphone from the desk, she was shocked to find something other than what she was looking for. Or rather, someone. Chloe sat at Quentin's desk, wearing a formal dress.

"What are you doing here?" Montana asked. Her question was more surprise than accusation, but Montana could see by the dark look that came over Chloe's face that she took it to mean the latter.

"What am I doing here? I should've asked you that the first day you stepped into this mansion."

Chloe got up from the desk and walked around it. Montana took a few steps back. The last thing she wanted was a confrontation, but Chloe seemed to have been waiting for one.

"I must say, I underestimated you," Chloe said. "If anyone had tried to tell me I was about to lose Quentin to a domestic employee, I would've laughed in their face."

"I'm not the reason you and Quentin broke up," Montana said.

Chloe walked closer to Montana. "Let me see. Before you start working here, I'm going on trips and shopping sprees and to every high-society function in Atlanta. After you start working here, my credit cards are canceled and you're on his arm. Explain how you aren't the reason."

"Maybe God didn't want you together."

Chloe threw her head back and let out a cackle. "I just love how church folk get so mystical when they've done dirt. You stole my man and you just blamed it on God."

"I didn't steal him," Montana said.

Montana felt herself get annoyed with Chloe's accusations. She knew that what she and Quentin had embarked upon was more spiritual in nature than what he and Chloe had shared. It was unfortunate that Quentin was still seeing Chloe when they met, but what had happened wasn't done on purpose.

"Well, it doesn't matter now," Chloe said with a shrug. "I got what I wanted from Quentin anyhow, even in the midst of your treachery."

"Your money."

"Yes, honey. He gave me a twenty-million-dollar settlement for my five years of standing in the gap for him."

"Standing in the gap?" Montana asked. "When did you expose yourself for Quentin's protection? When did you raise up a defense for him? You don't know what it means to stand in the gap."

"I protected him from his grief. When he was with me he wasn't thinking about his first wife, I guarantee it," Chloe said.

"He wasn't healing either. Actually, he was spiritually dead."

Chloe rolled her eyes and walked back to the desk to retrieve her purse. "I don't like you, nanny, but I'm gonna give you a word of advice. Don't believe Quentin's promises. He has no intentions of keeping them. Five years from now, you'll be standing in a room looking at your replacement."

"I don't believe that."

"I know you don't. I wouldn't believe me either, if I was you."

Chloe walked out of the office with her head held high. But she left Montana with more questions than answers. She knew there was no treachery on her part with Quentin, but what if the rest of what Chloe said was true? How did she know she'd be any different? How did she know her love would be enough for Quentin?

Lacking the answers she sought, Montana went back downstairs with the microphone in her hand. Quentin caught her before she went on the stage.

"Is everything all right?" he whispered.

Montana closed her eyes. She wanted to tell him about her conversation with Chloe, but what good would that do if Quentin's intentions were poor? He wouldn't let on now if they were.

"Chloe's here," Montana said. "Or she was. She might be gone now."

"Do I need to call security?"

Montana shook her head. "I don't think so. I think she was waiting to talk to you."

"Are you okay? What did she say to you?"

"Nothing. I'm fine. Let's start the auction, okay?"

Microphone in hand, Montana stood in front of the crowd on the band's stage. She tried to push Chloe's warning out of her mind while she addressed the partygoers.

"Thank you to everyone who came out to this event to support Transitions! I have had the opportunity to visit there myself, and it is truly God's work that Quentin Chambers is doing there. You are in support of a worthy cause."

"Bring on the hunks!" shouted a lady in her mid-sixties. Her husband, who was seated next to her, shook his head in embarrassment.

Montana had to restrain her giggle. "Yes, indeed! It is definitely time to bring on the hunks."

First on the stage was Tyler Prentiss. The catcalls started as soon as he started up the stairs. He was very handsome, with long locks that he wore tied neatly in back and a muscular physique. His skin was the color of cream, and he had light eyes like his mother. Montana watched the ladies swoon.

"Well, first, we have the very fine bachelor Pastor Tyler Prentiss. He's the assistant pastor at Freedom of Life, where he serves with his father Bishop Kumal Prentiss. He enjoys tennis, bowling, and spending time at the beach. His favorite foods are Italian and . . ."

"I will start the bidding at one thousand dollars!" yelled Dorcas, one of the sisters at Freedom of Life. Montana saw Emoni roll her eyes and again had to keep from bursting into laughter. There was no love lost between the two of them.

Another one of the church sisters said, "I've got two thousand on him, baby!"

Tyler looked tickled at the attention as if he wasn't used to it. He was Freedom of Life's most eligible bachelor. Everyone expected him to take over Bishop Prentiss's position one day as senior pastor at Freedom of Life.

After some furious back-and-forth bidding on Tyler, his mother, First Lady Diana Prentiss, rescued him by making a final bid of fifteen thousand dollars. The ladies, of course, were disappointed, but he gave all of the highest bidders a hug, so they were somewhat pacified.

The bachelors walked onto the stage one by one, each one nabbing thousands of dollars for Transitions. The auction was a great idea. Montana was going to recommend that they make it an annual tradition.

Quentin winked at Montana as he took the stage. He was the final bachelor and the one everyone wanted for an afternoon lunch date. Montana herself couldn't afford to bid, so she hoped one of the thirsty elderly ladies won a lunch date with her tall drink of water.

"All right, everyone! Our final bachelor is the founder of Transitions, my boss and your host, Quentin Chambers! I think it's only fair if we open the first bid at two thousand dollars!"

The bidding took off in a noisy frenzy, until there were six women contending for that date with Quentin. When the bids surpassed twenty-five thousand dollars with no signs of stopping, the room went loud with noisy catcalls and cheers.

"Twenty-five thousand going once! Going twice . . ."

"One hundred thousand dollars."

The bid came from Estelle. All the women in the room groaned. If Estelle was going to get in on the bidding, they'd never win.

When no one countered, Montana said, "Well, that's one hundred thousand from Mrs. Chambers going once . . . going twice . . . going three times . . . Sold!"

Estelle burst into laughter. "I have done my duty as a mother, protecting my son from all of you barracudas!"

"You can't watch him all the time!" someone yelled, causing everyone in the room to join Estelle in laughing.

Quentin took the microphone from Montana. As he did so, he stroked the side of her face, a very public gesture that shocked Montana.

Quentin said, "I hope you ladies have fun on your outings with your bachelors. I'm almost one hundred percent sure my mother has something up her sleeve for me. So if I may solicit one more thing from you, I would appreciate your prayers."

"Can everyone give the beautiful Ms. Montana a round of applause," Quentin continued. "She came in and really pulled this event together at the last minute. She's been such a blessing to me and this household."

Montana could've died of embarrassment. Many of the high-society ladies gave her a head nod of approval, and some of the church members, Emoni included, shouted "Hallelujah" like Quentin was preaching a sermon.

"Are you all enjoying yourselves?" Quentin asked. "Give it up for the band! As some of you may know, I dabble a little bit musically."

Quentin paused while everyone chuckled. Then he said, "Well, lately, I've been writing again. For some reason . . . I've been inspired."

Montana watched as three staff members pushed Quentin's white baby grand piano into the ballroom. Was Quentin going to play?

Quentin said, "I wrote a song I'd like to share. I was saving it for another, more private occasion, but one thing you learn by losing someone is to seize the moment."

Quentin set the microphone down and left the stage. He squeezed Montana's hand as he walked by, making her wonder what was going to happen next.

Quentin spoke into the microphone set up near his piano. "Y'all pray for me again. I'm a little rusty."

"It's all right, baby!" Ms. Levy said from her table.

The room was completely silent when Quentin started to play. The way his fingers flowed over the keys, he didn't seem out of practice at all. Then he started to sing.

Time stopped, when you walked through my door.
It's like the Lord answered my prayer with an angel.
You make me feel like a man again, ready to live,
And if it isn't love, then I don't know what it is.
Caught me by surprise feeling you.
But I can't fight it anymore, and I don't know if I want to.

If this isn't real, let me believe, 'cause only God could orchestrate this picture-perfect dream.
I found you, you found me. Neither one of us was ready, for what God had in store.
I found you, you found me, let's just go with it.
What are we waiting for?
Heaven sent you to me, when I didn't believe in love anymore.
Didn't know what my heart was for.
Heaven sent you to me, when I didn't believe in love anymore.
Didn't know what my heart was for.
Heaven sent you to me.

Montana could hardly catch her breath when the song finished. Of course, it was about her. She could tell by the way Quentin stared at her over the top of his piano. Obviously, he was ready to go public with his feelings. He'd just serenaded her in front of all his friends.

Montana wanted to cut and run, as she couldn't stand being the center of attention, and it seemed that everyone was looking her way. She didn't run, though. She tried to smile and not look too awkward.

Then Quentin got up from the piano and started walking toward her. Montana trembled with nervousness. She didn't know what Quentin was about to do, but it was clear that it would be *something*—the look of resolve on his face was unmistakable.

Quentin walked faster as he neared Montana, and then to hers and everyone else's surprise, Quentin lifted her from the floor and spun her around with a hug. When he set her down on the floor again and smiled down at her, Montana was sure her face was every shade of red known to man.

"Did you like your song?" he whispered.

All Montana could do was nod. Quentin gave her a huge smile and hugged her again.

Montana hugged him back amid a room full of applause. It seemed that just about everyone was thrilled about her and Quentin, so she allowed herself to share in that joy. There was nothing Chloe could do or say that could make her feel any differently about Quentin than she felt in this moment. She loved him and he loved her too. Now all of Atlanta knew their secret.

CHAPTER 53

Montana awoke just before daybreak. She had a full day ahead of her and runs to make for Reese's small wedding. She had to pick up his reserved tuxedo from the tailor and get the corsage from the florist. Some of what she did extended beyond her nanny duties, but she didn't mind. She loved the children dearly and would do anything for them.

She jumped out of her bed and started a pot of tea. Montana liked to pray and meditate before she started her day, and she'd been especially diligent following everything that had transpired with Quentin.

After she finished her cup of tea and Scripture meditation, she felt ready to face the day and any pitfalls that might be before her.

Right before she got ready to take her shower, Montana's doorbell rang. Immediately, her hands went to her hair, which was standing up in multiple directions, having yet to be tamed with her arsenal of styling products and brushes.

It had to be Quentin. No one else would be up this early, knocking on her door.

"Who's there?" Montana asked.

"It's me. You wanna go running?"

"I can't, Quentin," Montana said, through the door. "I have to run errands for Reese."

"I know. I'll help you do them if you go running with me first."

Montana smiled. She couldn't resist him. "Okay, give me a minute."

Montana took about ten minutes to shower, brush her teeth and hair, and throw on her workout clothing. Every time she tied her running shoes, it made her smile. Buying her the running shoes was the first romantic thing Quentin had done, and he hadn't even known he was being romantic.

She opened the door, and Quentin waited for her. He looked as gorgeous as ever. The sun kept playing with the light brown in his eyes, and it made them look like jewels.

"Come on," Quentin said. "I need to go hard today. I have to work out some stress."

"What's wrong?" Montana asked.

Quentin touched her fingertips and pulled her down the steps. "Oh, it's the good kind of stress. Either I sneak in your cottage at night to cuddle with you, or I run."

Montana laughed and took off down the path. "Well, you better get running, sir."

After her initial dash, Montana slowed to a jog so that she could warm up properly. Quentin had taught her how to pace herself so that she'd be able to run the entire distance. Twice she'd done the entire two miles without a break. She was getting into the best shape of her life.

Once she was done warming up, Montana fell into her pace. She counted her footfalls, in sets of twos. It helped her to concentrate.

About halfway through the path, when she was just starting to feel the burn, Quentin yelled out, "Hey, Montana. I need a break."

Montana stopped in her tracks and turned around. Quentin never needed a break, but he was leaning against a tree and breathing hard. She ran to him. Something was wrong.

"Quentin, are you okay?" Montana asked as she approached.

He nodded. "I just wanted to stop for a minute. Look at you. You're going harder than me."

"You're not the only one with pent-up energy."

Quentin rested the back of his head on the tree and laughed. "We're both anxious."

"Yeah."

Quentin rose up from the tree and brushed his lips across Montana's. It was a sweet, unassuming kiss. Not the kind of kiss that started something they weren't ready to finish.

"Are we running or kissing?" Montana asked.

"I'm okay with either," Quentin said. "Right now, I'm resting."

"Okay, I'll rest too." Montana leaned on the tree next to Quentin.

"Montana, do you think I'm doing the right thing letting Reese marry this girl?"

"He says he loves her, and they have a baby on the way, so I think you're fine."

"They're so young, though. It scares me. What if he can't handle being a husband or a father?"

"He has no choice about the father part, and you may have to help with the husband part," Montana said. "But I think he has a good example."

"I want to be a good example for him."

"You are. You're a great example for all your children."

Quentin sighed. "I haven't always been. The last five years, I've been incredibly selfish. God helped me see that."

"It was only five years. Not their whole lives. Your relationships will recover."

"That's why I love you, Montana. You are so positive. You've got a light inside of you. I don't want anything to hurt that light. I want it to just shine brighter."

"I love you too, Quentin."

Quentin turned to face Montana. His facial expression was now intense. It made her heart flutter. When he reached his hand into his pocket and pulled out a box, Montana thought she might faint.

Quentin took Montana's left hand and kissed each finger before dropping to one knee. "Montana. You don't know what you've done in my life. You've made me feel like a man again. You make me want to live again. I wasn't living before, I was slowly dying. You've introduced me to God again. Your love brought me back to life. You've . . . you've resurrected me."

Montana swallowed back the lump that formed in her throat. "Quentin, I don't know what to say to that."

"Say that you'll let me return the favor. Let me love away all the mistakes I've made. Let me give you a life that you maybe thought you'd never have, but that you definitely deserve."

"I don't care about the money, Quentin."

"I know, but you'll have it anyway, and you'll have all of my love too. All of my heart."

He opened the box, and a sunbeam illuminated the most beautiful princess-cut diamond that Montana had ever seen. Her hand trembled as he placed the engagement ring on her finger.

"Will you marry me?"

"Yes. Yes, I will!"

Quentin hugged her at the waist and then jumped to his feet. "You've made me happier than I ever thought I could be. I need you, Montana."

Those three words solidified it for Montana. She needed Quentin too. She needed to feel safe, loved, and cherished. Quentin was the man she'd been waiting for.

"I need you too, Quentin. I can't believe God has blessed me with my very own prince."

Montana sealed her declaration with a kiss of her own. A kiss full of possibility and hope for the future. There was more than passion in her kiss; there was a promise. There was a vow of love. Love that would cover anything and everything life would hurl at them. Love that would resurrect them both, as one flesh, as new creations.

God had put them together, and there was nothing or no one that would tear them apart.

A READING GROUP GUIDE

THE REPLACEMENT WIFE

Tiffany L. Warren

About This Guide

The questions that follow are included to enhance your group's reading of this book.

Discussion Questions

1. What was your initial take on Quentin and Chloe's relationship? Was Quentin leading Chloe on, or was she living in her own fantasy?

2. Why do you think Quentin started Transitions? Was his purpose fulfilled?

3. If you were Montana, would you have done things differently with Quentin? Was she a man stealer, in your opinion?

4. Discuss Job 13:15. Have you ever had a "though He slay me, yet will I trust Him" experience? How was your faith restored?

5. Do you believe a person can have more than one soul mate?

6. Do you think this is the last Quentin will see of Chloe?

CHAPTER 1

PAM

Isn't it weird how the very best things can happen to you at the very worst times? I just got off the phone with an editor at Gideon Publishing. Her name is Carmen, and she wants to give me a book deal. It's for my second book, a fictional version of the story of Jesus and the woman at the well. I never sold the first one that I wrote, which is probably a good thing, because there is too much of my own life in its pages.

My second book, called *The Chance Meeting*, took me only a year to write, but it took another year for me to get replies back from my query letters. Now, finally, eight years into my publishing journey I'm being offered the opportunity of a lifetime.

It is the best thing that could happen in my life, but I hate that it's happening when Troy is at absolute rock bottom with his music thing. He's lost nearly every penny of the three and a half million dollars he earned after discovering a powerhouse vocalist named Lisa with an incredible voice.

"Hey, babe. Logan is coming over in a few. Are you gonna cook something?"

Troy's voice pulls me from my thoughts, and I gaze directly into my husband's ruggedly handsome face. That very appealing face, those incredibly sexy light brown eyes, and his undeniable swagger caused me to postpone every single last one of my dreams while he pursued his music career.

Not anymore. I feel God moving me in a different direction, one that doesn't include feeding his friends. I've got to write a proposal for my *next* book. Carmen wants to offer me a two-book deal, but I've not given any thought to another project.

"I think *you* should cook something or order out," I say.

He blinks, as if blinking will help him hear me better. "Come on, Pam. This is important. He's going to collaborate with me on some music. He's really well connected, and I think he can help get Aria's project off the ground."

I roll my eyes. I should've stopped myself from doing that, because it makes me seem like an unsupportive wife. But I've been hearing that singing harlot's name for the past eight years.

Aria is Troy's big project. He's spent almost a decade trying to blow up with this girl. She's in my home so much, she might as well be my sister-wife, except I can't ever see that chick lifting one of those acrylic-nailed fingers to do a dish or a load of laundry.

"Pam?"

I shake my head and the negative thoughts about Aria. "No, Troy. I can't do it tonight. I've got something really important to do, and then I have to go to a Sister to Sister meeting."

"What can you *possibly* have to do that's more important than handling my business? Your job is to take care of home. Me and the kids, Pam. You been chilling for the past eight years, so the least you could do is be hospitable when I have guests."

I know he did not just reduce everything I've done in the past eight years to "chilling." I didn't know raising three children was chilling. I didn't know that the upkeep of a five-thousand-square-foot house was chilling. If I was chilling, then what was he doing in all the years before he made the three million dollars? Sounds like if I am in chill mode—which I am not—then it's my turn.

Besides, Troy knows dang well that if something doesn't give in the next six months, then I definitely am going to have to go back into the corporate workforce. He hasn't even asked me about my writing career—not since he bought me a journal when I was pregnant with our son, TJ. I'm starting to wonder if he even meant anything he said about supporting my dreams.

I close my eyes and sigh. "What do you want me to make, Troy?"

"I can make some wings and salad, Mom. Do you want me to?"

That is my surprisingly capable fourteen-year-old Gretchen. She's been obsessed with cooking since the age of ten, and she can probably cook a better meal than I can. A month ago, I let her handle Easter dinner, with me supervising, of course, and she really did a wonderful job.

"I'll give you an extra ten in your allowance if you do, honey. I sure appreciate you," I say and give Gretchen a kiss on the cheek. Then I give Troy a dry peck. "Gotta go."

"Your Sister to Sister meeting is not until seven. It's only five o'clock. What are you doing between now and then?" Troy asks.

I was wondering when he'd ask what I had to do. I almost thought he wouldn't. Troy barely notices anything that doesn't impact him directly.

"A publisher offered me a book deal, but I have to come up with a proposal for my second book."

Troy's eyes widen, and he hugs me tightly. "That is great, Pam! When were you going to tell me?"

When you stopped making requests. "I wanted to make sure I'd be able to come up with a second book proposal."

"That shouldn't be a problem. All that gossiping y'all do at those women's meetings, you ought to have plenty of story ideas."

"I'm not going to write about my friends."

Troy shakes his head. "I don't know why not. They would if they had the opportunity. How much money is the publisher offering you?"

"Um, she said seven thousand dollars for two books."

Troy frowns and scratches the back of his head. "Is that all? I thought publishers were handing out six-figure deals and what-not. That's what we talked about when you were sending out all those letters."

"I did some research, and what they offered me is pretty standard for a brand-new author."

"So when do you get the money?"

"I-I'm not sure."

"You're not sure? Pam, if you don't know the right questions to ask these people, you need to put me on the phone."

"I'm sure I have to sign a contract first."

"Well, we could sure use those thousands, Pam. We're getting low on funds, just so you know."

I lift an eyebrow and fold my arms across my chest. "How low?"

"We've got about two hundred thousand left, but it won't last long if we don't get some additional funds up in here."

See, this is exactly what I'm talking about with him. I'm sick of Troy living from one gig to the next. We've got about two hundred thousand dollars left out of the three and a half million. That's barely enough to get us through another one of Troy's ventures.

First, there was the Aria record project. He finished that one and sold about twenty-two copies. Okay, it was more like ten thousand. But he spent more money marketing and creating that record than he earned in profits.

Then there was the Aria tour. I guess Troy thought since he had all those CDs stacked in the garage that they should probably go on the road and try to sell them. Yeah, that wasn't such a good idea, either. The concerts—mostly in shopping malls and hole-in-the-wall clubs—didn't move many records. Just money from the assets to the liability column of our family balance sheet.

Finally, there was the Aria video shoot. Get the pattern here? The singing harlot and *her* career have sucked our blessing dry.

"And by additional funds, you mean the money from the book?"

"That and some more. I was wondering if you'd mind getting a part-time job, just until we get done with this project."

"You're kidding, right?"

"No, I'm not. I mean, it's not like I'm really marketable in corporate America, and you know I can't do no factory work. You were a VP at Ellis Financial. They'd give you something."

Anger simmers in the pit of my stomach, like a tea kettle full of near-boiling water. Troy told me I'd never have to go to work again. That I could take care of our family and that he'd take care of me.

"I've been out of the workforce for eight years, Troy. It won't be easy for me to get a job, either. Plus, I'd like to see where my book career could go."

"Both of us can't be starving artists."

"You're right, Troy. One of us has to be *responsible.*"

Troy touches my arm lovingly, but I snatch it away. "Pam, baby, it's only for a while. Just until Aria's new record takes flight."

"Don't you think you should find a new artist? You've been trying with Aria for years, and she's not a young twenty-year-old anymore. I think her time has passed, and you need to move on."

"You always want to give up before we break through."

"That's the problem, Troy. There's no *we* in this conversation. It has always been about you."

"You'd think that after all these years with me you would've learned something about teamwork."

Teamwork? Teamwork! I can't believe what I'm hearing. Troy is on a team, all right. Only I'm not on it, too. Aria is his partner and has been for eight years.

The teapot is on full boil now, and the whistle is ready to blow.

Then the doorbell rings. Troy looks as if he wants to say something else to me before opening it, but then he gives me a soft look and turns the knob.

"Logan! Man, it's about time!" Troy exclaims as he gives Logan a one-armed hug and fist bump.

"What do you mean? I'm early," Logan says.

"No, man. I mean, where have you been my whole life? It's time to get this thang popping."

I suppress the urge to cringe at Troy's slang. He keeps forgetting that we're almost forty years old, and that it sounds a lot better for grown-ups to use standard English.

"Man, God's timing is always perfect. This is our time!" Then Logan looks at me. "You must be Pam. You look exactly how Troy describes you."

In my opinion, there's nothing more handsome on a man than a smile, and Logan's smile is contagious. I can't help but give him one in return. His pretty white teeth seem to gleam in contrast to his blackberry-tinted lips and ebony skin. I can't believe he's standing here in our living room. He could be on a movie screen.

"Nice to meet you, Logan. Troy speaks highly of you," I finally say as I shake Logan's outstretched hand.

"This is my wife, the *writer,*" Troy says. "Doesn't she look like a writer?"

Logan chuckles. "Sure, she does."

"Yeah, well, she needs to write some song lyrics or something, 'cause that's how we're gonna get to stack the dough. Nobody black is about to get rich off writing books."

"I only know music, not books," Logan says. "And this sounds like a discussion I wouldn't touch with a ten-foot pole."

"Troy doesn't know, either," I say, hoping Troy can hear the venom in my voice.

I spin on one heel and grab my purse. I storm out of the house, knowing that this isn't over. As a matter of fact, it's only just beginning, because if Troy thinks he's going to throw my dream away like it belongs to him, he's got another thing coming.

This dream is mine, and God opened a door that no man can shut. Especially Troy.

If you enjoyed *The Replacement Wife,*
don't miss Rhonda Bowen's

Hitting the Right Note

On sale in April 2014 at your local bookstore!

CHAPTER 1

"He asked me to marry him! We're getting married!"
According to a recent report on ABC's *Nightline,* 70 percent of professional African American women over the age of twenty-five are unmarried. As JJ held the phone away from her ear to avoid Sydney's screams, she realized that her older sister had joined the 30 percent and left her stranded.

JJ Isaacs set the phone on hands-free and began applying mascara to her lashes. Though the news was not entirely surprising, it was not what she had expected to hear when she saw her sister's number pop up on the caller ID. Not on this night, anyway.

"Ohmigosh, JJ! He wants to marry me. Hayden Windsor wants to spend the rest of his life with me. Can you believe it?"

Could she believe that ex–NBA star Hayden Windsor, one of the first professional basketball players to figure out how to retire from the game and not go broke, wanted to marry her sister? Of course she could. Who wouldn't want to marry her tall, gorgeous, successful-business-owning sister? In fact, if they weren't related, JJ would have married her.

"Congratulations, hon," JJ said, pushing back a thin layer of irritation to find the genuine happiness for her sister that was camouflaged underneath. "I'm guessing you said yes?"

JJ grimaced and reached for her lipstick as Sydney screamed her response in the affirmative. She had never seen—okay, heard—Sydney like this. Her older sibling was usually the sane one in the craziness that was their big, dysfunctional family. Whereas everyone else was content to fly by the seat of their pants, Sydney was always the one with the plan. Getting married to a man she had dated for less than a year was not like her at all. But that's what happened when people fell in love. Or so JJ assumed. Having had no firsthand knowledge of the being-in-love experience, she couldn't say for sure.

"That's great, Syd," JJ said, reminding herself that she was happy for her sister. "Hayden's a prize."

"He is amazing, isn't he?" Sydney said, managing to modulate her voice to a less ear-splitting volume. "JJ, you should have seen his proposal..."

JJ rolled her eyes and mouthed a silent *no, thank you.*

"It was perfect," Sydney began. "He took me to..."

A banging on wood saved JJ's sanity.

"Five minutes to curtain, ladies," a booming voice called from the other side of the dressing room door.

JJ had never been so happy for a curtain call. She loved her sister and really was happy for her, but the last thing she wanted to hear from her sister, who had yet to remember what JJ was doing that night, was how her perfect boyfriend had done the perfect proposal to set off their perfect engagement.

"Syd, I gotta go." JJ jammed her feet into heels and swiped a layer of gloss over her lips as the scramble of women around her picked up speed. "I'm about to go onstage."

"Oh, honey, I'm so sorry! I completely forgot you had a show tonight."

JJ tried to ignore her annoyance.

"It's okay." JJ stood and straightened her dress. "I wouldn't have wanted to wait till tomorrow for this news. In fact, you can call me back later tonight and tell me all the details."

By then she wouldn't be as anxious and cranky as she usually was the last few minutes before a performance.

"Okay, sure," Sydney agreed.

A hand tugged at JJ's arm.

"We gotta go, JJ," Torrina said, nodding toward the door.

JJ picked up the cell phone to end the call. "Gotta go, Syd. Love you."

"Love you, hon. Have a great—"

JJ didn't hear the end of her sister's sentence. She barely got to toss her phone on the dressing room vanity before Torrina, her fellow backup singer, dragged her through the door and down the narrow backstage passageway. Sturdy iron beams holding the stage in place, and swiftly moving black-clothed men and women holding the show in place, barely registered with JJ as she hurried behind the other singers to her place near the second curtain.

"Everyone on your marker Curtains go up in five, four, three, two..."

JJ didn't hear the end of the countdown. Just the drummer's intro as the band started up Jayla Grey's "Sunday to Sunday." JJ was already up onstage with the rest of the backup vocalists as the curtains rolled up. Jayla would make her entrance in only a few seconds as she sang the first verse to one of the most popular songs off her Juno Award–winning album, *Desire.* JJ remembered when the "Sunday to Sunday" single first started blowing up the airwaves a couple years back. She never dreamed that she would be part of the performance for that song, but here she was at the Festival Place with hundreds of eyes watching her perform. Okay, so they weren't really there for her, but she was part of the show.

Jayla's strong, sultry contralto voice came in with the first few lines of the song, about a woman who was willing to slave for her man because she loved him. The crowds began to clap in rhythm and cheer.

JJ's own hips began to move to well-choreographed steps as the song progressed. Beads of perspiration began to dot her forehead and chest as the hot strobe lights shone down on her and everyone else onstage. But it just energized her and set her blood pumping as her voice came in strong for the pre-chorus. Her body began to feel the music, catching its own rhythm, making the steps her own. The sweet melodies curled out of her, blending with those of her fellow singers to bring a rich, lush harmony that cushioned Jayla's flawless voice. The screams of the crowd soaked into her like a light, warm drizzle on a humid day. JJ was in heaven and she never wanted it to end.

But eventually it did. Much quicker than she expected, with the fifty-minute set feeling like only fifty seconds. Her body still buzzed with energy as she skipped down the steps from the stage, her five-inch platform heels clicking gracefully. At first she could barely walk in the things. But after four months of wearing them onstage, she could manage a sprint if she needed to.

"Good show tonight, guys," Coley, the show's producer, said as he met JJ and the rest of the singers at the bottom of the steps. He pushed the mouthpiece of his headset up to his ear. "You guys were awesome, as usual."

"Good to know," Donald, a fellow singer, commented as he uncapped a bottle of water. "Especially since I felt like I was melting underneath those lights up there."

"Yeah," Torrina agreed, with a cheeky smile. "Plus I almost broke my neck on the wires on the floor back there in our little area."

"I guess it's a good thing I work with professionals then," Coley said, returning his mouthpiece to the right position as he began to walk away. "Lesser singers would have complained."

They all laughed as they headed back to the dressing rooms. Jayla, who was already in her robe, met them at the doorway.

"Thanks a lot, guys," she said, hugging each of them. "I was just telling Philip and the rest of the band, everything was almost perfect tonight. Couldn't have asked for a better show."

"Does that mean we get a raise?" Mark, the other male singer, asked with a grin.

Jayla smiled. "You better talk to Todd about that. He's the one signing your checks, not me. I just dish out the praise. You guys enjoy the rest of the night and this week. On Monday we'll start rehearsals for the tour."

JJ smiled but said little. Though everyone had been really nice to her, as one of the newest members of the team of backup singers, she still felt a little on the fringes. Truth was, she was only there because one of Jayla's original singers, Amina, got in a tiff with management and quit. Torrina had shared the dramatic details with her not long after JJ joined the crew.

However, her newness meant she didn't get all the inside jokes and she didn't always get invited to all the social events. But over the past two months, as she spent more time with the team, she was starting to feel like one of the family.

"I'm gonna head out but just wanted to say you were amazing tonight, Jayla," JJ said, squeezing the older woman's arm. She was about to turn away when Jayla grabbed her.

"You weren't too bad yourself," Jayla said with a smile. "I caught you doing your thing out there. You're coming on tour with us, right?"

JJ's eyes widened. She knew Jayla was going on a major tour in a couple weeks, but she had assumed that the main three would be going as backup. No one had talked to her about being a part of that team, and she honestly hadn't even considered it.

"Uh, I... I don't know," JJ stammered.

Jayla nodded thoughtfully. "Let me talk to my people and have someone get back to you. But keep your calendar open."

JJ opened and closed her mouth a couple times to answer and just ended up nodding.

Jayla chuckled. "See you next week, JJ."

JJ stumbled through the dressing room, barely able to focus as she gathered her things and exited the building. As soon as she stepped through the door into the cool, dark night, a hand grasped her upper arm, yanking her forward.

"Did I just hear what I thought I heard?" Torrina asked, her voice several pitches higher than usual and her eyebrows arched several inches higher than normal.

"She wants me to come on tour with her!"

Both women squealed and jumped around in the parking

lot, holding on to each other. JJ wasn't normally a screamer, but maybe there was something in the water tonight. She couldn't help herself.

"Jayla Grey wants me to come on tour with her!" JJ shrieked again. "She told me she was going to talk to her people. She invited me to rehearsal on Monday. She wants me to come on tour with her!"

"Oh, that's amazing," Torrina said, still bouncing even though her feet were planted firmly on the ground. "It would be so much fun to have you with us. I mean the other guys are great, but it would be great to have a girlfriend on the bus."

"I know," JJ said. "And, girl, I'm gonna need you to have my back. Someone's gonna have to keep me from making an absolute fool of myself when I see Angie Stone."

"Girl, I don't know if I can help you there," Torrina said, slapping a hand on her hip. "Last year I saw John Legend backstage at a show I was doing and I near lost my mind."

JJ burst out laughing.

"I'm serious!" Torrina said, eyes widening and hair flashing in the normal dramatic way in which she told her stories. "I was trying to climb over the barriers from our backstage area to his, nearly ripped my thousand-dollar dress. I almost got to him too, except his security guard got to me first."

"Oh no!" JJ covered her mouth. "That must have been embarrassing."

Torrina grinned. "Just a little. But I could take a little embarrassment for some John Legend. You know what I'm sayin'?"

JJ laughed. Only Torrina.

The door swung open again, letting out a blast of sound and another round of musicians and performers, some of them from Jayla's team.

"JJ, Torrina, you guys heading out with us?"

"Where's everyone going, Sam?" Torrina asked the short, stout guy wearing a spiky Mohawk and sunglasses.

"Probably going to grab a bite to eat in the hotel restaurant, then hit a couple bars downtown. One of the other guys says he knows a spot where they have a live band all night. Wanna come?"

"Sure," Torrina said with a nod. "I could eat. You too, JJ?"

"I'll head back with you guys to the hotel, but I've gotta crash," JJ said. "I'm exhausted. I think my body's still reeling from the excitement of these last couple nights. Plus I feel a headache coming on."

"Not used to life on the road yet, are you?" Donald asked. He threw an arm around JJ, tugging her against him as he joined their circle.

"No, not yet," JJ said with a tight smile as she casually eased herself out of Donald's uninvited embrace. "Still a newbie."

JJ followed the group over to the two huge, black SUVs that would take them back to the hotel where they had been staying for the past two days, making sure to be seated between Torrina and the door. As the vans pulled out of the parking lot, Torrina leaned over and whispered in JJ's ear.

"It's okay. You can come with us tonight. I'll keep Donald out of your way and make sure they lay off you at the bars. No one will give you a hard time."

JJ was grateful for Torrina's concern. She knew that Donald's unwelcome attention created an issue for JJ, especially when they all hung out socially. In any other situation JJ would have just told him to back off. But she was trying to make a name for herself in the industry and didn't want to stir up drama over what might just be a minor issue. The fact that she opted not to party like a rock star already made her stand out. She didn't want to be called a whiner on top of it too.

"Thanks, but I really am tired," JJ whispered back. "Three shows in three days is crazy."

Torrina's lip curled. "I know that's right."

"Plus my sister got some big news today and she's supposed to call me back tonight, so I really want to catch her," JJ added.

"Gotcha." Torrina nodded. "If you change your mind though,

just text me and I'll let you know where we are. We'll probably be out till four a.m. anyway. When we finish a set of shows like this, these guys like to go hard and then crash for a couple days."

JJ chuckled. "I can imagine."

The SUVs pulled up to the hotel entrance and they all got out. JJ waved to the others as they split up in the lobby; she headed toward the rooms, they headed to the hotel restaurant.

"Call me if you need someone to scrape you off the bar floor," JJ called.

She grinned as the sound of Torrina's laughter followed her across the lobby.

Pushing the door to the stairwell open, she began her trek up the steps to the sixth floor. She spent most of her life bypassing elevators for the stairs, so her thighs were used to the workout. Once inside her room, adjacent to Torrina's, she slipped off her jacket and sank down onto her bed to take off her strappy shoes. She had just freed her toes from their confines when she heard a knock on the door.

"Room service."

She grinned and hurried to open the door. Her bellhop was dressed in a gray ribbed sweater and leather jacket instead of a uniform, and carried several take-out containers and a bottle of something sparkling instead of pushing a hotel dinner cart. Plus she was sure it was illegal for someone to look that deliciously handsome.

She grabbed the lapels of his jacket and pulled him inside.

"Perfect timing," she murmured before his lips met hers. He managed to kick the door closed and wrap his arms around her without dropping any of his packages.

JJ snuggled closer, slipping into the familiar place where her body fit in his arms. Okay, so she may not be getting married, and her sister may have just abandoned her in the single zone. But at least she wasn't hanging out there alone. Being in the 70 percent might not be so bad after all.